The Curse

What was the secret shame that had driven India's proud father from England—and made him so fanatically determined to shield his daughter from all knowledge of the world?

What inner torment had turned India's Aunt Maude from a legendary young beauty into a hideously obese aging woman living out her days in bitterness and self-hate?

What demonic danger now threatened India herself, as she discovered that she was torn between two handsome, iron-willed suitors—each warning her of the other, and each demanding that she surrender herself body and soul to him alone?

Somehow, the answer lay in the depths of the glowing black pearl necklace that held India in its hypnotic spell . . .

Look for the forthcoming books
in the great new BLACK PEARL SERIES!

And—also by Willo Davis Roberts,
available in Popular Library editions,

WHITE JADE
CAPE OF BLACK SANDS
HOUSE OF IMPOSTORS
THE JAUBERT RING

Willo Davis Roberts
The Black Pearl Series - I
DARK DOWRY

POPULAR LIBRARY • NEW YORK

Published by Popular Library, a unit of CBS Publications, the Consumer Publishing Division of CBS Inc.

May, 1978

ISBN: 0-445-04224-9

1

The necklace lay across my palm, shimmering in the faint light that was all that penetrated the cramped ship's cabin. I stared down at the pearls, my breath catching, as it had done the first time I saw the maharani's jewels, at the sheer beauty of them.

Not white pearls, nor creamy ones, nor the rosy ones from Ceylon, which I had sometimes seen on visitors to our house in Calcutta, but black pearls. Very rare, very valuable.

They were not truly black, of course, but a glowing, satiny gray. Always fanciful, I wondered again how they had come into Papa's possession, and thought of why the maharajah had given them up—the maharani had died and the maharajah, heartbroken, had disposed of them because he could not bear to be reminded of her.

It did not matter, of course. Now they were mine. I, India Stuart-Brice, who had nothing else in the world save the responsibility for two younger sisters and a brother, held what had to be one of the most exquisite pearl necklaces in existence.

A dowry, Papa had said. A dowry, so that I should not have to go into a marriage penniless. At times, that took my fancy—that there might be a husband waiting for me in the strange new land of California whose coast even now lay off our starboard bow. But at the moment, all I could think of was that the pearls were certainly not spendable for necessities, should we fail to be met by Aunt Maude Stuart-Brice Graham when we landed.

"India! What are you doing? Didn't you hear the shout? We're in sight of land!"

My sister Caro burst into the tiny cubicle, almost knocking me onto the nearest bunk, and I had no time to conceal the necklace. I would certainly have done so had I heard her coming, for I had told no one, not even Caroline, about the pearls.

Caro was the beauty of the family, shorter than I by several inches, and with a more womanly figure for all that she was only fifteen to my nineteen years. Instead of the brown hair that I considered to be so ordinary, Caro's hair was long and like pale spun silk, and as she did so often she was now brushing strands of it off her face.

She stared in amazement at the necklace in my hand. "Oh, how pretty! Where did you get it, India?" Automatically, she reached out for it, and only when she had taken into her own hand did the green eyes widen. "Is it—real? Not beads, but—"

Her soft lips formed the word but did not say it, as she waited for me to confirm the incredible.

After a moment, I reached to retrieve the necklace and slip it back into its pouch. "Black pearls. Papa gave them to me for a dowry."

"Genuine pearls? But they must be worth a fortune! Especially that peculiar color—I've never seen anything like them! They can't have come from our part of the world, surely?"

I lifted my skirt and secured the bag in place beneath it, snug against my waist where the folds of material would, I hoped, keep it from detection. "Papa said they were worth a king's ransom."

"But why didn't you tell me we had them? You've been going about all these months with a long face about what would happen if Aunt Maude didn't get our letter or doesn't want us, and all the time you were carrying those! Oh, I know, you didn't say it, but I know all the same you're worrying—you always worry so much, dear India! And all the time we were rich!"

I sighed as I looked at her. So like Caro, not either to

6

worry nor to realize that our circumstances remained just as she had described them to be. "I thought it best to keep the necklace a secret," I said quietly. "We had a long journey, and we knew nothing about our fellow travelers, nor even about the sailors. They're a rough-looking lot, and —"

Caro's mouth quirked slightly. "And you think I talk too much. You may be right. But isn't it marvelous, we aren't the penniless orphans we thought we were! Tell me all about the pearls, everything Papa said."

"No. There's no time now. I'll tell you later—and no word to the twins in the meantime, mind. Nine is much too young to be expected to keep exciting secrets. How long will it be before we reach Monterey?"

"Oh, the mate says several hours before we can actually land, but we can see it now! Think of it, to have solid earth under our feet instead of the sea! Oh, come up and look, and help me keep Brice from falling overboard—he's so anxious to get there he keeps leaning over the rail!"

"And you left him up there by himself!" I forgot about the necklace, and even my apprehensions about landing and finding the relatives we had never seen vanished in the urgency of making sure Brice had not fallen into the sea.

Caro followed me up the ladder to the deck, chattering as we went; she was positively glowing in anticipation, as, indeed, she had been even before she learned of our wealth.

A wealth we could not spend, I thought, and wondered if it were true that, as my sister had sometimes accused, I was a born pessimist, a worrier-about-nothing.

Well, within a few short hours our long journey would be over, and then I would know whether it had been for nothing or not.

The land that only a short time ago had been spotted from a perch high in the rigging was now a bluish smudge on the horizon. We found the twins at the railing, but not, thank heaven, hanging over it.

"I see it!" Brice announced unnecessarily. "Will Aunt Maude be there to meet us, India? Will we go directly to her house? The mate says there are Indians in California, but they are not like *our* Indians at all, but have reddish skins, and they talk a peculiar language we will not be able to understand!"

Since he had asked these same questions, and made the same observations, numerous times before, I found it pointless to reply. I stood between the twins at the railing, an arm around Bethany's childish shoulders, hugging the little girl against me. A bit of their excitement began to touch me, too, for perhaps they were right—perhaps life in this new land, while different from what we had known with Mama and Papa in Calcutta, would be good.

The twins were quite unlike Caro and me in coloring, for they had dark eyes and dark brown curls that tumbled about their rosy faces—Papa's coloring, while Caro had Mama's; and I—poor India, I thought—I had Mama's hazel eyes (not so bright a green as Caro's, but touched with brown) and completely undistinguished brown hair. Not even the maharani's pearls could make a beauty of me.

They might, however, help to win me a husband one day. There could have been comfort in that thought, but there was not. A husband bought by pearls was not what I had in mind for myself at all, for I had read the novels Mama adored and I knew that the important thing was romance. A true romance would not be affected by a string of pearls, nor the lack of them, surely.

We stood at the rail of the ship that had carried us so far, for so many weary months, and I wondered what was to come, and remembered what had gone before.

I had always wished my parents had named me some ordinary thing, like Mary or Jane or Alice. I had almost no experience of girls my own age, but I read as many books as I could lay hands on, and I knew from those that *India* was an extraordinary thing to call a daughter. It set

8

me apart from the others (or it would when I had the opportunity to mingle with anyone other than my own family) and I didn't want to be set apart. I wanted to melt into the background, to be the same as everyone else.

Yet I knew that I was different.

Why this should be I was not sure, for Caro, I was certain, would fit well into any group of young ladies, and she had been reared the same as I, except for those early years in England which Caro did not remember.

I remembered England. Long ago when I was a small child, we had lived in Suffolk, at Willows Hall. Even now I could bring to memory the thick stone walls, the dim, cool corridors, the well-kept gardens bright with English flowers, although the memories evoked in me no longing for "home." England had remained home to Papa, to the very end, but it was not home to me.

Calcutta, where we had lived for most of the life I remembered well, had been home. And now there was nowhere I belonged, no house, no family, no country to call my own.

My father, Judson Stuart (he had dropped the *Brice* from our name, although he gave it to his only son years later) had been obsessed with India since boyhood; hence my embarrassing name. How he persuaded my conventional mama, Mary Ellen, to leave England and a life of luxury to go halfway round the world, I didn't know. Mama had been sickly from as far back as I could recall—though perhaps not while at Willows Hall? Although the way we were waited upon by a horde of servants there, it might not have been so obvious to a small child that her mother did very little—and she had died shortly after the twins' third birthday.

If Mama had explanations for the things Papa did, she never made them to her children. Certainly she deferred to him in all things, and I could not believe that the many moves of our early days were to her liking, for moving a household inevitably becomes the responsibility of the

9

woman in the family, and is a considerable chore no matter how many servants there are to assist her.

I remembered England, but I had no desire to return there after all these years. When we were left alone, we had two choices—England, or California. Grandparents, or Aunt Maude. Papa had told us, almost literally with his dying breath, to go to Maudie.

I had no memory of Aunt Maude. She had left England before we did, or perhaps I had seen her but, since she was not one of the people who made a fuss over me, she had simply not made any impression on a small child.

My grandparents I could bring to mind quite easily, although not entirely because of any fuss they had made, for Lord and Lady Stuart-Brice were not demonstrative people, even with their grandchildren. Grandmama was a gentle, white-haired old lady who always wore a string of pearls when she worked in her garden, supervising the dozen gardeners who did the real chores. She never raised her voice, and she had sometimes held me upon her lap and told me stories about Papa and Aunt Maude when they were my age. The scent of lilac would always bring to mind Grandmama's comfortable lap and her quiet voice.

Lord Stuart-Brice was a different case altogether. No one would have dreamed of addressing him as *Grandpapa*. He was a very tall, very stern gentleman who never displayed any affection for anyone, least of all to a tiny girl who spilled her milk and dirtied her frock by falling into mud puddles. The servants spoke to him with respect, of him with awe, and stayed out of his way as much as possible, since he was quite capable of bringing his cane down on an unsuspecting head should things not be to his liking. I had known that cane myself, on an occasion when I broke some object in his study. I had long since forgotten what the object was, but I could still feel the sting of the cane on my four-year-old shoulders.

It was Willows Hall, however, more than my grandparents, that meant England to me. It was a great stone castle, with a moat and swans and extensive gardens noted the length of England for their beauty and perfection.

I wasn't sure how much I actually remembered of Willows Hall and how much the imagery in my mind depended upon Papa's stories of his childhood there. That he loved his home and his homeland no one could have questioned. And when the restless years were over, when we had lived in Delhi and Kampur and Bombay, and had finally settled into the pleasant walled villa outside of Calcutta, Papa named the place *Willows,* for all that its gardens were far different from those of his Suffolk home.

All those years, I thought, I had lived at Willows, which was an imitation of Willows Hall, and now I was neither English nor Indian; I was an alien wherever I went, for India had remained a foreign country in spite of our years there.

"What is my homeland?" I had once asked, and Papa patted my head and smiled and told me that I was a Stuart of Willows, and that that was a fine thing to be and sufficient for any small girl.

It might have been enough, had Willows any relationship to the outside world—what I thought of as the "real world"—but it had not. Oh, there were dark-skinned servants who cared for the motherless children and tended the house and grounds. They spoke their careful English to us, since Papa insisted upon it, and we were not even allowed the opportunity to learn their language, which might have given us a sense of belonging somewhere. At night the servants went home, with the exception of Rajindra, who slept in his own small house on the grounds.

We lived, the four of us, as pampered yet restrained English children might have done in Suffolk, provided with everything we needed except companionship with other English children. That there were some in Calcutta I had no doubt, for many of the employees of the British East India Company had their families with them. There must have been schools for those children, and, shy

11

though I was, I longed for school and contact with the world those other children lived in.

I hadn't minded too much when I was very young, for there had been books aplenty and Papa spent a good deal of time with us. He taught us games and songs, and to play the piano, and he always read to us, long after I had reached a fluency in reading on my own.

Caro was born when I was four (while we were still at Willows Hall in Suffolk), and I delighted in her pink-and-white-and-gold beauty and took her for my own. Indeed, in our early years in Bombay, when Mama did not feel well and often slept through a good part of the day, Caro fell to me. Certainly there was always a servant about with a watchful eye, but it was to me that Caro came when she was hurt or needed comfort, and Papa used to laugh and call me "the little mother."

When Bethany and Brice were born, and Mama's health declined still further, I was a matronly ten and quite capable of changing nappies and bringing up bubbles after a feeding (the wet nurse was a fat Indian *amah* who had plenty of milk for two more babies after her own chubby son had been fed) and managing their naps and their outings. These latter consisted of riding about the grounds of Willows in an enormous carriage, brought all the way from England at considerable expense before the twins were born, since Mama had said that she was too weary to carry about another infant.

I never minded being "the little mother," for all the babies were good and sweet-tempered, except that Caro occasionally had flashes of temper which had to be controlled. We loved Mama, but she played less and less a part in our lives. By the time she died, when I was thirteen, we scarcely missed her, since she had by that time come to spend almost all of her time in her own room, and we only saw her once in a while when she felt well enough to join us for dinner.

By the time I was fourteen, however, I was aware of an increasing restlessness. The twins were old enough to play by themselves—Bethany, especially, was a very self-sufficient child—and Caro needed nothing from me, either. I longed for friends of my own age, and, most of all, I began to dream about going beyond the walls of Willows. Only a child so totally immersed in books would have waited so long to seek freedom—that was the way I thought of it. Freedom to move about in the world, to *live*.

We were prisoners there at Willows, however beautiful a prison it might be. We saw almost no one except the servants and each other, and it was no longer enough, no matter how many books Papa managed to obtain for us.

"Why can't we go out, Papa?" I would beg. It didn't matter where, I simply needed to go *out*, but he only laughed and ruffled my hair. "You are happier where you are, my love! The world out there is dirty, and sordid, and dangerous for such a precious young lady as you. One day, perhaps, we will go home, and then things will be different."

Home, to Judson Stuart, meant England.

Yet it wasn't *my* home. I knew that, had known it for a long time. I had none of Papa's yearning for England—certainly none for my grandparents and the castle with gardens where a little girl was punished for pulling up a single flower when there were thousands of them and one blossom could not have been sorely missed. I'd been shut up in a walled garden far too long already.

Still, even England would have meant freedom of a sort. The people would speak my own language, their skins would be the same color as my own, and there would surely be other young people my own age.

"When?" I pressed. "When will we go home to England?"

I suspected, seeing the pain in Papa's eyes, that the answer was *never*. His indulgent smile faded and he spoke softly. "One day," he said. "One day we will go home."

The answer did nothing to comfort me. Because there was no one else, I revealed my desires to Caro.

"We could run away," she said at once, with all the wisdom and logic of almost ten years. "We've seen

13

through the gates that there are horses and carriages and ladies and gentlemen going by, and lots of natives. We'll simply wait until a delivery is made through the tradesmen's gate, and we'll slip through and investigate for ourselves."

And so that is what we did—or, rather, tried to do. For we got only a short distance beyond the gates before we were discovered and brought home in disgrace. For once there was nothing genial nor tolerant about Papa; he frowned down on us from his superior height and spoke in almost as stern a manner as Lord Stuart-Brice himself would have done.

"I hold you responsible for this, India. I can't imagine what you thought to accomplish, beyond getting lost and frightening your family out of our wits. There are all sorts of dangers out there, and you don't even speak the language so that you can communicate with the natives."

And whose fault was that, I thought, but did not say it. Sometimes I could talk back to Papa, but not today. He was genuinely angry and upset.

"I thought you understood that the wall is for your protection. You are young ladies with no understanding of the evils of the world, and I have done my best to keep you safe from them. I will have to punish you for such an unwise action, because I must impress upon you how wrong it was to leave the grounds. You will go without your suppers and spend all of tomorrow each in your own room. You will talk to no one while you think about your disobedience, and I sincerely trust it will never be necessary to punish you for such a thing again."

If he thought that he had put out of our heads the longing for freedom, however, Papa was much mistaken. If anything, the tantalizing glimpse we had had of strange new faces had only strengthened our determination that we should somehow escape from our nursery and join the rest of the world. Out there, we were convinced, lay adventure and romance and all the things of which we dreamed.

I was shy of meeting people—how could I not be,

when I met so few?—but I knew that life could not begin to be lived until I moved beyond the confines of my own home and family circle. Papa had occasional visitors, mostly men who came to Willows in the evening and drank brandy in the study and smoked fragrant cigars. They were always pleasant to me, and called me *Miss India,* as if I were a young lady.

But they were Papa's friends, not mine. Everyone in the stories I read had friends of their own, confidantes, lovers.

All I knew about lovers I had learned from books. They swept one into manly arms and kissed a girl until she swooned. And then there would be a wedding, and a house of one's own—one without a walled garden?—and perhaps the freedom to come and go in a carriage, to visit other ladies and play whist or some other card game, and drink tea, and gossip. And of course, eventually, there would be babies of one's own.

I was quite aware that at the age of nineteen I was hopelessly ignorant in the matter of husbands and babies. The relationship between my parents had been warm and loving, but even I, estranged as I was from normal relationships, knew that because of Mama's frail health, it was not quite as a normal marriage should be. Mama always had her own room, always slept during the day, was always cosseted and waited upon and deferred to in tiny ways though Papa's will took precedent in the greater things.

When I tried to learn something about how babies came into being, I had been shushed by the female servants who told me this was not a proper thing to ask. Yet at some time it was apparently proper to produce infants, so there must be a time when questions became permissible, when they would be answered.

Most girls, I was sure, had learned those answers at a far earlier age. The heroines in my books were invariably younger than nineteen. They giggled with their friends and learned all the right things for a girl to know, such as how to act when a young man came calling. Some of

15

them had earnest and informative conversations with their mothers. But Mary Ellen had died without telling me anything at all except to be a good girl.

Caro shared my restlessness. She began to plot ways to escape from Willows, to scale the walls, to avoid being caught and brought back before we'd even seen anything.

"There are men out there," Caro said bluntly. "How are we ever going to find husbands if we don't meet them?"

For an interminable time, I thought that finding a husband was not to be a part of my life, that Papa intended us to stay shut up like one of those poor papist creatures in black habits; I had seen some of them once, years ago, when a gate had been inadvertently left unlocked and Caro and I glimpsed briefly the shaded street and the people who trod it: Nuns, they were.

I wondered, if we had been Catholic instead of Church of England, if Papa would have deposited us all in a nunnery.

But a nun was a simple soul without ordinary longings, who would not know the emotions that stirred ever more intensely in my breast as I grew older.

And then, six months ago, I had in quiet desperation approached Papa one night as he sat over the brandy, smoking his solitary cigar, and knelt at his feet to press a cheek against his leg, to reach for his hand.

"Well, well, why aren't you sleeping this time of night? What is it, love, too hot for you? Or are you ill?"

"No, Papa, although it is very warm." For a moment I was unable to speak, and then the urgency broke through my reserve. "Oh, Papa, how long is it to go on?"

My anguish must have reached him, for Papa put down the cigar and clasped my hand in both of his. "How long is what to go on? You sound quite—distraught."

My lower lip quavered with the intensity of my need. "Papa, how long are you going to keep us here? In this—prison?"

"Prison? Willows, a prison?" His astonishment brought

16

him forward in his chair. "India, is that how you see it? When all I've tried to do is protect you—"

"From what? Surely other girls aren't locked up, away from the world? The girls in England?"

There was a flicker of some unnamed emotion in his eyes in the lamplight. "Perhaps their fathers don't know as much about the world as I do, my dear. I don't want you hurt."

And finally I could say it, the thing I had never been able to voice. "But I *am* hurt, Papa! It hurts me not to have friends, not to do all the things other young people do! I never see anyone but the servants and the family, never!"

"You see Miss Telsman—"

I made a sound of wounded outrage. "Miss Telsman! A dried up little spinster paid to teach us to be English young ladies. But we aren't in England, we'll never go back to England—and we don't belong here, either! Papa, am I never to marry? Never to make a life of my own? Am I not entitled to that?"

He looked down on me, his first-born, and gradually a smile came over his features. Amusement—and relief, perhaps? "Is that it? You're worrying about romance? Well, the time will come, love, your time. You are not such an ancient age, not yet nineteen—your mother was twenty when we married. And there will be a young man for you, I swear it. Look, I even have your dowry, I'll show it to you."

He got up, leaving me sitting there on the floor with my skirts sliding immodestly up to show both ankles and calves, and moved to the safe hidden behind the painting of Willows Hall. After a moment he came back and sank again into his chair, with the lamplight making a golden pool across his lap and upon my upturned face.

He carried a small pouch that closed with a drawstring. He opened it carefully and allowed its contents to slide out onto my hand.

I stared. We had always had jewelry; Papa considered

17

it appropriate that his womenfolk be adorned according to their stature in society (although we never moved in that society, not even Mama) but I knew at once that this necklace was different.

Pearls were not a rarity in this country, and I had seen them occasionally on lady visitors as well as on some of Papa's business acquaintances who were natives of Calcutta. But I had never seen any such as these.

They were not the rosy-tinted pearls of Ceylon, nor the creamy-lustered ones of Japan or the Persian Gulf, but a deep shiny gray, the iridescence seeming to come from deep within each globe. They were perfectly matched and perfectly sized, and it seemed to me that they conveyed a faint warmth, not reflected from my hand but a warmth, a life, of their own.

It was a necklace fit for a queen.

"There are earrings, too." Papa said, and tipped the pouch again. "These are tear-shaped, yet true mates in color to the others. Would you like to try them on?"

I was mesmerized by the simple magnificence of the jewels in my hand. "Pearls? Are they genuine pearls?"

"Black pearls. Among the rarest in the world. These were fashioned for a maharani who died before she could wear them—I don't know the entire story, but her husband disposed of them after her death, and there's no bad luck attached to them, don't think that. You needn't be afraid to wear them."

Afraid—no, that was not the emotion the pearls evoked, not fear. I had never seen anything so lovely.

"Are they—mine?"

Pleasure lit his face as he touched one of the drop-shaped earrings with a forefinger. "They're worth a king's ransom. And they came to me, to hold in trust for a dowry for my daughter. No matter what our fortunes, when that young man comes along for you, you won't go to him empty-handed, but with a fortune of your own. Here, put them on."

He lifted the necklace and put it about my neck, fastening the clasp at my nape, then pulled me to my feet. "Come into the hall, I'll bring the lamp, and you can see yourself in the mirror. You can fix the earrings best yourself, no doubt."

The pearls were cool against my skin, but it seemed that they warmed at once. I stared into the glass, wondering how even such gems as these could so brighten my ordinary face; for the moment, I looked almost as lovely as Caro. I touched the pearls with my fingertips, wonderingly.

Black pearls. A king's ransom. My gaze lifted until my eyes met Papa's in the mirror as he stood behind me, smiling.

"How did you get them?" We had never wanted for anything, but we were not truly rich. Surely the price of the maharani's pearls was beyond the reach of ordinary people.

Papa squeezed my shoulder affectionately. "A father is entitled to his secrets, eh? Let's only say that they are perfect for you, and they assure that you will never go penniless to the man you marry. Whatever his fortunes, you will have one of your own. And perhaps when the time comes for the others, for Caro and little Beth—well, might they not grace each of you, at least for a wedding?"

My eyes moved back to the mirror. "They're so beautiful. They seem almost—alive."

"Alive. Yes. Pearls *are* alive. They are not minerals from the earth, like diamonds or rubies, but were once part of a living creature. And they will, in time, die. But not in your lifetime, my pet. They will live as long as you do, as long as your grandchildren. Longer, if you take proper care of them—for several hundred years."

I turned slightly so that the lamplight fell more directly upon the silvery-gray globes. "And how do I take care of them, Papa?"

"Pearls are soft, and the first thing to remember is that they can be damaged if they come in contact with hard or rough surfaces. When you aren't wearing them, they should be kept here, in this special pouch. And after each time you wear them, they should be washed and carefully dried, to remove all perspiration from them. Some say they should be washed in sea water, but others are horrified at this; the maharajah who had them fashioned into the necklace felt that simple washing and careful drying would be best. They can be damaged by high temperatures, so it is best to be prudent about where they are kept. And perhaps they should not be locked away from the air for long periods—take them out occasionally, even if only to look at them. They are fragile, but exquisite, are they not?"

"How do they die?" I asked, fascinated.

"They simply begin to deteriorate until they no longer have their beauty, their luster. But you need have no fear of that. They should, I'm told, last at least a hundred and fifty years, and probably will be beautiful for far longer than that. I have been saving them for you, but I think that now is the time to give them to you. Keep them safe, India."

"Yes, Papa." It was an overwhelming gift, and for a moment had distracted me from my primary concern. "But when do I meet a young man to impress with them?"

Papa laughed. "Oh, you are like your mother was, like a burr that will not be pulled from the horse's tail! You have made up your mind to it, you are a woman grown, eh? Very well. It may be that you are right, that I have protected you from the harshness of the world for too long. It may be time for you to emerge from the safety of this cocoon. Very well. We'll see. We'll see."

And I had to be content with that. At first I expected that, any moment, Papa would bring home some handsome young man, probably someone from the British East India Company, where he had many connections.

But nothing happened. Life went on at Willows as it had gone on before, with dressing and eating and sleeping and walking in the gardens, and playing silly games with

20

Caro and the twins, and reading the books Papa brought me.

When I brought up the subject again, Papa was unruffled. "Of course I promised you, love. But it must be the *right* young man. One doesn't produce a suitable fellow at the drop of a hat. I will find him, and when I do, you will know about it. You have my word for it."

And so I waited, impatient, dreaming, going off into a romantic world of my own until Caro said crossly, "What's the matter with you, India? You don't hear when I speak to you!"

I hadn't told Caro about the pearls. At that point I wasn't worried about her speaking carelessly about them; she had no one to speak to, any more than I did. But the pearls were my secret. Twice I took them out of the safe and looked at them, then fastened them briefly around my neck to admire before gently replacing them in the safety of the pouch.

How had Papa come by them? Worth a king's ransom, he said, but I had little idea of their monetary value. My every physical need was always met; Willows was luxuriously appointed, a dressmaker came twice a year and Miss Telsman directed the sewing of our simple garments. Grandfather Stuart-Brice was a lord and a wealthy man, and Papa was his only son—and his heir, I assumed, although I was unaware of any contact between them since Papa had removed his family from England. No doubt Papa was wealthy, too. It was not something with which I had ever concerned myself.

I waited for the expected wonder to happen.

Something happened, all right, but not what I had been anticipating. For Papa died, the bottom fell out of our world—and yes, now I knew how safe and secure Willows had been, after all, just as he said—and I could look back on it as a haven rather than a prison, for I had been thrust without warning into the icy world of grief and fear.

The grief was beginning to recede behind me, although I knew that I would never stop missing Papa.

But the fear remained.

It would take more than a necklace, however valuable, to give me the courage to face the unknown future, and I was afraid.

2

The end of life as we had known it came without warning. One night we went to bed as usual after spending the evening playing an indifferent game of chess, Caro and I; we had been bored, and we speculated upon the young men whom Papa was supposed to produce for our benefit. Caro, of course, took it for granted that she was included in the promise.

"I suppose you'll have to marry first, since you're the oldest, India, but I don't intend to wait until I'm nearly twenty," she said.

I laughed in protest. "I'm not nearly twenty, I've just turned nineteen. But you're very pretty, I'm sure there will be young men wanting to marry you if they're ever given a chance to meet you. Lady Featheringill is giving a party next month, and I think she's invited me. I heard Papa talking about it, and he told Miss Telsman I must have a new frock. Perhaps there will be young men there and I will meet them. At any rate, I'll meet someone new, and I'll tell you all about it when I come home, if you can manage to stay awake until then."

Caro's lower lip protruded slightly, the way it had when she was small and wanted her own way. Strangely enough, it only made her prettier. "I don't want to hear about it, I want to go too. I'm fifteen. That's old enough to stay up for a grown-up party, I should think."

"But you weren't invited this time, dear. No doubt that's because I'm the oldest and should have a chance to

23

go out into society first. But your turn will be coming soon, I'm sure."

"It had better," Caro said dangerously, "or I shall do something drastic."

I was amusedly intrigued. "Such as what?" I asked.

"Throw a temper tantrum, perhaps. Papa can't stand screaming females, I've heard him say so."

"Quite so." My amusement deepened. "But I shouldn't count on his giving in to your demands because of a tantrum. More likely he'd turn you over his knee and spank you the way he did the time you wore Mama's new gown and tore it beyond fixing."

"But I was only seven then! He can't treat me as a child any more, I've grown up!"

"I hardly think you'll convince him of that by having a tantrum. Come on, let's stop playing, I'm tired of chess. Even going to bed sounds more fun. I'll make up a story before I go to sleep, about Lord Horace Dillingfrothen, who will be terribly handsome and terribly rich, and will want to marry me the moment he sees me!"

Caro scowled. "I'm tired of making up stories. When is something *real* going to happen?"

I sighed in sympathy with my sister. "Soon, I hope." For I was tired of make-believe too, and I'd had four more years of it than Caro.

I looked in on the twins before I retired to my own room. Bethany lay sleeping like a cherub, her dark curls spilling across the pillow, her favorite doll within the circle of her arm.

It will be better for you, Bethany, I promised silently. I won't let you remain as isolated from society. When I am a married woman with a home of my own, I will give parties that you will come to, and you won't be lonely as I have been.

Brice slept in the adjoining room, and he, too, had taken a toy to bed, but his was the engine of a model train Papa had had brought from England, part of a set Papa himself had owned as a boy. Brice was never dearer than when he was asleep. Awake, he got into the normal small-boy scrapes, although he read well and was beginning to spend more time in the library the way the rest of us did. But I remembered him well as an infant, when I had held him and rocked him to sleep, and I loved him deeply. It had never occurred to me until that moment that if I married and moved into a home of my own, I should have to leave the twins behind. I stood for a moment, looking down on him. It would be hard to do. But of course we would visit back and forth. I wouldn't stop seeing my family altogether.

I turned away, closing the door gently so as not to waken him. I had barely slipped into my own bed when I heard the commotion at the front door. Alarmed, I got up and shrugged into my wrapper.

Papa was out, as he often was in the evenings. I did not know where he went; he did not usually volunteer and I did not ask, following the pattern my mother had set before me. A man with an invalid wife must find some diversion beyond his own family, she had once told me, and it was best not to inquire what it was.

At the time I had no idea what she meant. Even now, I was only vaguely aware of what those diversions might be. Certainly I was not disturbed by the possibilities, for I was secure in my conviction that whatever his interests might be, Papa put the welfare of his family above all else.

There had been a few times when Papa returned late at night and I knew that he had had more than his customary libation. I had never, however, known him to be drunk, or to cause any disturbance.

We were alone in the house except for old Rajindra, who always waited until Papa returned, no matter what the hour, before retiring to his own small hut. I was moving toward the front door when something fell against the side of the house, making a sound I recognized as ominous even before I knew what it was.

Rajindra appeared, walking straight and slim for all the weight of his seventy-odd years, a frown forming on his dark face. "Ah, Missy India, this can be no matter for a young lady—"

There was another thump, a muffled curse, and Rajindra threw open the door, the light from the lamp in his hand spilling out across the veranda.

For a moment I didn't recognize the face there, it was so white and so distraught. My attention was caught by the figure at his feet, a man in evening clothes, his chest soaked in blood.

"Papa!" I fell forward on my knees, avoiding Rajindra's outstretched and restraining hand. "What's happened?"

"He's been shot." The voice, if not the face, was instantly recognizable as that of my father's friend, Sir Roland Trask, an important official at the British East India Company in Calcutta. "India, my dear, please don't—let us carry him into the house, and Rajindra must send someone for the doctor, although I fear it may be too late for that. He's lost an appalling amount of blood, poor chap. Here, that's the way, get his feet and I'll manage his shoulders—can you lead the way to the bedroom, India, there's a good girl."

Caro appeared as I hurried down the passageway, her fair hair falling about her shoulders as she had been brushing it, clad only in a thin nightshift.

For once I wasn't concerned about immodesty, not when Papa was dying. Dying! Impossible—Sir Roland must be mistaken. Yet there was blood, blood that soaked Papa's shirt and dripped upon the parquet flooring so that poor Rajindra slipped in it and nearly lost his footing.

They put Papa upon the bed, and Sir Roland bent over him, loosening his clothing, while Rajindra scurried away for help.

"Hurry, hurry!" I cried after him.

But when I stepped close to the bed and stared down at the savage wound, my heart sank.

"If you're going to faint, dear girl, please do it over there," Sir Roland said grimly. "Judson, can you hear me? Judson!"

Papa moaned faintly but did not reply, and I swallowed my fear and took a firm grip on the bedpost.

"What must I do, Sir Roland?"

"Towels, cloths, something to hold against the wound. If we can stop the bleeding he may have a chance," Papa's friend said, and I ran to do his bidding.

Caro stood in the doorway, not approaching close enough to look, as I had done, at Papa's injured chest. She was still there, pale and with a beading of perspiration on her upper lip, when I returned with an armful of toweling, which Sir Roland and I pressed against the terrible hole.

For a few moments it seemed that we might assuage the deadly bleeding, but only for those minutes. The scarlet warmth crept wetly through the towels, staining my hand as I held it there, and I struggled against the need to be sick.

We asked no questions. It didn't seem to matter, for the important thing was whether or not the bleeding could be controlled. I stayed beside the bed, willing myself to have the necessary strength, praying that the doctor would come quickly.

Only after the man had arrived to make his examination did I retreat to the doorway near my sister, whose eyes pleaded for something I could not offer her.

The doctor grunted and straightened, rubbing at his back as if he'd bent over too many beds already this day. "Mortally wounded, I'm afraid. Very little I can do. What happened?"

Sir Roland didn't look at Caro and me, huddled together, waiting. "We'd been out together, at the Morriseys', and I was bringing him home. I let him out of the carriage at his own front gate, as I often do, and had started on down the street when I heard the shot. I came back at once, of course; my driver was armed, but we saw no one to fire at. Judson's purse had been dropped only a few feet off, turned inside out, and the ring ripped off his finger. A ruby—he wore a heavy gold ring with a ruby in it. His pockets turned out, too: the thief wasn't missing anything. Poor chap, he'd been shot at close range, just as you see him; he was bleeding furiously, but he spoke to me, said he thought he could get to the house with my help. I got him here, but only just. It must have taken incredible effort to walk so far, even with help; if I'd known how bad it was I'd never have let him try."

"The streets aren't safe at night these days," the doctor said, pursing his lips. "Deuced shame, a man can't go about his business without being set upon by thieves. I'd say any family he has should be notified at once."

In the stillness we could hear the ticking of the clock in the corner of Papa's bedroom, the clock that was a twin to the one in the room he had had at Willows Hall when he was a young man. Ticking, ticking out the final minutes of his life—I fought the urge to scream a protest.

"His family is in England," Sir Roland said. "His wife died some years ago, and there are only his children here in Calcutta."

The doctor shot a quick look at me from under brushy eyebrows. "And they are all very young? Some family friend should be notified, then."

"I am a family friend," Roland Trask said gravely. "I will attend to—everything."

The older man nodded. "Very good. I am most terribly sorry, but I don't think he can last more than a matter of hours, if that. I have a baby to deliver; I'll be on my way. I'll check back in on my way home, later."

A matter of hours, he said. I turned toward Caro, whose beautiful eyes were welling great tears, and we held each other while the convulsive sobs shook us both.

Mama had been so little a part of our lives—only a pretty but sickly lady to whom we spoke briefly once a day—that her death had been sad rather than tragic. Papa was altogether different. He had taught us to read, and held us on his lap while he read aloud, and tucked us into bed at night, and heard our prayers. He had played games, and talked to us by the hour, making our family a cohesive whole.

And now he lay dying, and there was nothing we could do about it. Nothing.

After a time Sir Roland drew us apart and wiped our faces and said that we should try to rest.

"Rest! When Papa is—no," I said with determination, "we will stay here with him."

And so we sat for the rest of the night, beside the bed, holding the hand that until so short a time ago had been strong for all of us. We watched as his life ebbed away in a crimson stream, for even though the wound had been packed with toweling the blood soaked through it and onto the bed.

About two in the morning Papa stirred and opened his eyes. They were glazed with pain, but he recognized me; I felt the faint pressure of his hand against mine.

"Papa?" I leaned forward with a leap of hope; perhaps the doctor had been wrong? "Papa, I'm here."

"India." My name was no more than a whisper on his pallid lips. "India."

"Yes, Papa. I'm here," I echoed.

"Go—to Maudie. She'll—"

He couldn't say the rest of it. His eyelids fluttered, but the effort to keep them open was too much. He sighed deeply and a froth of red bubbles appeared at the corner of his mouth, so that I turned in alarm to Sir Roland, who had kept watch with us.

"Maudie—his sister Maude?" he said, and I nodded blindly, making no attempt to control the silent tears. "She's in America, isn't she?"

I didn't know. I didn't care. All I cared about was Papa. Caro, on the other side of the bed, looked at me with red-rimmed eyes.

Papa spoke once more. At dawn, when the gray shadows began to creep across the polished floor, before the color came back into the room around us, when we had all begun to drowse from sheer exhaustion, I felt again the faint movement of his hand.

He spoke my mother's name. "Mary Ellen," he said softly, and then he died.

Sir Roland didn't have to tell us it was over. We both knew, for Papa's hands went slack, and the final reddish bubbles at his lips were stilled.

It was not until that great burst of anguish within me

had been somewhat alleviated by our shared tears that Caro and I took time to consider our predicament.

Except for relatives scarcely remembered, far across the oceans, there was no one to provide for the twins and ourselves. We were completely alone.

Sir Roland took charge of the things that had to be done immediately. Burial took place within hours of death, as it must in a hot climate. I tried to listen as our benefactor attempted to make clear our position here, and to suggest what we ought to do.

"Your grandparents are still alive in Suffolk, and your Aunt Maude is in this place—" He consulted his papers with a frown. "California? On the west coast of America?"

"I don't know. Papa talked about his sister, but only of his memories, the things they did together as children. He hadn't heard from her in years. We only know from an occasional letter from my grandmother, Lady Stuart-Brice, that Maudie married and went to America. She's never written to us."

"Well, getting a letter halfway round the world is a formidable task. Quite possibly she's written missives that never arrived, as happens so often. Your father wanted you to go to Maude, and I think that's what you ought to do."

Numbly, I nodded. "I suppose so."

"I'll make arrangements for your passage on the earliest ship. It will take a short time to dispose of the household goods and see that you're ready to travel. In the meantime, I believe there may be a ship leaving sooner that might get a letter to your aunt to tell her of your circumstances and your plans. If you could get off a message to her at once, I'll see that it's sent on its way. And you shall follow after it as quickly as we can arrange it."

How did I compose a letter to an aunt we did not know, to tell her that not one but four orphans were about to descend upon her? The only good thing about having to do it was that it distracted me somewhat from the other activity in the house—the house that I had regarded as a prison and now knew had been a sanctuary.

I knew a good bit about Aunt Maude as a child. She had been two years younger than Papa, and they had been close friends, she forever getting into mischief and Papa just as frequently rescuing her.

It was perhaps not altogether an altruistic attitude on his part, although he did love his sister. But as he was the older, he was expected to "know better" about everything, and to keep Maudie out of trouble. When she was caught out, both of them were punished by stern Lord Stuart-Brice, who had quite definite ideas about how children should behave.

Even with Papa's clever intervention, they suffered many a day locked in their respective rooms, missed many a meal, and were thrashed from time to time with a willow switch, or even, when their misdeeds had been particularly wicked, beaten with Lord Stuart-Brice's cane.

There was no denying that Papa and Maude had sometimes merited their punishment. They waded in forbidden muddy ponds, walked the parapet of the old wing at Willows Hall (and since they didn't fall and break their necks, they were soundly whipped) and rode dangerous horses after many warnings to stay out of the stables unless accompanied by a groom.

Aunt Maudie had also displayed a deplorable tendency toward joking pranks. Since Lord Stuart-Brice had no sense of humor whatsoever, the results were often disastrous. One morning he broke his breakfast "boiled" egg and had it slither sickeningly down his new buff kerseymere trousers; only the fact that moments later he was called to the stables to deal with a seriously injured groom saved the children from violence. By the time Lord Stuart-Brice got around to dealing with his offspring, his temper had somewhat cooled; they were simply sent to bed supperless and confined to their rooms for all the following day with nothing but bread and milk to eat.

And the time that young Maudie lost a particularly

valuable snuffbox, of which my grandfather was an avid collector (it was not really lost, Papa confided, for they knew where it was—Maudie had dropped it into the moat as she wrestled Papa for it), Papa had been accused of taking it. His denial meant nothing; perhaps he should have put the blame off onto Maudie where it properly belonged. But she was so little, he told us, and her chubby legs were too tender for willow switches; Papa took the switching in her place.

But all those things had happened years ago, before I was born. Papa had a picture of his sister, painted when she was sixteen—a lovely, dark-haired girl in a pink dress—and I thought she must have been a lighthearted, charming person. Only what was she like, now? She had a family of her own, and a husband. The husband might object to us, even if Maudie did not. We knew nothing about him save his name—Henry Allington Graham.

How did one write to an aunt one did not know? Particularly with such unwelcome news—the death of a brother, the impending arrival of his orphaned children upon her doorstep.

Caro sat beside me, trying to help, and no doubt as much in need as I of some diversion from the tasks being carried out in Papa's room.

"Remind her of the affection Papa had for her, and how he spoke her name—" Caro's voice broke, but she quickly recovered. "Surely she remembers Papa with that same affection, and she will take us in."

And so, with a good deal of crossing out and writing over, which of course necessitated an entire rewriting of the finished copy, we produced between us a letter to be sent.

We did not want it to sound cold or too formal, nor yet to presume an intimacy that did not exist. Caro read it aloud with what satisfaction we could muster at this stage of things. " 'Papa has told us all about you and we feel that it is only right that we should do as he wished, and rely upon you for guidance and support.' Surely that will do? Oh, India, how are we going to break it to the twins—that Papa is gone? I cannot bear to tell them!"

In the end we did it together, with considerable difficulty. All in all, that day was the most dreadful of my life, and when at the end of it I fell into bed, I was grateful for the exhaustion which made it possible to sleep.

It did not occur to us, initially, that we would go to our relatives without funds of our own for keeping us. That humiliating fact came into focus only after the letter had gone off to Aunt Maude Stuart-Brice in California.

Only a little over twenty-four hours after Papa's death, the servants were already preparing to close the house. I had given no thought as to what would become of it, leaving that in the capable hands of my father's friend. Sir Roland came to us in the sewing room, where Caro and I were sorting out garments to be packed or to be given away. We knew nothing of the climate in California, nor of the type of life we would be expected to lead, which did not aid us in making decisions.

"I expect everything we have is hopelessly out of fashion," Caro said, but listlessly, as if the matter were of no great importance. "We will probably be a disgrace to Aunt Maude. Perhaps the thing to do would be to take only a few things, and have new ones made when we reach California. It would save a good deal of work."

I turned then and saw Sir Roland in the doorway, his face even more grave than it had been when he left us the previous day, if that were possible.

"Come in, sir. Pray sit down, and Rajindra shall bring you something to drink—" I tried to make myself think, to be hospitable, to maintain the normal courtesies.

"I think we should all sit down, India," he said. "The letter has gone off to your aunt, and with any sort of luck it will arrive before you do. However, getting you off isn't the only problem we have."

The room was very warm, and I brushed a strand of hair back from my face. I waited wearily to learn what the problem was.

"I have spent the morning going over your father's affairs, and I'm afraid the news isn't as good as I had hoped." He cleared his throat, then inhaled as if gathering his resolution to do an unpleasant task, as indeed it was. "There is almost nothing in the way of money. I had thought the house, at least, could be sold for enough to keep the four of you for some time. But I've just learned that it is heavily mortgaged—your father borrowed against the value of it only recently, and selling it for anything like what it's worth still won't return much to you, scarcely more than enough to secure your passage to California. That, of course, I am happy to advance to you now, so that you may lose no time in reaching your family, where you belong. I had also thought there were some pieces of jewelry, things that belonged to your mother, but I find that those, too, have been sold. Rajindra says they have been gone from the safe for quite a long time. And when I investigated the trust Judson drew upon from Lord Stuart-Brice, I learned that his allowance ends upon his death. No provision whatever has been made for your father's dependents."

We stared at him stupidly. "Allowance?" I said after a moment. "But Papa earned his own way, did he not? There is surely money in the bank?"

He shook his head. "Very little, I'm afraid. I believe Judson was consolidating his holdings in anticipation of a business venture with Mr. Morrisey, but the fact of the matter is that he hadn't consummated the business. And no one quite seems to know what he did with the monies he raised; certainly they are not in any bank account of which I've been able to find a record. He did leave a will, with his estate to be divided between the four of you, and I myself was designated to administer the estate. However, so far as I can determine, there is precious little estate to administer. The bulk of your father's funds came from the remittance from England, and that is now at an end."

He talked on for some time, but it was only the word *remittance* that truly registered. The phrase was vaguely familiar, and I repeated it, parrotlike. "Remittance? Are you saying Papa was a remittance man? Surely that term is applied to one who has left his homeland in disgrace and is paid for staying away so as not to disgrace the family as well?"

"Anyone who is supported on remittances sent from home would be so called. There is no reason to assume that the recipient left home in disgrace," Sir Roland said, but I knew at once that he was smoothing over something he did not want to discuss. It was there in his tone of voice and in the way his eyes suddenly refused to meet mine. "At any rate, he received a quarterly stipend, and it seems that this is what primarily supported this household, for it was a generous one, as befitting the only son of an English lord. I will correspond with your grandfather, of course, in the hope that he will be prepared to assume your support. But we cannot expect him to make such arrangements, should he desire to do so, soon enough to take care of your immediate needs."

He went on at some length, explaining and asking if we understood. I merely nodded, although most of the time I had no idea what he was talking about. I don't think Caro even nodded. The only time she moved was to rise for fresh handkerchiefs when those she had were completely sodden.

Papa, a *remittance man?* It was impossible to imagine Papa leaving home in disgrace.

But it would explain a lot of things, things I had given little thought to until now. Our hasty departure from Willows Hall at dawn, the fact that we were seen off only by the servants, with neither of my grandparents showing up to say farewell although they were both early risers by nature. It would explain why there were no letters from any of Papa's family except for those few from Lady Stuart-Brice which had twice come at Christmas time.

It would explain that longing in Papa's voice when he talked about home. A longing he could never assuage because he knew he could never, at least as long as Lord Stuart-Brice was alive, return to England?

And again the thought: It was impossible that Papa

should have been banished from England. I could imagine nothing he could have done to warrant such banishment.

It was not for some time that it occurred to me that some of the money that ought to have been in the bank and was not might have been spent on the maharani's black pearls.

When it did, I went immediately to the safe and removed them, letting them spill out across my hand where they caught the light with a soft, shimmering radiance. Should I turn them over to Sir Roland? Suggest that they might be sold to pay our expenses?

I had no real idea of the value of the pearls. They might or might not be worth enough to support us for a long time.

Papa had said they were a dowry, and my romantic readings had impressed upon me the importance of a good marriage. Surely, if I were to make such a good marriage, would I not then be in a position to see to the welfare of Caro and the twins?

I had little time to consider the matter. It was either tell Sir Roland at once or remain silent about the pearls.

I remained silent.

Partly this was because I thought Papa's family would surely see that we were provided for. And partly, perhaps, it was that I could not bear to hand the pearls over to anyone to be sold for cold cash for such things as routine living expenses. At a later time I would question my own selfishness in this matter, but at that moment I acted upon impulse. I slipped the pearls back into their pouch and hid them in my room. When we packed to leave Willows, they were secreted upon my person, as they had been ever since.

3

Willows was a large household, and there was a great deal of work to be done before it could be closed or put up for sale. Rajindra was invaluable; he helped me make the decisions that had to be made, involving disposal of all sorts of things. Mama's belongings were still in the bedroom that had been closed upon her death. Caro and I went through them, saving what we could; Caro was about the size Mama had been, but very few of her dresses were suitable for a fifteen-year-old girl. There were more garments suitable to the bedroom than to public appearance, for Mama had been almost a complete invalid for years before her death. There remained some evening gowns from the earlier, better days, but I would have blushed to wear them even had they accommodated themselves to my taller, slimmer figure. For Caro they were completely out of the question.

"Dreary-looking wretches we're going to be," Caro commented, "in the sort of thing we have of our own to take with us. Neither of us has a single really exciting gown to our name."

"No. But no one will expect us to be modish, coming as we do from India. Sir Roland is quite right about the jewelry; there's nothing left except a few trinkets. It's hard to believe Papa would have sold those things—the diamond brooch, for instance. Yet it isn't here."

"I'd like the cloisonné bracelet," Caro said, "unless you want it, India." And then she stared at me over the small collection of keepsakes, her eyes suddenly brimming.

"What difference does it make what happens to these things? How can we stand here dividing up bracelets and rings when Mama is gone, and Papa is dead, too? What else matters?"

I had been feeling the same way myself, but my response came out of a native common sense. "What matters is that we are still living, and will have to make the best of it, for the twins' sake if not for our own. Everything in this house must be disposed of, and we'll take with us only what we can conveniently carry. So we must sort it out, for all that it's a painful task to do it. Sir Roland said to limit ourselves to one trunk apiece, and a small satchel for the things we'll need aboard ship, so we'll have to leave most of it behind."

Passage was booked for us aboard the *Essex*, a sturdy vessel under the command of a Captain Spacy, who was known to Sir Roland to be trustworthy. There were few ships leaving Calcutta which would reach North America, but the *Essex* was bound for the city of Los Angeles to pick up a cargo of hides destined for England.

"It's a British ship," Sir Roland said. "Which will leave my mind more at ease about you. There are a few American ships, but the masters as well as the crews of those vessels tend to be a surly, rough lot. At least on Captain Spacy's vessel I can be certain you will not be molested."

"Why should we be molested?" Caro asked innocently.

Sir Roland shook his head. "I knew that Judson kept his children sheltered from the world, and for the most part I agreed with him that the protection was necessary. But perhaps it would have been wiser to include in your education some information about the dangers young ladies are subjected to when they leave home and family to travel, especially aboard a ship. Sailors are a rough lot; it takes a good captain to keep them under control on a long voyage when there are young ladies aboard. Indeed, many captains would not even consider taking females with them, for whatever price."

"Why? What would they do to us?" Caro was not alarmed, but rather intrigued at the prospects of a journey

38

among strangers, even sailors. "We've no money, so they couldn't rob us. So what did you mean about being molested?"

But Sir Roland at that point, despite his recently stated belief that our education had been neglected in some areas, refused to be drawn out about the particulars. He reiterated the statement that it was his concern to see that we arrived safely on the doorstep of our Aunt Maude, and that he had done his best to that end. He would, of course, deliver us to the docks himself.

We were leaving Willows in deep grief, but there was no denying that the moment we passed through the gates in Sir Roland's carriage a certain excitement began to be generated within us all. The twins bounced on the seat and peered out at the surrounding traffic, never having seen so much activity in their lives as on the streets of Calcutta.

Caro and I were more decorous, but we, too, gazed avidly upon the throngs of people, the shops and carts and carriages and horses, and then upon the ships. The noise and confusion, even the smells, were exciting.

I retained a vague memory of the ship upon which we had sailed from England all those years ago; it had seemed to be huge, far larger than anything I saw at the wharves today. Yet that must be because I had then been so much smaller, I thought. The *Essex* was certainly safe or Sir Roland would never have entrusted us aboard.

The sailors who hauled our possessions up the gangplank were English sailors, the first English males, outside of Papa's older friends, whom we had ever seen. They looked at us with curiosity, and I must admit the interest was mutual. Caro brightened perceptibly and spoke to me in an undertone.

"They don't look any older than we are, India! Just think, there will be someone our own age to talk to during the voyage."

Behind us, Sir Roland, with a twin by each hand, had overheard. "I am certain that Captain Spacy will see to it that his men do nothing to annoy his passengers," he said dryly.

Caro made no response to that, but there was a becoming color in her cheeks and the look she gave me made it clear that being annoyed by the sailors she considered to be the least of her problems.

"Ah, there is Captain Spacy now," Sir Roland said with satisfaction.

I glanced up to see a man of middle years with grizzled hair, a weather-beaten face, and a slight paunch. He was in conversation with two other men, both of them much younger, and we could not help overhearing their words.

The taller of the two men was dark, well dressed, and extremely handsome. For all my inexperience with young men, I knew at once that his appearance was quite exceptional, except for the fact that he was at the moment irate about something.

"But I tell you it's imperative that I book passage on this ship! There isn't another scheduled to sail for California for months!"

"I've already informed you, Mr. Millay," Captain Spacy said evenly, "that the last cabin has just been given over to Mr. Peltier, here." He gestured with a broad, tanned hand at the second of the two men, and I took time for a better look at him, since we did not wish to intrude before their business had been settled.

At first glance, Mr. Peltier was less imposing, for he lacked several inches of Mr. Millay's height; his fair-haired looks were nothing out of the ordinary, although his features were pleasant enough.

"I'll pay you double what you've given over for your passage," the darker man said. There was an air of authority about him that almost compelled one to give in to his wishes.

Mr. Peltier, however, regarded him calmly. "You might pay me triple without gaining my berth, sir. I have every intention of going to California on this ship." The pleasant look remained about his mouth, which, now that I exam-

40

ined him more closely, appeared well shaped, attractive, and surprisingly firm.

Caro was watching them both, her lips slightly parted. The young men who had carried up our luggage were sailors, and had intrigued her interest. These men, however, were older and quite obviously gentlemen.

"Surely on a ship the size of this one, space can be made for one more individual," Mr. Millay insisted.

"Mine is a cargo ship, gentlemen," the captain stated. "We can accommodate only a few passengers, and those we accept first come first served. I'm afraid I cannot help you, Mr. Millay, unless Mr. Peltier should choose to share his cabin with you. He has paid for the entire cabin, as he carries a good quantity of personal belongings with him and wishes his privacy. Possibly space could be found for enough of his baggage, however, to leave the second berth available for you, sir. It is a matter you will have to settle between yourselves."

It was obvious that begging was not Mr. Millay's usual style, but he controlled himself and assumed a conciliatory manner. "I should be quite happy to take upon myself the expense of the accommodations, if you would be so good as to share them, sir," he said.

The captain had turned away, spying us and moving in our direction, but my attention remained with young Mr. Peltier; it would undoubtedly make our voyage far more interesting to share it with these young men. They did not fall into the category of crew, so presumably the captain would not prevent our becoming acquainted with them.

Mr. Peltier, however, was not to be won over. "I'm sorry, Mr. Millay. I require the entire cabin for my own use. I cannot possibly share it."

He walked away, leaving Mr. Millay with an angry, flushed face.

Captain Spacy put out a hand. "Ah, Sir Roland Trask, I believe. And these are the last of our passengers, I take it?" His keen gaze swept across us, and it was easy to believe that Sir Roland had been correct in saying that ships' captains preferred not to carry females. He was

41

courteous, as befitted a man in his position toward Sir Roland, but there was certainly no joy in our presence.

"Quite so," Sir Roland said, and nudged us forward.

There was no business to transact, since our passages had already been arranged and paid for. Captain Spacy beckoned one of the young sailors and turned us over to him, for the captain himself was busy with the loading of his ship; we would sail with the tide, only a few hours away.

Needless to say, Caro and the twins had no memories of shipboard, and were interested and entranced by everything we saw. Caro didn't even wrinkle her nose, as I did, when we were introduced to the quarters that would be our home for the months of our journey.

"Best quarters on the ship," the sailor said. His eyes rested boldly upon us, lingering longest on Caro. "Except for the captain's, o' course."

There were four bunks that scarcely looked large enough to accommodate an adult-sized person. But that, our guide informed us, was deliberate.

"In foul weather, makes it easier to brace yourself, hang on, like. I'm to bring along your small bags; the rest will go in the hold. I'll be back directly with 'em."

Caro gazed after him. "He was rather good-looking, wasn't he?"

"He was bold to the point of being rude," I said. "Caro, I'm as avid as you for company, and especially that of someone our own age. But Sir Roland is right. I think one does not make friends with common sailors, especially those who lack even the rudiments of good breeding."

She wrinkled her pert nose. "Oh, pooh! India, you're a stick-in-the-mud! The poor boy can't help it that he wasn't reared as we were. And why are we so high and mighty? We're penniless, aren't we? And may well be forced to grub for our own living if Aunt Maude decides not to take us in."

"And why would she decide that? We're her only brother's children. She'll accept us as he would have done

42

her children, had our positions been reversed," I said with a conviction I did not quite feel. "Here, you two are half monkey, anyway, so you might as well sleep in the upper bunks. Brice, take that one over Caro, and Bethany can have the one over mine."

We stayed below only long enough to stow away our meager belongings. We were all of us eager to go back on deck, the twins to observe anything and everything to do with loading a ship and getting it under way, Caro and I simply to thank Sir Roland and tell him good-bye, and at the same time to meet our fellow travelers.

Sir Roland and the captain had taken the time to share a glass of brandy; I could smell it when Sir Roland bent to brush his lips across my cheek.

"Good-bye, dear girl. I trust that you will have a safe journey, and that your aunt will be in good health and you will find yourselves in good hands. And you, miss." He turned to Caro with a rueful smile. "I suspect a warning is in order. Your sister will observe the proprieties, and I urge you to follow her example. There will be suitable young people aplenty, I'm sure, when you reach California and have the benefit of your aunt's guidance."

He turned again, this time to rest a hand upon the shoulder of each of the twins. "And you two, mind what India says, and don't fall overboard!"

I was grateful to Sir Roland for all he had done for us, for indeed I would not have known how to manage on my own. But I was glad, too, when he had gone—when we were on our own, now that our voyage was about to commence.

We knew that it would be a long and arduous journey, for we must cross the entire breadth of the Pacific Ocean. Even with the best of weather and good luck, we would be months at sea. Yet it was an adventure, and we were eager to meet the people with whom we would share it.

"I wish we had kept out something prettier to wear," Caro said, fixing a critical eye upon my plain gray cashmere. "I wonder if both those gentlemen obtained a passage, those two who were discussing it with the captain when we came aboard."

But we were destined to be disappointed, for the only other passengers who also appeared at the captain's table for our first meal aboard were an older couple whose name was Forsman, whose apparel was certainly as dowdy as ours.

Captain Spacy introduced us to one another, gruffly, as a chore to be gotten over. He was not comfortable with his passengers; he would be courteous, but not friendly.

The Forsmans, it appeared, were missionaries bound for California to see their daughter who had married, incomprehensibly and to their horror, a Catholic.

"Heathen country, it is," Mr. Forsman informed us. "All those Indians—not the sort we have here, of course, but regular savages—and then there are the Mexicans, a different sort of Indians, and the Spanish who've intermarried with some of the Mexicans—and the entire lot of them Catholic! Queer sort of place it must be, scarcely a Christian to be found!"

Caro turned her head, startled. "But the Catholics are Christian, surely!"

Mr. Forsman fixed her with bright blue eyes that held a fanatic's zeal. "Don't you believe it! 'Infallible' pope! As if any man is infallible! Oh, my, the things that have been done in the name of the Catholic church! No, no, disabuse yourself of the notion that you are traveling to a Christian country! I trust that *you* have Christian family there!"

"Yes, of course," I murmured, with an admonitory glance at my sister.

"Of course," Caro echoed, and addressed herself to her food, which was tolerably good. We had been warned that once we set off across the Pacific Ocean our fare would become less varied and appetizing, but while we were able to take on fresh provender the *Essex* served the best.

"And the young gentlemen," Mrs. Forsman said, leaning forward to address Captain Spacy. "Are they not joining us for dinner?"

She was a short, round person who might almost have been a twin to her husband, so alike they were with their wreaths of white hair and their bright blue eyes.

"We have no other passengers," Captain Spacy said shortly.

Mrs. Forsman's mouth formed an *O* of surprise, and I'm sure Caro felt the same inner lurch of disappointment that I did. "But there were two young gentlemen, were there not? One had booked passage and the other wished to share his quarters. A Mr. Peltier and a Mr. Millay, surely?"

"Mr. Peltier had booked passage." It was a grudging admission from a man who clearly did not enjoy small talk. "He is not on board, however."

"No? Why ever not? Did he change his mind at the last minute?"

Captain Spacy had cool gray eyes under tufted gray brows. He stared directly at the lady. "Mr. Peltier did not see fit to inform me of his state of mind. He simply did not board before we sailed, madam."

She swept the assembled group with her look of consternation. "But how dreadful! You mean you did not wait for him, after he'd paid his fare?"

Color mottled the captain's face, faintly visible through his tan. "A ship sails with the tide, madam. There can be no waiting for tardy passengers. Perhaps he will make an effort to travel after us. I learned just before sailing that a sister ship follows us in a matter of a few weeks. That, however, is up to Mr. Peltier." He bit down hard on a crust of bread, and I had the impression that he had concluded his remarks on the subject.

"What a shame," Caro murmured beside me. "I thought Mr. Peltier was quite dashing, didn't you, India?"

Mrs. Forsman, while managing to eat her share, continued to chatter. "But what a shame! Such a nice young man he appeared, and now he's simply lost his passage money! Was he going to Los Angeles, or on to Monterey like the rest of us?"

For a moment I thought the captain would not answer,

or that he would point out that Mr. Peltier's business was none of *hers*. Then he said gruffly, "His destination was Monterey, madam."

"And the other young man, Mr. Millay, he missed out, too? When he might have had Mr. Peltier's stateroom had he known Mr. Peltier would not appear?"

"But Mr. Millay was on deck just before we sailed," Brice popped up. Papa had usually joined us for dinner, and even the twins had always felt free to interject their own comments into adult conversation. Before the voyage was over, Mrs. Forsman would make her somewhat acidulous comments upon that, but tonight, when he had information, she turned to him eagerly.

"Did he come with us in Mr. Peltier's stead, then?" she demanded, ignoring the deepening color in our captain's complexion.

"Not at all, madam. Mr. Peltier had paid for his quarters, his belongings are aboard, and it is possible that he may arrange to catch up with us at Canton or even, conceivably, at the Sandwich Islands. I could not, therefore, in good conscience allow anyone else the use of the cabin he had booked. And that, Mrs. Forsman, is what I told Mr. Millay." There was a finality in his tone that brooked no further questions on the subject; even Mrs. Forsman finally grasped *that*.

So neither of the so promising young men was aboard after all! Our disappointment was great, but we were allowed little time to brood over it, for Mrs. Forsman turned to us. "So young to be traveling alone, and so far. Do you leave your parents behind, or perhaps you go to join them?"

"Our parents are no longer living," I said with a reminding stab of emotion. "We go to join our aunt in Monterey."

"Oh, how sad for you! But marvelous that you have relatives to take you in. It can be a real tragedy to be left alone so young, particularly if one is without a fortune of one's own." She looked hopefully at me, waiting for a report on my finances.

46

I felt a warmth in my cheeks that ought to have warned her she was treading on someone else's ground. I had no experience in handling such inquisitiveness, but I had no intention of making all known to casual fellow travelers. "It is such a short time since Papa died that it is difficult to talk about it," I said.

I lowered my eyes, but not before I intercepted a glance of approval from Captain Spacy, who was attacking his food as if it were alive and needed slaying.

"India," Brice said eagerly from his place across the table, "one of the sailors is going to teach me to braid ropes."

"Not braid," Bethany corrected. "He said *splice*. I'm going to learn, too."

"You can't. You're a girl."

This challenge had been flung at her many times, and somehow Brice never seemed to learn that it did not deter her in the least. In fact, I was certain that my younger sister tackled many things simply *because* she was a girl.

"I shall," Bethany said with a serene confidence, so that everyone except Mrs. Forsman had to smile.

Mrs. Forsman kept a tenacious grip on her efforts to prise information from us. "What did your poor unfortunate Papa do, Miss Stuart? Before he died, of course?"

"He never made it a point to discuss his business with us at home; Mama said it wasn't something ladies needed to be aware of," I said, and again noticed that the captain's lips twitched.

And so it went; Mrs. Forsman did her best to learn things that were none of her business, and we resisted giving information. Indeed, it was to become a game that lasted the length of our voyage, for she was never rebuffed sufficiently so that she stopped trying.

Caro and I took turns frustrating the poor lady in her quest for knowledge about ourselves. It was Caro who managed the final *coup* that evening, although it was not a verbal one.

Mrs. Forsman had leaned toward her, oozing sympathy, to pat Caro's hand. "What a shame, such pretty things you are. But how difficult to make good marriages, perhaps, if there are no dowries?"

Caro moved her hand, and in so doing somehow managed to upset the glass beside her. Its contents were emptied into the ample lady's lap, causing her to gasp in consternation and leap at once to her feet.

Mrs. Forsman's words were swallowed up in her husband's concern; he would immediately take her off to their cabin to remedy the damage.

Captain Spacy regarded us for a long moment in silence, then grunted. "I think you scored one point, Miss Caroline," he said, and rose from the table. "And it is time I returned to my duties."

Brice swiveled to look up at Caro. "Did you do that on purpose? Empty your glass in her lap?"

"Of course not. What a wicked thing that would be to do," Caro said, and immediately spoiled the effect of her words by giggling.

"What did Captain Spacy mean, that Caro scored a point? Is there a game?" Brice wanted to know.

"A game," I decided. It would give us something to do on what could only be a tedious journey. "If Mrs. Forsman learns anything about us, she gets the point. If we thwart her attempt, *we* get it."

It was soon evident that there was no subject so sacred that Mrs. Forsman would hesitate to delve into it. We sought to fend her off with words, but several times during the voyage she was distracted from her questioning by an act of desperation on our part. Once a pudding was sent skidding in her direction, which also necessitated a change of clothing, and once Brice stepped upon her foot with sufficient force so that the lady limped for several days.

Yet with all this, Mrs. Forsman remained undaunted until the end.

Captain Spacy, whom we saw only at the dinner table for the most part, did his best to look after us. However, he proved less agile with his tongue than we, and I could tell that it pleased him when we bested our adversary.

We had wondered if we might be plagued by illness, for it was common knowledge that the motion of the sea could have a disturbing effect upon the stomachs of land-lubbers. No such sickness occured, however; not even Mrs. Forsman succumbed to an indisposition which might have provided the rest of us some relief from her tongue.

The early part of our voyage, when we were sailing through the Bay of Bengal and into the South China Sea, was relatively interesting, for we touched at several ports and there were new people and activities to observe. In Canton we were delayed interminably as we awaited important documents to be delivered by an official of the company that owned the ship line. Captain Spacy fumed and sputtered impotently until the documents were handed over. His relief at being finally allowed to continue was matched by our own.

Once we headed straight out across the open sea, however, for the Sandwich Islands, the days assumed a sameness and a monotony worse than anything we had endured at Willows. For at home we had had books, and music, and Papa to entertain us. On board the *Essex*, we had only ourselves.

There were sailors, of course. But we soon learned that they had been given their orders. When Caro tried repeatedly to engage a young fellow called Jake in conversation, he was forced to tell her.

"I'd like to talk to you, miss, but captain's orders is, stay away from the passengers, especially the young ladies. It's worth my skin to be caught out, miss."

For a time Caro raged about it to me. "What harm is there in our talking to the sailors? We're going to be on this wretched ship for months! How will we pass the time if we can't talk to anyone?"

"No doubt how we will pass the time is exactly what Captain Spacy is concerned about," I said, sighing. "Sir Roland warned us. Maybe Mr. Peltier will join us before the voyage is over, and surely the captain can't keep us from talking to *him,* should Mr. Peltier seek our company."

"He didn't catch up in Canton, which was the last likely place. So how would he get to the Sandwich Islands ahead of us?"

"The sister ship Captain Spacy spoke of might gain on us, if they don't stop in so many ports or for so long, especially since we ourselves were delayed," I said, but really I had little hope of it.

Of the voyage itself, the less said the better. Once away from land, the food became as uninteresting as the journey itself. Brice loved simply watching the sea, and several times he was brought down from the rigging by a sailor who secretly sympathized with him and did not report it to the captain.

The rest of us read the few books we had (Mrs. Forsman had only a Bible, so we did not even trade off with our fellow passengers for variety). We walked the deck for exercise, and certainly Caro and I watched the crew and wished that we might talk to at least a few of them.

At the Sandwich Islands the last hope that we might be joined by our missing passenger was abandoned. The *Durham,* sister ship to the *Essex,* had sailed only two days before our arrival in port, having indeed gotten ahead of us during our delay at Canton. A customs official confirmed that both Sherard Millay and Nathan Peltier had been on board, the latter recovering from injuries that resulted from being set upon by thieves. So we knew at last why Mr. Peltier had not come on board before the *Essex* sailed from Calcutta, and that both young gentlemen were now ahead of us on the journey to California.

We would go on the rest of the way to our destination with only the Forsmans for company, and by this time we were all thoroughly sick of both of them. From Mr. Forsman we got a sermon at each meal (in addition to grace, which was so lengthy Bethany said even God must be tired of the sound of his voice); from his wife the probing questions, the motherly concern our own mother had never displayed in such lavish proportions, and of which we appreciated nothing.

But at least we approached the end of our travels, for

the shores of California were sighted and once more our spirits rose; there was something new to think about.

We were not allowed to leave the ship at Los Angeles, although we were in the harbor for several days while our cargo was unloaded and a new one taken on. The smell of it prompted us all to attempt to breathe through our mouths, and Brice was the one who asked.

"What is it? It *stinks*!"

"Hides," the first mate told us. (He was an older man, and presumably safe for us to talk to; at least he had always answered all the twins' questions, and never announced that he was forbidden to be friendly.) "Lots of cattle in California, and hides worth two dollars apiece here, more than that once they've reached England and can be made into leather goods."

"How much is a dollar?" Brice wanted to know, and then became totally confused by the relationship of dollars to the familiar pound.

And then at last we left Los Angeles and moved on to our final destination.

We dropped anchor in Monterey Bay on the twenty-fifth of August, 1842. And at last we were allowed into the boat going ashore, with the promise that our luggage would follow within the hour. I allowed my fingers to close over the lump beneath my skirts that was the maharani's black pearls, and I wondered what our fate would be on this strange, unfamiliar soil.

4

Captain Spacy, of course, was much too busy to bother with us. Now that we were parting company, it was deemed safe to assign us to the company of the sailor Jake.

Monterey was much smaller than I had somehow anticipated, for it was the capital of California, and I had thought to see something on the order of Calcutta. By comparison Monterey was but a village, yet my heart warmed at the sight of it.

The bay was only a gentle indentation in the shoreline, relatively unprotected, but the water was a jeweled blue reflecting the sky overhead, and we landed on firm, clean sand. No tropic land, this, for the air from off the sea was refreshingly cool, combining with the sun to create a most pleasant climate.

"That there's the Presidio," Jake said, pointing. We turned our heads to look at the sizeable walled enclosure where there were men, animals, and buildings of the same material as the walls. "That's a Spanish word, means *fort*. The military runs the place."

"Have you been here before?" Bethany asked, tipping up her small face with its halo of dark curls.

"No. But the first mate has, he told us about it. Everybody speaks Spanish here, or one o' them Indian tongues. Can't understand a word o' it."

We were walking across the expanse of beach, leaving footprints in the damp sand; Brice had dropped to his knees to dig into it in delight, and we paused to wait for him. To feel solid ground after weeks of rolling decks made us feel almost drunk, as if we had to learn to walk all over again.

Caro regarded the sailor with alarm. "You mean no one speaks English?"

"Only Spanish," Jake said. "That's what the first mate says."

"Aunt Maude will speak English," I told them. "And her husband, he's English, too. For the rest, no doubt it is possible to learn to speak their language."

"We already know one word," Brice said. He was heaping up sand into a mound around his feet. "*Presidio.* Fort. Learning Spanish will be easy, won't it, India?"

"There's no one here to meet us," Caro said. We stood for a few minutes, looking up into the town.

The buildings were quite different from anything we had ever seen before, even in illustrated books. They were built of *adobe* (our second Spanish word) which was, Jake informed us with his secondhand knowledge, simply brick made from mud, which was then whitewashed so that the newer buildings gleamed in the sunlight. The roofs were of red tile which was most attractive, so that our impression of Monterey was at once a pleasant one.

It was situated upon low, rolling hills, with the white sand sweeping off around the curve of bay, then rising to tree-covered slopes. The trees were of a variety unfamiliar to me, and the scent of them gave the air an invigorating tang.

"It's very different from India," Caro said slowly, swinging in a circle so that her skirts formed a pale gray bell and the breeze lifted her fair hair in a sunny halo.

"And from England," I agreed, with a growing sense of excitement. I liked the look of this land; it was open and clean, and the air was fresh and, except for the stink of hides, which we perhaps carried with us, sweet smelling.

After all those years of living in a walled garden, might we not now walk upon this glorious beach? Climb the windswept dunes?

"We shall have to determine where our aunt lives," I

said at last, gathering my wits. "Perhaps"—I addressed our protector—"you might ask where the Grahams live? Henry Allington Graham? He was, I believe, an officer in the British army at the time he and my aunt were married. But I suppose there would not be British officers here?"

"Only Mexican army in Monterey," Jake supplied. "If you'd care to wait, I'll see what I can find out, miss."

We had no objection whatever to being left on the beach. Men came and went from the ship in the small boats, unloading the cargo they had brought for Monterey, taking on more of the smelly hides.

The children had soon whisked off their shoes and stockings and were wading in the edge of the surf; only a horror of what Aunt Maude might do were she to catch us emulating the twins kept Caro and me from joining them.

Still, even without walking in the water, we were enjoying the freedom of movement, for all that we dared not wander too far away. Naturally no one had met us, for it would have been impossible for them to know the exact time of our arrival. But surely, if our letter had arrived, they had made preparations for us.

"India, look!"

Caro's indrawn breath drew me around to where she gazed toward the town, which sprawled beyond the Presidio walls. From the doorway of a large two-story building, which we subsequently learned to be the customhouse, a figure in white shirt and dark trousers had appeared, a figure we recognized even at this distance.

"Mr. Peltier!" Why should it give me such a surge of pleasure, as if Mr. Peltier were someone I knew? "No doubt he's waiting for the *Essex*; his belongings were on board, remember?"

"And he speaks English," Caro said. "It's an odd feeling, to be amongst people who speak another language, even if we haven't met any of them yet. I wonder if it will be difficult to learn Spanish?"

My gaze remained on the man coming toward the

beach. I remembered that he had not been as tall as Mr. Millay, yet now, approaching us with athletic strides, he seemed strong and well proportioned.

He came to within half a dozen yards of us before he spoke. "Good afternoon! You're off the *Essex*, are you not?"

"Yes, that's right. We've only just landed." It made me slightly breathless just speaking to him.

His fair hair blew in the wind. Surprisingly, his eyes were brown, as dark as the twins'. "Is that their boat, just making off?"

"Yes. It will be unloading for hours, I believe."

Caro's mouth curved in a smile. "One of the crewmen has gone to determine where we should be going, or if there's anyone about to meet us. Our aunt is Mrs. Henry Graham. Do you know her, sir?"

He shook his head. "I'm sorry. The only family I know here is the Alvarados, unless—perhaps it's a Graham girl that Ramón is engaged to marry? Is there a daughter, Amalie?"

I had to confess that we did not know the names of the Graham offspring. "We only know there are children, who are probably our ages. We are India and Caroline Stuart, and the children playing there are Brice and Bethany, our brother and sister," I said, feeling very bold at introducing ourselves to a perfect stranger. Yet it seemed only a sensible thing to do, under the circumstances. Jake had disappeared, and I did not think he was very bright, anyway; this man might well be of far more help should he choose to be.

"I'm Nathan Peltier. I was to have traveled with you on the *Essex*, but I missed the sailing and came on the *Durham* a week later. You must have been delayed somewhere, or you'd have gotten here ahead of us."

"We spent over a week in Canton," I confirmed. He had stopped gazing out at the ship and was looking directly into my face. For some reason this produced in me a queer sensation, as if my bones had suddenly turned to liquid. Or perhaps it was only that my limbs, having adjusted to the rise and fall of the sea, must now readjust to firm ground.

"We heard you'd had an accident, and that was why you missed the sailing," Caro chirped. She moved closer to me, and, incidentally, closer to Nathan Peltier. "We hoped it wasn't serious, Mr. Peltier."

He transferred his attention to Caro. "Not as serious as it might have been. I lived."

Brice burrowed through the sand to our feet. "Were you robbed, Mr. Peltier?"

A muscle jumped in the man's cheek. "No, strangely enough, I wasn't. At least I didn't lose anything of value. Look here, surely you aren't to be left standing on the beach until the ship is unloaded. It may be hours, or even until tomorrow, before your baggage is brought ashore. Did you say someone was making enquiries about your relatives?"

"Jake. He's one of the sailors from the *Essex*. He went up that way, toward the Presidio."

"Well, if your relatives were not expecting you just now, it may be some time before word of your arrival reaches them. My friend Ramón Alvarado is up there with a carriage, and whether or not it is your cousin to whom he is engaged, he will surely know your aunt. Monterey is not a large community. The best thing would be for Ramón and I to see that you reach your destination, and arrangements can be made about your belongings later."

I hesitated, for if Aunt Maude had grown to be anything like the parents she had left in England, she might well insist on all the proprieties. Getting into a carriage with two young men to whom we had not been properly introduced would not be among them.

"Oh, India, do let's!" Caro urged. "It will be ever so much easier that way, and if our cousin *is* engaged to Mr. Peltier's friend, why, no one can object to that, surely."

I was not all that sure of it, but seeing a small boat returning from the *Essex* with the Forsmans helped to make up my mind. I had no wish to be standing on the beach when they reached land, for I was quite sure what *their* reaction would be.

"It is very kind of you, sir. It would, indeed, be much easier. We will, of course, have to tell the sailor to whom we were entrusted, so that he knows where we've gone."

"Good. That's settled, then. Come along. No doubt we'll find your Jake at the customshouse—it's where most information is dispensed."

We called to Bethany, who reluctantly put her shoes and stockings back on, and Brice, who carried his, and all climbed the slope toward the town.

"Are those Indians?" Brice wanted to know, indicating two old men who sat against a shady wall watching us. They were dark-skinned and brightly dressed, with broad-brimmed hats decorated in gold and silver threads.

"There are many Indians about, but those two are Spanish gentlemen. I don't suppose any of you speak any Spanish?"

When we shook our heads, Nathan Peltier was reassuring. "It is a small matter. There are enough English-speaking people here now so that both languages are used, and you'll be able to make yourselves understood to almost anyone. Many Americans are coming in, and while their English is a coarser version of our own, it's readily intelligible."

"Are there English people here, too?" Caro wanted to know. "Besides my aunt and uncle, I mean?"

"A few, certainly. I haven't been here long enough to learn a great deal, but there were two English couples at the Alvarados' last night, for dinner and a social evening. It's a leisurely country; there is a good deal of social activity."

Caro looked at me and grinned, appearing younger than her fifteen years. "I do hope we'll be invited to join in some of it. Sea voyages are terribly tedious, aren't they? Unless you're a man, perhaps. Then you can talk to anyone and do as you please."

Mr. Peltier was amused. "Is that how it seems to you, that a man can do anything he likes? Well, I suppose we

57

do have the advantage, most of the time. But think of all the things you get out of doing, because they're considered a man's job—all the hard, dirty, messy things."

"Even those would be a change from being walled up in a garden," Caro said. "Even the grandest garden palls after a time. This is so different, so—sort of wild, and open, and free! Are you going to stay here, Mr. Peltier? To live, I mean?"

I opened my mouth to reprove her, for she sounded exactly like Mrs. Forsman, but our new benefactor was already replying.

"No, I'm only visiting old family friends. Don Esteban was a friend of my father's many years ago in Spain. When I've worn out my welcome—or another ship comes through, going in the right direction—I'll return home."

We had left the beach now and were passing among the inhabitants of Monterey, most of whom regarded us with as much interest as we regarded them. There were very few women, and those were all dark-skinned—Mexican and Indian, our guide told us—but men aplenty. All those bold, dark eyes upon us made me glad that Mr. Peltier was with us, an obvious protector.

"Where is home, sir?" Caro asked, and while I knew I ought to repress her exuberant curiosity, I was as eager as she to hear the answers. Already I was regretting that Mr. Peltier was not to be a permanent resident of Monterey.

"My home is called Eagleton, it's in the north of Essex. My parents are there, and two younger brothers and a little sister, about the age of your Bethany." He smiled down at the bouncing child beside him.

"Essex," I echoed, trying to remember my geography lessons. "Is that anywhere near Suffolk? Aren't both on the east coast of England?"

"That's right. They're adjoining counties. Do you have family in England too, Miss Stuart?"

"Yes. My grandparents are in the family home. It's called Willows Hall. Do you know it?"

"I'm sorry to say I know it only by reputation; it has extensive and beautiful gardens, I believe." A frown creased his forehead. "You are related to the Stuart-Brices, then?"

It established a bond between us at once. We, who had come from Willows Hall, were not-too-distant neighbors of the Peltiers, at Eagleton. Surely nothing here that Aunt Maude could object to. I even formulated a response to Mrs. Forsman, should I be unlucky enough to be on the receiving end of her tongue again: I would say that our families were neighbors in England. No need to admit that they were unacquainted with one another. Let her assume something less than the worst that she would prefer.

We had reached the customshouse, which was full of busy, impatient men, for with the *Durham* preparing to sail and the *Essex* unloading, there must be great activity. Mr. Peltier left us briefly, near the door, to determine what might best be done with us; we saw him speaking to a startlingly handsome young Spaniard, who looked in our direction and smiled.

"Is that the one who's engaged to our cousin? Ramón?" Caro sighed noisily. "Did you ever see anyone so attractive in your life?"

I had to agree that he was, but my mind was on something else. "Isn't it a coincidence, that Mr. Peltier comes from *Essex*, and that was the name of our ship?"

"Well, it's a county in England, isn't it? I suppose the name is common enough. Won't it be fun if there are cousins our own age? And parties to go to? Oh, India, I've so longed to go to parties!"

"Will we get to go, too?" Bethany asked. "Or will we have to wait until we grow up? Why do only grown-ups get to do anything interesting?"

A shout behind us brought us around, our attention on the street, and I stifled a cry. For our Brice, dawdling behind us and engrossed in something in the dirt at his feet, was directly in the pathway of an oncoming horse and rider!

Before the child became aware of his danger, however, a figure moved from among the drifting natives—a tall, dark-haired man whose face and clothes were clearly English; he moved swiftly to snatch Brice out of the way, only moments before the rider would have run him down.

My thanks were already begun when I realized I had seen the rescuer before. He was the Mr. Millay who had attempted to book passage on our ship.

"You'd best be careful about squatting in the street," he said with a severity I took to mean that he, too, had been frightened. "A drunk on a horse is not all that unusual in Monterey; there's too little else to do here."

Brice, who had not had time to be frightened, brushed the dust off his trouser knees. "I'm sorry, sir. I didn't notice him coming, and there's all that music from over there." He gestured toward a building from which issued forth laughter and men who walked none too steadily. "I didn't even hear the horse until it was too late."

"Thank you, sir," I said quietly, and Caro, too, voiced the same words in as grave a tone. We all knew that Brice might easily have been killed.

Mr. Millay looked down upon us with a slightly puzzled frown. "You're quite welcome, I'm sure. I beg your pardon, but surely we've met before? Somewhere other than in Monterey? I've only been here two days, and I couldn't forget having met you here, but surely I remember—"

"On the *Essex*, sir," Caro said, smiling now that our fright was over. "In Calcutta. You were attempting to book passage when we boarded the ship."

His face cleared. "Of course! And you sailed, while I had to wait for the next ship! Only it seems we passed you somehow, and reached California first! Are you alone? Are you in need of assistance?"

"Mr. Peltier is making inquiries for us. His friend, it seems, is engaged to our cousin, and will see that we get to our aunt's house." I gestured to the two young men, so different from one another in coloring, who were approaching across a crowded room.

Was there a flattening of Mr. Millay's voice? "Ah, Peltier. I did not know you were acquainted."

There was no time to make explanations, for the two

60

had reached us. I heard Caro's indrawn breath and felt the urge to laugh; she had thought Mr. Peltier quite the thing, and now, only a few moments later, she was entranced by his companion.

Ramón Jesús Alvarado was in his middle twenties, about the same age as Nathan Peltier. But there all similarity ended. For he was dark-skinned, smiling, and dressed in a fashion that made Peltier, in his simple white shirt and dark trousers, look like a sparrow next to a peacock. Ramón too wore a white shirt open at the throat, but it had a ruffled front. And his jacket and trousers were of a rich bright blue with silver embroidery all over the jacket, the whole topped off by a silver-spangled black hat with a wide brim, and his boots were clearly intended for riding, not walking.

The effect might have been absurd, but somehow it was not. Ramón Jesús Alvarado acknowledged the introductions with a smile that revealed white, even teeth.

"I am so happy to meet you all. My Amalie has told me that there was a letter from cousins in India, but she did not know you would come so soon. It will be my pleasure to see that you reach the Graham *hacienda,* which is called Casa del Mar, which means 'house by the sea.'" His English was delightfully accented but perfectly comprehensible. "I will bring the carriage around for the ladies, if you would care to wait here."

It was only after he had gone that I realized Mr. Peltier and Mr. Millay were regarding one another in a guarded fashion. "I have not been formally introduced to the young ladies," Mr. Millay said.

For a moment it seemed that Mr. Peltier would resist making him known to us now, so I spoke quickly.

"We owe this gentleman thanks. He rescued Brice from being trampled by a horse only a moment ago; my heart is still pounding from the fright it gave me."

"Mr. Sherard Millay," Peltier said reluctantly. "The Misses Stuart. You will excuse us, Millay. The young ladies are tired and eager to join their family, and Ramón comes with the conveyance."

His words barely missed outright rudeness, and Mr. Millay's face flushed. He, however, kept a civil tongue and bowed to each of us. "It was my pleasure to meet you both, and to serve you. I'm sure we will meet again. *Adiós*."

Brice looked after his retreating back. "What is *adiós*? Is that another Spanish word?"

"He's been here two days and already is impressing us with his grasp of the language," Nathan Peltier said dryly. "*Adiós* means good-bye. Ah, here comes Ramón!"

It was the only carriage we had seen; everyone else was either on foot or on horseback. Even we, in our ignorance, knew that the Alvarados must be well-to-do, to possess such equipage.

We were handed in by Mr. Peltier, who then took the seat beside Ramón, and we were off. I caught a glimpse of Mrs. Forsman's astounded face and was glad that the clatter of our horses drowned out whatever it was that she said.

We passed the church that was part of the Presidio, and a cluster of adobe buildings and several frame ones, and then we were out in the country, on a well-used track.

"Is it far?" I asked, leaning forward toward the two men ahead of us.

"A few miles to the north," Ramón said cheerfully. "Amalie will be delighted that you have come in time for the wedding. We are to be married in three weeks, and then she will come to live on El Rancho Hermoso. You must come often to visit her, since not everyone there speaks English, and she will long for her own tongue."

We climbed the hill, and Caro touched my arm so that I looked back. The cargo was being unloaded from the ship at anchor in the sparkling bay, onto the pale crescent of beach that rimmed the harbor. Beyond lay the ocean, far more beautiful now than it had seemed while we crossed it. The people scurrying about were no more than ants, indistinguishable from one another, but I thought that the tall figure in English garb on the steps of the customshouse might be Sherard Millay, looking after us.

There was a breeze off the ocean, smelling cool and fresh and clean. We moved along at a good pace behind the matched bays, and I wondered why Papa had deprived us of the privilege of riding this way, when it was so enjoyable.

And then I settled back to do just that, to enjoy every unfamiliar tree and shrub, to drink in the refreshing air, and to speculate upon what we should find at the conclusion of our journey. At least we knew now that we were expected, and that there was a cousin named Amalie, and my spirits rose as we traveled.

Surely we would be welcomed, with or without any resources of our own. Almost, I forgot my fears.

Almost, but not quite.

5

Casa del Mar was a beautiful house that sat atop one of the rolling hills, with a magnificent view of the serene Pacific. It was not built in the Spanish manner, but in the Tudor style of England, and an attempt had been made to recreate the gardens of England, as well, although I did not recognize many of the profusion of flowers except the roses, and the sand encroached upon what were intended to be lawns.

I watched eagerly for my first glimpse of our new family, ignoring the questions which bombarded us from the twins. A curtain moved in an upstairs window, and a face appeared. Ramon lifted a hand in greeting, and a handkerchief fluttered, and then the curtain fell back into place.

Our driver looked back over his shoulder, laughing. "Amalie will be running down the long stairs to meet us. It is not ladylike, her mama says, but when one is seventeen, one runs to meet one's beloved, no?"

Seventeen. Two years younger than I, and in three weeks my cousin would marry this handsome young man and go to live on his family's ranch, and live happily ever after. Would such a fate be mine, as well, here in this strange and beautiful land?

Nathan Peltier, also seeing the house for the first time, spoke my own thoughts. "It's a lovely house—but it doesn't seem to belong here. The style is not right for California."

Ramón laughed aloud this time. "Ah, you are right,

amigo! The *Calfornios* call this house *La Tontería*, what you would call folly, perhaps, or foolishness. They have given it a Spanish name, but it is an English house, and this is not the climate for that, although since it is close to the sea they have not the need for thick adobe walls which are necessary away from the coast."

He guided the horses off the main track onto a drive of crushed shell, and a slender girl in a pink dress came out of the wide front door and stood waiting for us. "You will see, señoritas, that to enclose one's house with walls, as in the Presidio, is a wise precaution in this country. Not only does it provide for family privacy, but the walls are capable of keeping out invaders. This is a reasonably civilized country, but our government is far away in Mexico City and sometimes I think they forget about us. There are less than eighty soldiers to protect us against whatever forces might move upon us, and they are underpaid and poorly equipped. Often there are deserters; there is little to inspire their loyalty. *Amalie, see what I have brought you!*" The last was a shout to the girl who was coming down the steps, the pink skirts swirling around her ankles.

My first envious thought was that Amalie was beautiful. The second was that Caro was right, we were sadly out of fashion, if her gown was anything to judge by.

Amalie was small and fine-boned, with rich dark eyes and hair and a ready smile. The pink dimity molded small, high breasts and a tiny waist surely unburdened by stays; her feet, in soft kid slippers, were neat and dainty.

"Ramón! I did not expect you! And with all these guests!" Her dark gaze turned to us, prepared to envelop us in the warmth that radiated toward her betrothed. "I have told Teresa to prepare tea in the drawing room, and Carlos will be here in a moment to take your horses."

"These, my love," Ramón said as he swung down and took her hands in his, "are your—how do you say?—your cousins from Calcutta! They have arrived on the ship today, and my friend Nathan called upon me to see that they were delivered to you."

Nathan Peltier handed Caro and me down, and I felt a

65

tremor run through my hand as it rested briefly in his, and then Ramón was making introductions, and my new cousin kissed us all and truly made us feel welcome.

Teresa, a brown-skinned, smiling woman in a loose-fitting red cotton dress, brought us tea in a large, high-ceilinged room with elegant furnishings. English tea—with tiny sandwiches trimmed of their crusts, and scones such as I remembered from my early childhood, and small cakes that tasted doubly good after our limited shipboard fare of the past months.

"No one else is here to welcome you," Amalie apologized. "Papa has gone to Monterey to talk to the governor on business. Hester is visiting a friend for a few days, the little Castro girl, and Mama is taking a nap."

Ramón bit into one of the cakes with obvious relish. "Excellent. I hope you have learned how to instruct a cook in the making of these, my love? And you will never be one of the Californios if you say *nap*. We take the *siesta*."

"Mama," Amalie said positively, "takes a *nap*." They both laughed, and our pretty cousin turned to us. "How strange, that all these years we have been cousins and did not know it! And how sad, that you must lose your own papa before we could come to know one another. Ramón and I are to be married in three weeks, and you must both be members of the wedding party! Ramón's sister Manuela was to have been my maid of honor, but it is only right that a member of my own family have that honor since you are here! My own sister is only ten, and too young to be anything but a flower girl."

"I'm nine," Bethany said around a mouthful of cake. "Can I be a flower girl, too?"

"Of course you shall be! We will all have new dresses, everything will be in the palest of pinks, white gauze over pink satin, and—"

"Stop! Stop!" Ramón commanded. "There will be time to talk about clothes when you are alone. Nathan and I have no wish to hear about them; we will be content with seeing you at your most beautiful. Nathan has consented

66

to stay on and visit with us until the next English ship touches our shores, and who knows, that might be months! We will have a round of fiestas and fandangos, music and dancing! And Nathan, who has already proved adept at learning our dances, will help us entertain the new cousins, no?"

"Of course," Nathan agreed. "I'd be happy to join in your celebrations."

I grew warm at the thought. But Caro leaned toward me when the men were engrossed in a conversation about horses, to whisper for me alone. "Our clothes, India! We have nothing to wear to these parties, nothing like Amalie's!"

I was only too aware of our lack in this matter. But Amalie had mentioned having new dresses made for us all, and I could only trust that Aunt Maude would see to the paying for them. It could prove to be a humiliating business, this part of the penniless cousins.

Ramón selected one more cake and stood up. "It is time we go, my friend. I did not conclude my father's business, and the customshouse will not stay open all night, even with ships in port. No doubt the little cousins are weary and would like to rest and refresh themselves. And we will surely see you all tomorrow evening, when we dine together."

We were both sorry and glad to see them go. It was true, we had been long without rest, and Amalie took it upon herself to play hostess. We were shown about the house, to the kitchen where a smiling Teresa was already preparing for the dinner to be served late that evening. And there was a library with the familiar scent of leather bindings, and a music room with a grand piano finer than the one we had left at Willows, and a private sitting room which was Aunt Maude's. The latter had a heavy, musky scent that I found slightly unpleasant, and the blinds were drawn against the sun which had now dropped toward the sea so that it blazed against Casa del Mar's western windows.

"We had not thought you would arrive so soon,"

Amalie said as we climbed the graceful stairs. "So perhaps the preparations are not quite complete. We have not so large a house as Willows Hall, but we have given you, India, and you, Caro, the room next to mine. Perhaps when I have gone, Caro might move into that, if she likes. And we thought that Bethany might have the smaller room across. And Brice—well," —she laughed down at the boy beside her—"we were running out of space, so we are converting the nursery for him. It is a large room, but rather bare. Furniture is a problem, you see. It must be shipped from Boston, in New England, all the way around South America. Most of what we have here came from England, which took much longer yet, but Mama wanted her own things about her." She shot me a curious glance. "You are old enough to remember Lord and Lady Stuart-Brice, are you not?"

"A little," I murmured. "I was six when we left Willows Hall."

She sighed. "I don't remember them, of course. Mama says she has no intention of ever going home to England. This will be our home forever. Of course I don't mind, now that I'm going to marry Ramón, but I had always wished to see Willows Hall. Is it very beautiful?"

"Yes. If you don't mind drafty floors and corridors in the winter, and untouchable gardens in the summer. Your father's home was in England too, surely?"

"Oh, yes. Although he was in the army for many years and he did not live at home. His health was destroyed by years in the tropics, and then he found that England did not suit, either. He was to have taken on a new post in India, where your papa was, but when the ship was delayed in Los Angeles, he found that he felt much better here than anywhere else he had been. So he resigned from the army and eventually found this place, where he built Casa del Mar. Is it truly like an English house?"

She spoke with the longing of one who does not expect ever to learn at first hand.

"I think so," I told her. "Although my memories of England are almost entirely of Willows Hall itself."

"Ah, of course! You were only six. Here, this is the room we have prepared for you. I hope you will like it."

She threw open a door and ushered us into a massive and somber bedchamber that took me back, at once, to Willows Hall. The walls were paneled in dark wood, which had begun to warp, probably from the dampness of the sea air. Its furnishings were elegant but heavy, with a massive four-poster bed, a carved armoire, and a desk such as might have been appropriate for a prime minister.

The windows had been thrown open, however, to let in sunshine and fresh air, and there was a view of the sea beyond the padded window seat. And there were books. Shelves and shelves of books.

Amalie smiled at my exclamation. "Mama loves books, she always has. And your papa, too? Lonely children often read, do they not? And I think that our parents were rather lonely at Willows Hall—Grandfather Stuart-Brice did not often invite in families with children for them to play with?"

"I don't think he especially liked children at all." Not even his own, I thought, and was amazed to hear my cousin say the words aloud.

"Not even his own, I suspect. Mama's fondest memories are of her brother Judson, not of her father. My own papa is rather reserved, too, but Uncle Judson was an affectionate man, was he not?"

And then, seeing the tears that sprang to my eyes, she put a hand on my arm in contrite apology. "I'm sorry. It is too new a thing, losing your papa, is it not? Come, I will show you the bath. We keep it in the room across the hall, the sewing room, which is most untidy at the moment because Miss Strang is supervising the making of my trousseau. Only three weeks to go, and so much to be done!"

We followed her dutifully across the hall, after pulling Brice inside the window, for he was nearly out upon a roof before we noticed him.

"He will no doubt break his neck," Bethany commented complacently.

"He will learn not to climb on roofs," Caro corrected. "Oh, my, look!"

We all admired the tin bath, which Amalie assured us would be moved to our room whenever we wished to use it; the servants would bring up hot water for it if we gave them sufficient notice.

And then we had to admire, as well, the wedding gown, an exquisite creation of white satin and lace—"brought all the way from England"—which was being fitted onto a likeness of Amalie's slender figure.

"Look at the sleeves," Caro murmured. "I knew we were totally out of fashion with these leg o' muttons. Sleeves have gone small and dainty."

"I don't know if we're in fashion or not," Amalie confessed, holding up for our approval a lavishly embroidered nightshift of softest, sheerest India muslin. "I suspect we are rather behind the times. But Miss Strang is copying these things from Paris creations; she was there two years ago, and she has an excellent eye for style. At any rate, I will be as well dressed as any bride in California."

Caro watched her with envy. "Have you know Ramón long?"

"No, although I've seen him from afar for years. But he's so much older, to him I was only a child, you see. He's nearly twenty-six, and one day Don Esteban will turn over the rancho to him; in fact, Ramón is very nearly in charge of it now. I consider myself most fortunate; Ramón and I fell in love, and our parents were delighted that we had chosen one another. My best friend was married to a man she did not even know, because her father arranged it. He is much older and does not even like to dance, and she is shut up in a great house with no parties and not even her own piano to keep her company."

It was a chilling thought, we all agreed. Amalie was very lucky.

"When are we going to meet Aunt Maude?" Brice demanded, turning his attention from the mannikin which held the wedding gown. I hoped Amalie had not noticed

70

when he stuck a pin into the mannikin's bosom, and I maneuvered to extract it when no one was looking.

"She usually sleeps until about three, but today she hasn't come down yet. I will see if she's awake," Amalie offered.

But then, before she could do so, we heard horses' hooves, and she turned instead toward the stairs. "I think it must be Papa. We'd better tell him you are here."

There was no doubt that Amalie herself had sincerely welcomed us, but from her tone when she spoke now I wondered uneasily if our uncle, Henry Allington Graham, would take a different view of our arrival. We followed her down the stairs, at a far more sedate pace than she had set when she knew Ramón was arriving, and we were at the door when our uncle dismounted.

My unease increased at once, for there was something about Henry Graham, about his bearing and his tall, lean figure that reminded me uncomfortably of someone else I had once known—Lord Stuart-Brice.

His iron-gray hair suggested that he was approaching sixty; far older than I knew Aunt Maude to be. Had it been a love match, I wondered? Or had her marriage, like that of Amalie's friend, been arranged by her father? It was enough to make one shudder, to imagine a husband chosen by Lord Stuart-Brice.

He wore conservative and sober clothing, conceding nothing to either the climate nor the customs of the Californios; he was drab and proper and I knew at once that he did not welcome us at all.

Not that anything he said was discourteous. He greeted us with the correct words, but they were spoken without warmth. "Which of you wrote the letter to my wife?" His eyes were blue, a pale, glacial blue, and seemed to see quite to the inside of one. It was an effort not to squirm before his gaze.

"I did," I admitted. For some reason my voice had gone almost breathless.

"I will speak to you after dinner in the library," Major Graham said. Although he was no longer in the army,

71

and had not been for years, he was still addressed by everyone as *Major*. The cool eyes swung in the direction of the twins. "I trust these children are well trained, that they know how to behave themselves. I do not believe in children being a nuisance."

I felt the heat in my face but replied steadily. "I will try to make sure they are not, sir."

"Amalie, has your mother met our guests yet?"

"No. Papa. She is still sleeping, I believe. Do you think I should wake her?"

"I scarcely think that would be to anyone's advantage," he said, and walked past us through the foyer and into a room at one side.

Amalie's smile reappeared as soon as her father had gone. "Do you want to rest for a time? Or would you like to see the grounds? We have our own private beach where Hester often likes to go. And I, too, sometimes walk there with Ramón."

Since our luggage had not arrived so that we could unpack (and indeed, we were not at all anxious to reveal our outdated dresses in this household), we elected to see the beach.

We started for it decorously enough. However, once we were out of sight of the house, over the edge of the hill, Amalie sat down and removed her shoes and stockings and urged us to do the same.

"It's ever so much nicer in bare feet," she explained. "Mama never comes outside, so she won't know."

We had never in our lives walked barefooted upon a sandy beach. It was truly a marvelous experience, and when Brice waded out into the lazy surf I wished that we, too, might do so.

"Don't you think that Mr. Peltier is exceedingly handsome?" Amalie asked, looking directly at me. "We did not know he was coming, either, but it will be great fun having him here. I believe there is another young gentleman, too, who came on the *Durham*. I don't think Mr. Peltier likes him, for some reason. But I know he's been invited to the fiesta at the Alvarados. Everyone is invited, most especially all the newcomers."

"Us, too?" Caro asked uncertainly.

"Yes, of course! Most especially you! You will have dancing partners aplenty, for every man will want to dance with you. There are far more men that women in California—isn't that a pleasant state of affairs?"

"It would be," I said, "if we knew how to dance. We have never danced."

Amalie's astonishment might have been amusing had it not been caused by so painful a fact. "Never danced? What did you do, then, for entertainment?"

Clearly she was shocked when she learned of the life we had led, behind the protective walls of Willows. "Why, even Papa—" she began, and then stopped, but her meaning was clear. Even Major Graham had not cut his children off from the outside world. "Did you never know why he found it necessary to isolate you in that way?" Amalie asked, unable to conquer her curiosity.

"No, only that he said it was for our own good," Caro told her. But I wondered, with a small, unspoken doubt, if it had anything to do with Papa's having been a remittance man for all those years.

It was difficult for me to conceive of my father doing anything for which he would have been banished from home and country; but now that I was given a glimpse of the way other families lived (aside from what might or might not be true to life in my books) it was even harder to understand why he had kept us as apart from life as if we'd been in a convent.

That he loved us was never in doubt, for there had always been warmth and affection, with time as well as money lavished upon us. If he had, indeed, been protecting us, then what had that protection been from? The evils of everyday life, as he had said? Or from learning anything about his own past that might have been disturbing to us?

The difference between Papa and Major Graham was strongly in evidence at the dinner table that evening, our first meal at Casa del Mar. It was served, formally, in the large dark-walled dining room; only a spectacular crystal chandelier, lighted with dozens of candles, detracted from the depressing atmosphere.

Major Graham asked the blessing in a dry, emotionless way; unlike Mr. Forsman, he was brief and perfunctory. The meal itself was well prepared and tasty, including several things we were unaccustomed to; we had had fresh provender since touching at Los Angeles some days ago, but the food aboard ship did not compare to this. Fresh vegetables and fruits were a treat indeed, and at first it was not so obvious that there was no conversation to speak of, because we all concentrated on eating.

Gradually, however, I became aware that what I already knew to be Amalie's customary chatter was silenced. Aunt Maude had not come to the table; she was indisposed, but would see us later in the evening. I wondered if she, like my own mama, was wasting away in poor health.

Even the twins were not inclined to speak under the icy eye of our newly-met uncle. By the time Teresa served the fresh melon for dessert, the silence had become oppressive, and we were all relieved to be excused from the table.

Major Graham had requested—no, commanded—that I join him in the library, and it was there that Amalie ushered me while he smoked his evening cigar.

The room would have enchanted me had I not been so apprehensive about the coming encounter. It was large and paneled in dark wood, like the rest of the house, with heavy leather-covered furniture. But here the carpet was a rich, deep crimson in the lamplight, and there were books. More books than I had known existed in any one location.

I ran a finger over the leather backs, loving the very smell of them. Would I be allowed to partake freely of this feast?

"India?"

I spun guiltily at his voice, unable to control the tremor in my knees. "Yes, sir."

"Sit down. There." He indicated a chair and sank into another, one clearly his own, for his box of cigars was beside it, as well as a bottle of brandy and a glass on a silver tray.

"There are things we must discuss," he said. In the diminished light it seemed to me that the glacial eyes were sunken in shadow below the heavy gray brows; he reminded me of nothing so much as a great, predatory bird, and I would not have been surprised to find talons at the ends of his fingers.

"Yes, sir." In spite of myself, my voice was barely audible.

"You wrote to my wife."

He waited for my acknowledgment of this, as if I were to confess to each statement he made as to my sins before a confessor, although why anything yet said should be a sin I couldn't imagine.

"You stated that your father had told you all about her."

I swallowed. "Quite rightly so, surely? They were, after all, brother and sister."

"Do you remember your aunt at all? From when you were at Willows Hall in Suffolk?"

"No, sir. We left when I was only six. If I met Aunt Maude, I do not recall it."

"But you do remember stories your father told about her?"

"Oh, yes. All of them."

"And he spoke to you of Maude, on his deathbed?"

"Yes." I was glad the light was insufficient for him to see the tears that prickled in my eyes. Major Graham would be contemptuous of tears. "He told us—to go to Maudie."

"Maudie. Not your grandparents."

"That's right, sir."

"It would have seemed more natural, perhaps, to have sent you to your grandparents? To Lord Stuart-Brice?"

75

"I believe that Papa had—had severed connections with his father. At any rate, I remember no communication from him in all the years we spent in India, and only a few from my grandmother."

For a long moment he sat staring at me, until it was an effort not to squirm in the big leather chair. I was conscious of my old gray cashmere with its unfashionably large sleeves, and of my hair style which was also undoubtedly years behind the times.

When he spoke again, his words were unexpected. "I am not a wealthy man, you know."

Astonished, I said nothing. What reply could one make to such a statement?

"This house may seem to you to be a grand one, although perhaps not if you remember Willows Hall. Amalie may have told you that we settled here because the climate seems to suit my health; I was forced into retirement from the army because of ill-health."

Again he waited, as if I could say some magical words to change the situation. I did not know what he wanted me to say, and so chose the safer course of saying nothing at all.

"We live on an income from England. From my family, and from Maudie's. It is not, however, large. It is enough to support this household, to pay for the few servants necessary to run it. That is all."

Humiliation washed over me in a scalding wave. Was that what he had called me in to say? That we were a burden, a liability that he was not prepared to accept? What in heaven's name could I say to him about it?

I had for the moment totally forgotten the pearls. All I could think of was that I had taken it for granted this branch of my family would come to our assistance, and it seemed that this was not to be the case.

"We have not the means to reach England, sir," I managed finally, in as steady a manner as I could achieve. "We have no funds of our own."

"Judson left nothing? Nothing at all?" There was a

sharpness, a disbelief in his tone; he even sat up straighter in his chair, waiting for my reply.

"No, sir. He said that Maudie—" I could not go on. It was too much to ask of anyone. I could not beg for his assistance. I did not know what I would do, Caro and the twins and I, but I knew that I could not go down on my knees to this man who looked at me as if I were something to be examined under a microscope.

"Maudie. Yes, he would have sent you to Maudie." A small sigh escaped his austere lips. "I came this evening from the governor's house in Monterey."

For a moment his change of subject left me trailing behind, so far it seemed from our previous topic.

"I speak to you of a confidential matter. Something not to be discussed beyond the family. Even Amalie does not know how I proceed in this matter, and I request that you do not discuss it with her."

He waited for my stiff nod before he went on; if a tear escaped and made its way down my cheek I could only hope that he did not see it.

"I do not know how much you know about California. It was settled by the people from Mexico, the Spaniards and the Mexicans. The latter are for the most part a shiftless lot; they live from day to day and have little desire to better themselves. The Spanish are a different thing altogether. Families like the Alvarados are aristocrats, powerful, influential, many of them wealthy. We are most honored that one of these families have welcomed Amalie into their midst."

Was that why the major was pleased about the engagement? I wondered. Not because Amalie had fallen in love with Ramón, and he with her, but because the Alvarados were wealthy? But I had no time to wonder long.

"At present we are governed by one man, sent here from Mexico City. Oh, he has soldiers, but they are of little consequence. Mexico City is many days' journey to the south; the government there has little awareness of our problems or our needs, and should the necessity arise for a quick decision, there is no one but a local man to make it. It is a situation that does little to further progress in California."

I had no idea why he was telling me this. It seemed totally removed from my own situation, and that was uppermost in my mind. If he was going to reject us, to send us on to England and Lord Stuart-Brice, why didn't he say so, instead of prolonging the torment with all this talk I didn't understand nor care about?

"California is a vast land, a valuable one. Quite possibly it is one of the best-suited places in the world for raising cattle. The hides are enormously profitable for those who produce them. It takes many acres of land to raise cattle, *ranchos* of hundreds and even thousands of acres, such as the one belonging to Don Esteban Alvarado and his son. One day California will come into its own, and whoever governs it will have power, recognition, and—quite possibly—wealth."

He leaned toward me so that the lamplight fell across his face, lighting an almost fanatic zeal in his eyes.

"I intend to be that governor. No, not under the Mexican flag—the day of the power of Mexico is fast coming to a close. The Mexicans are too far away, they are too careless. The Californios—those who live here now—are a proud and independent people of mixed backgrounds, but they have one thing in common. They like the life they lead, and they will not be swayed from it. Mexico City will not help them in the direction they wish to go, and I do not think the Californios will consent to be exploited by a government that does nothing for them."

Fatigue was creeping over me for all that I was still tense with apprehension. What was he leading up to? What did he expect from me?

"Several of the world's great powers are aware, more so than Mexico City, of the potential of California." He looked at me as if expecting me to deny it, so that he could then refute my denial.

"The United States?" I suggested timidly.

He made a sound of derision. "Oh, there are Americans wandering in, but they, too, are a rough and shiftless

78

lot. They don't look for anything so stable as establishing homes and towns and ranches. They're looking for quick riches, for adventure. Well, I assure you, there are riches in California, but they will not be taken quickly. They will be won by those willing to live here and work here.

"No, it won't be the United States that lays claim to California. Their government is far away, farther than Mexico City, and they have too much land to claim closer to home, easier to get. There are mountains and deserts between California and the United States that make a joining of the two virtually impossible. France is interested, but France is also far away, and she has no ships to amount to anything. It will be England who steps in, one day in the not-too-distant future, and once the British flag flies over Monterey, I expect to be named as governor."

I forebore to mention that England, while undeniably having ships, was also a great distance away. I wished he would end this conversation, if that was what it was, and give me permission to go. I was still burning under his implied reluctance to accept us as his responsibility; I wanted only to crawl into a hole and nurse my wounds.

"When that time comes, and it approaches rapidly, I think, then I will no longer be a foreigner on foreign soil. I will be a man of power and substance, the latter far beyond any compensation that may be expected from the Crown. But until then, I am not a man of wealth. Should any scandal attach itself to my name, it is most unlikely that I would ever gain the governorship. I would remain as impecunious as I am now. Being Governor of California is my only opportunity to improve my financial situation beyond what it is today."

I sat there as he waited for my reaction to this. Perhaps, had I not been so exhausted and so near to tears, I might have thought of something sensible to say. As it was, I could scarcely think at all.

Major Graham stood abruptly, so that he towered above me. "I think," he said in a stiff voice, devoid of the animation he had displayed while telling me about the government of California, "that we understand one another now, do we not?"

With that he strode from the room, leaving me with my mouth slightly open.

Understood one another? Perhaps he understood something, but I certainly did not. Were we to stay? Or go on to England? And if the latter, who would provide our fare?

I was still sitting there, bemused, bewildered, when Amalie poked her head around the edge of the door. "India? Mama has asked to meet you. Not all of you tonight—she is feeling badly with a toothache—but you, at least. She is distressed that she hasn't welcomed you before."

I rose slowly, hoping that my own distress was not evident to Amalie, for I had no doubt that it would upset her, as well. "I want very much to meet Aunt Maude," I agreed, and went with her.

I carried the memories of Papa's stories, and of the portrait he carried with him halfway round the world, of a young and lovely woman. I knew Maudie would have aged, of course, and perhaps her health was not of the best.

But I was in no way prepared for the woman I met in that dimly lit, overcrowded, heavily scented room. When Amalie pushed me gently ahead of her toward the figure in the bed, I felt my breathing suspended as I stared in horror.

6

The air was so thick with some cloying scent that in an instinctive movement I tried to back out of the room. There were two lamps lighted, one on each side of the big bed, and the crimson draperies were drawn over all the windows. It was a large room, but cluttered with odds and ends of furniture and personal belongings; without Amalie's hand gently insisting in the small of my back, I would never have wended my way between the obstacles to approach the room's occupant.

Maude Stuart-Brice Graham.

She sat propped on various colored pillows, and as we entered she lifted a chocolate from a box beside the bed and popped it into her mouth.

She was the most grossly fat woman I had ever seen.

Her hair was still untinged with gray, and her eyes were the same dark brown that Papa's had been. But there all resemblance to any human being ended.

Fat spilled over the grotesquely bridal nightgown she wore, great rolls of fat so repellent that without Amalie behind me I would not have been able to move toward her.

Aunt Maude looked like nothing so much as a monstrous, bloated toad.

"Come in, come in." Her voice, astonishingly, was beautiful, like the young girl that I knew she had once been. "India? Is it India?"

I wet my lips. "Yes, ma'am. I'm India."

She chewed and swallowed the candy and reached for

another piece. "Idiotic name for a child, I always thought. You were a pretty little thing, though. Looked a lot like your poor mother. Mary Ellen. I liked Mary Ellen."

Fascinated, I observed the mastication of the second chocolate. She did not offer the box to us, which was just as well; to have tried to eat anything, while looking at her, would have made me ill.

"Come, come, sit down. Amalie, love, pull up a chair for your cousin. In the light, where I can see her."

She smiled and revealed blackened, ugly teeth, with the incisors missing on each side. "I apologize for not coming to the table tonight. I often eat here by myself, especially when I have the toothache. But it was not because I wasn't eager to see you. It was a long voyage, but you all came through it all right."

"Yes." I was mesmerized. Close enough to see the chocolate that melted around her damaged teeth, close enough to smell the musky odor that emanated from her person. She put out a hand toward mine and I repressed a shudder.

Yet her touch was not unpleasant, after all. Her hands, once pretty, were now swollen like the rest of her, but her touch was gentle, soft.

"Ah, so young you are to be left alone. I remember how Judson doted on you! Tell me—" She shifted in the pillows, and took back her hand to reach for another candy. "Tell me about Judson. How he died. I know you wrote in the letter, but that was so formal, so cold. Tell me about him."

There was no doubting the emotion in her voice, the reality of her affection for the brother she had not seen in so many years. And so I related it all, and then fell silent.

Aunt Maude lifted a handkerchief to dab unselfconsciously at her eyes. "And so he has gone. Ah, well, sometimes there are worse things than dying to endure." She did not elaborate upon that cryptic statement, however, but consoled herself with yet another chocolate. No wonder she was so obese!

82

"You come at a good time, my dear. My Amalie is about to be married—to a very nice young man. She chose him herself, and that is a very nice choice to be able to make. The gay and handsome Ramón, who thinks the sun rises and sets in our Amalie. Does he not, pet?"

Amalie blushed prettily. "Ramón is very good to me."

"And that is as it should be. India's parents, too, made a love match." Maude sighed, and it was easy to conclude that this had not been the case in her own marriage. "We will have a beautiful wedding, which in the way of these Californios will last a week, two weeks, who knows? Amalie tells me, however, that you do not dance?"

"No, ma'am. There was no one to teach us."

"Well, that must be remedied. No one can live through several weeks of fiesta without dancing! Amalie is very light on her feet, very dainty. We will have lessons tomorrow. You may not believe it, but I once was a graceful dancer myself. I can still instruct."

"And clothes, Mama," Amalie said, leaning toward the bed. "They could bring only a few things, and Caro says they are out of style. They will need dresses."

"About the dancing—" I hesitated, then plunged on, recalling Mrs. Forsman's prim face. "It is so short a time since Papa's death. Do you think we ought not to be in mourning? We wore black armbands, but we had no other proper clothes to show our respect. And dancing, perhaps—" I stopped, because I *did* want to dance, but I did not want to be thought callous and unfeeling.

Amalie's face fell. "I hadn't thought about that. Oh, Mama, do you think they will have to wait?"

Aunt Maude flapped a puffy hand. "Bah! In England, you would wear mourning for a year. In Calcutta, too, perhaps. But this is California, and the people here are more realistic. Besides, no one knows how long ago you lost your parents, do they? Why tell them? It would be a cruel thing to young girls, especially since Amalie tells me you have been sheltered almost to the point of imbecility, to keep you from the festivities! Of course you will have clothes, and of course you will dance! There is even a young man visiting the Alvarados, an Englishman. Peltier? In spite of his name, he is English. He will be a welcome addition to the wedding party. And now I am tired, pet. I will talk to Miss Strang in the morning, and you may all find yourselves at work with the needle, for the time is short."

She turned on a smile that almost made me forget her blackened teeth. "I am glad you are here, India. Convey my welcome to your sisters and brother, and tell them I will meet them tomorrow. And oh, Amalie, hand me the oil of cloves, in case this cursed tooth begins to act up again during the night."

Amalie passed her mother a tiny bottle from the stand on the opposite side of the bed and bent to kiss Aunt Maude good night before we left the room. I experienced a peculiar feeling, watching that demonstration of affection, and wondered if I could bring myself to kiss that cheek.

Amalie closed the door quietly behind us and took up the lamp she had left on a table in the hall, holding it high to light our way.

"Poor Mama, she suffers terribly at times with her teeth. Papa says she should have them all pulled out, but she refuses to do so. I must admit the idea of having all one's teeth pulled is a terrifying one!"

She prattled on as we went along to my room, where she left me with a smiling "Good night."

I stood for a moment inside the doorway of the room I would share with Caro, and in spite of the inexplicable scene with Major Graham, I felt a little better about having come here. And I thought very well of Amalie, too, who must have recognized how repulsively fat her mother was, for Amalie had said no word of apology or explanation for Aunt Maude.

Amalie, whom I had already liked, went up another notch in my estimation of her.

"India?" Caro spoke drowsily from the bed. "Did you meet Aunt Maudie?"

"Yes. You'll meet her tomorrow, too," I said. I did not

84

light a lamp, but began to work at my buttons in the darkness, which was not at all absolute. Caro had thrown back all the draperies and opened the windows wide, so that we had the fresh, sweet air off the sea.

"Did you like her?"

My hesitation was brief, so brief that Caro did not notice. "Yes. I liked her."

"Good," Caro said comfortably. "Uncle Henry is rather . . . reserved, is he not? Not at all like Papa. But he told me we might have horses to ride, and that someone would go in the morning for our luggage, and if we needed anything we had only to ask for it. Wasn't that nice of him?"

"Very nice," I agreed, remembering that incomprehensible scene in the library earlier that evening.

I moved to stand in front of the window, leaning out to see the moonlight shining on the water below. Perhaps it was I, rather than they, who was slightly deranged.

Yet we were here in California, and the future seemed a bit brighter.

The small bag attached to my undergarments brushed the windowsill with an infinitesimal sound, and only then did I remember the black pearls. And I had told the Major that Papa left nothing at all!

Yet I could not consider the necklace as a legacy, certainly not a fortune left to turn over to our relatives in return for our keep. Major Graham had emphasized his impecunious state, although certainly nothing I had seen so far in this household indicated that there was a need for any great stinting of money. And though it was the common custom of the day for whatever branch of the family was at hand to take on the responsibility for the aged and orphaned, certainly Major Graham was under no obligation to do so if he chose not to.

The battle with my conscience and my own will was short and silent. I might have discussed it with Caro, but I was sure my sister would be as unwilling as I to hand over to Major Graham anything so precious as the maharani's pearls. If he took on our guardianship, his control over us could well be absolute, to the point that anything of value in our possession became his. to do with as he liked. And I remembered what he had said, that he supported the household on funds from *both his family and Maudie's*—so that Maudie was a contributor, too, through my grandfather. She had seemed genuinely welcoming, and I thought would certainly see that we were fed and clothed until such time as we could be settled in our lives as adults.

Also, there was the point that Lord Stuart-Brice would surely see to it that his grandchildren were cared for, no matter what his differences had been with his son. At the very least, I should wait until we had some word from my grandfather, once he knew of our predicament, before I was reckless enough to reveal my possession of the pearls.

For all I knew, Major Graham might decide to sell them to further his own ambitions! I had no idea whether his pretensions to the governorship of California had any basis in reality, or were only a figment of his wishful imaginings. And I was well enough versed in history to know that many a man had achieved high office through his financial resources, as opposed to his abilities.

No. Already my mind was made up. I would not mention the pearls—and I would caution my sister also to guard against a slip of the tongue—until we heard from our grandfather. That was time enough to make any further decision.

And so with that, feeling not content but somewhat more at ease, I climbed into bed beside Caro and fell asleep.

Several disturbing and unpleasant things happened on our second day in Monterey, but they were not to take place until the day was well advanced.

The breakfast room at Casa del Mar was a much more cheerful place than the formal dining room. Although it had similarly wainscoted walls, the upper part of them was papered in a woodsy hunting scene, with red-coated riders hurdling obstacles in pursuit of dozens of identical foxes. In addition to this, there were many-paned windows overlooking the sandy gardens and, beyond that, the sea.

"Papa ate hours ago, and has gone about his business," Amalie informed us as we ate greedily of fresh eggs and fruit. "And Mama never comes down for breakfast. She has hers at noon, in her room, and then if she feels well enough she will join us for dinner. I'm to introduce the rest of you to her in the early afternoon, and she will help us with dancing lessons. Until then, however, we can do as we please. Miss Strang is already here, and we will acquaint her at once with your needs."

"I am going to the beach," Brice announced, helping himself for the third time to the scrambeld eggs. "I am going to get wet all over."

"It wouldn't be wise to wade out into the surf more than ankle deep," Amalie advised, "unless someone is with you. We don't have an undertow on our own inlet, such as exists in some stretches of the coast. But the surf can be more powerful than one expects. Papa always cautioned us against wading alone."

"Bethany can come with me, then." He bit into an orange and the juice ran unheeded down his chin. "I don't intend to sit around while you all talk about dresses. Not while there's something else to do."

Bethany hesitated. "But *I* want to know about the dresses! Am I to have some, too?"

"Of course," Amalie assured her. "I'll tell you what. You come and meet Miss Strang, and she can see what needs to be done. And then you can join Brice on the beach. And my little sister Hester will be home sometime today, too, and she can join you in your games."

Morning, then, was spent in the small sewing room upstairs. It had been inadequate when Miss Strang, a thin lady of sixty years, had been working on Amalie's trousseau. Now that she was taking on the making of frocks for three more of us, it was clear that we should have to spill over into the adjoining bedrooms.

Bolts of cloth were brought out for our inspection;

while nothing would actually be cut until Aunt Maudie gave her approval. Amalie assured us that her mother would be most generous and let us have whatever we wanted.

The materials available were a far cry from those Miss Telsman had stitched on in Willows, half a world away. Oh, there were a few lawns and fine silks, but there were also rich velvets in vivid colors, and satins and brocades. Bethany ran her fingers reverently over a crimson velvet.

"Might I ever have a dress of this?" she asked.

"Why not? With your coloring, it would make a perfect dress for fiesta, would it not, Miss Strang?" Amalie asked.

Miss Strang was not a woman moved to excitement. "Velvet is very pretty. But it will take time to make up these additional gowns. Perhaps the young ladies would care to assist with the sewing?"

Neither Caro nor I particularly liked sewing. Yet our education had not been entirely neglected, and we could both place small, neat stitches. And what female would not assist in the making of a gown from such fabulous goods?

We watched, entranced and envious, as Amalie tried on the bridal gown. She was exquisite; there was no other word for her. This, the most important of the garments, was nearly finished; it remained only to be hemmed, which Amalie would do herself around the yards and yards of satin beneath the lace overskirt.

Bethany at last drew herself away from the finery; we could see her out one of the high windows, racing toward the inlet, her skirts held up with both hands so as not to impede her progress. Brice was in plain sight, so far obeying the admonition about wading, for he crouched in the sand, doing something we could not discern from this distance.

"We will entertain all the Alvarados here for dinner this evening," Amalie said. "What can we do about gowns for India and Caro for tonight? Unless you have something suitable in your trunks, when they are brought?"

We shook our heads in unison. We had nothing to

compare with Amalie's frocks, certainly nothing suitable for a dinner party. Our first grown-up social affair, and we with only drab or childish costumes! Nathan Peltier would be there. I thought, and felt the heat in my face at the thought of him seeing me as such a disadvantage.

"The trunks are coming soon, are they not? We will see what can be done with your things when they arrive," Miss Strang pronounced, and we had to be content with that.

When it came time for a midday meal, Caro and I had to bodily drag the twins back up the slope to the house. It was easy to sympathize with them, in this first delicious freedom; indeed, had it not been for a desire to appear before Mr. Peltier and the others as attractively as possible, I would have spent the day on the shore myself. As it was, however, there were other things to be done.

Amalie ate with Aunt Maudie, which gave me an opportunity to tell the children what to expect when they met her. I had already told Caro, who was round-eyed with curiosity after my description of our aunt, and I did not dare trust the twins to control their tongues at the sight of such a fat person unless they were forewarned.

"What's the matter with her?" Brice wanted to know.

"I don't know that. Only that she is poorly, as Mama was. She has great difficulty with her teeth paining her, I believe. The important thing is, you must not say anything about her looks."

"Why not?" Bethany asked.

"Because, stupid." Brice spoke scoffingly, "it would be rude. Wouldn't it, India?"

"Of course. It is always rude to comment negatively about anyone's appearance." I hoped I had conveyed this to their level of understanding.

We were not encouraged to dawdle over our food, since the household was busy preparing for the coming dinner party. The entertainment would not be on the scale we would encounter later at Rancho Hermoso, the Alvarado home. But, for Casa del Mar, it would be a major event.

Extra women had been called in to assist with the

cooking; the cleaning, of course, had been going on for days, and as many foods as could be were prepared in advance. Much cooking was still in progress, however, and none of the women wanted us underfoot.

These Indian women were quite different from our own Indians of Calcutta. For the most part they were round-faced, smiling people; they had little if any English (except for the regular house servants) but they bobbed their heads and nodded at us, and jabbered between themselves. Sometimes they laughed, and obviously at us, but since they were so evidently friendly we could not take offense; when Bethany asked why *they* should be able to comment upon our appearance, when we were not allowed to comment upon anyone else's, I explained that because they did not have the advantage of good breeding, they did not know any better.

Our first shock was the arrival of our trunks from the *Essex*.

They came in a conveyance called a *carreta*, driven by a young Mexican boy and accompanied by the sailor Jake. I went to the door when Teresa called, as Caro and the twins were with Aunt Maudie.

Jake was there on the doorstep, twisting his hat between his hands. At first I could make nothing of his hemming and hawing, until at last I asked him outright if there was something wrong.

"It's your trunks, miss." He twisted the cap even harder, then crammed it into his pocket where he usually kept it. "Captain Spacy's fit to be tied, he is. Never had such a thing happen before. O' course it didn't happen aboard ship, you understand, but still, since they hadn't been delivered here to you yet, the captain feels sort o' responsible, like."

"For what?" I asked, mystified. The Mexican boy was waiting to help unload the bulky boxes, smiling broadly whenever I glanced in his direction.

"For the damage, miss. You see, the boxes all sat on the beach overnight. No reason for 'em not to that we knowed of. 'S done all the time, when the contents ain't valuable, you see. Just clothes and the like, right?"

Alarm began to send out feelers along my nerve-ends, then. "What damage do you speak of?"

"Why, to your clothes and the like, miss. Somebody opened 'em up and scattered everything about like so much chaff. I had to run half a mile up the beach to get the last of it, I did." His youthful face suddenly colored, as if in recollection of the embarrassing article he'd had to retrieve. "I got no way o' knowing if it's all there, but I picked up everything I saw, miss."

My initial reaction was one of humiliation that my undergarments had been scattered along half a mile of Monterey waterfront. And then, gradually, it dawned upon me that this vandalism might have some more sinister import.

"I hope you didn't have nothing valuable in them trunks, miss," Jake pleaded. "Because I didn't find nothing but clothes to put back. And a few books and trinkets. Nothing like money or real jewels, like."

The cold spread through me; it was only with an effort that I refrained from touching the small pouch hidden beneath the folds of my skirts.

"No. There was little of value. But who would have done such a thing? Why?"

"I expect somebody thought there might be valuables, so they went looking, like. Captain Spacy will be most relieved, miss, to know there wasn't nothing to steal. Most put out, he was, when he heared. I'm afraid some of the things is in bad shape—torn, like. Not much dirtied, the beach is too clean for that. But torn, like."

Dear heaven! As if we hadn't been in bad enough shape already! But it wasn't the damaged clothes that concerned me. What if I had packed the pearls away in a trunk, thinking them safe? What if I hadn't had the foresight to keep them on my person?

For a moment, only a moment, it occurred to me to wonder if anyone knew about the necklace. But no. No, it was impossible that this should have been the case, for I had told only Caro, and she had told no one. Indeed, neither of us had had an opportunity to confide in anyone but Sir Roland, which we had not done. After we had boarded the *Essex,* even had we been careless in our speech and let it slip that we possessed valuables, our fellow passengers would have known that the trunks were in the hold. They had been among the last things loaded, so presumably would not have been all that difficult to find and search during our voyage.

No, I put that thought from me. It must be that someone had come upon the unguarded property waiting on the beach, and thought to rifle it. In fact, strewing it along the beach that way seemed to suggest that it might have been mischievous children rather than adults, I thought.

"Well, bring them in," I said, and Jake and the Mexican boy pulled and hauled the trunks into the front hall. Then, after a brief rest, they managed to get them up the stairs and to the nursery, where there was the space for me to inspect them. Jake murmured yet another commiseration, and then he was gone.

The others found me there, staring in dismay at what was left of our belongings. My newest dimity, the one I had thought might best pass muster for the dinner party this evening, had been torn past mending.

Caro's jaw dropped. "India, what's happened?"

Inspection proved that we had not lost everything, yet what remained brought Miss Strang's lips to a compressed line. "One is not given much to work with," she said.

Still, to her credit, she did her best. Caro and I each had a white India muslin she thought might be renovated, if we all worked at it; even Amalie was willing to be pressed into service.

"The sleeves are impossible," Miss Strang pronounced. "We will remove the sleeves. So."

This was a relief, since it was the enormously full sleeves that most differentiated our dresses from Amalie's, and we all set to work picking out stitches, even Bethany, for all her protests.

Miss Strang knew her business well. She took the discarded sleeves and ironed them out and recut them in the newer, smaller shape. Necklines, too, were adjusted; there was no time for permanent stitching, she said, but they were lowered and tacked into place in passable fashion. They should hold provided we did not become too athletic, she informed us, which sent us off into fits of giggles.

We had reached the stage where the dresses were being changed by the addition of ribbons and lace, and I had hopes that we would not be thought too peculiarly behind the times, when I was once more summoned by Teresa.

She was panting a little from the climb up the stairs, but she kept her smiling good humor. "Is ship's captain, miss," she said in her accented English.

"Captain Spacy? What ever for? He sent his apologies with Jake—unless he's discovered the culprit who broke into our trunks?"

I ran ahead of her down the stairs, but it was not Captain Spacy who awaited in the foyer below.

The man who turned at the sound of my approach was older, shorter, with wind-and-sun-reddened skin and a pipe clenched between his teeth. He was a perfect stranger.

I stopped almost in midstep, thinking there must be some mistake.

"Sir? You asked for Miss India Stuart?"

He removed the pipe and addressed me in a gravelly voice, touching the brim of his cap as he did so. "Aye, you'll be Miss India? I'm Captain Hull, of the *Durham*, now anchored in the bay. We're away for London with the morning tide, but I've just spoken to Captain Spacy and learned that you were here. I've come with another apology; it seems that we have neither of us managed well by you, young lady."

I was at a loss as to his meaning, and I must have looked it.

"Your trunks desecrated before they could be picked up by your family—of course, the responsibility of the shipper ends once delivery is made to shore, you understand. But even though the master of the *Essex* cannot be held responsible for what happened, he's sorry about it, as am I. My own business, however, is such that perhaps I am somewhat at fault. Although in my own defense I must say I could only use my best judgment at the time."

"I'm afraid I don't understand what you are trying to say, sir," I managed, wondering how the captain of the *Essex*'s sister ship could have anything to do with me. "Please, would you like to sit down in—in the library, and Teresa could bring you some tea? Or—or—" Was it proper to offer him a brandy, or could only another gentleman do that? I was hopelessly unknowing about such things.

"No, no, lass, there's no time for that. I only came myself to make sure the message was delivered to you, ungarbled. There was a letter for you, you see. From Sir Roland Trask, him as procured your passage upon the *Essex*. He learned that we were to sail a week behind the *Essex*, on the same general course, and touching at the same ports. He came aboard almost at the last minute to put it into my hands, with the admonition that I was to deliver it only to you, and at the earliest possible moment. He seemed rather agitated, and I took it to be a matter of some importance; indeed, the fee he paid me for the delivery made that only too clear."

"I see, sir," I said, although I was not sure that I did. What urgent message could Sir Roland have, when all our business in Calcutta had been concluded well before we sailed? "And where is the letter?"

He coughed and looked as if he intended to spit, but then remembered where he was, and strangled as he swallowed. After a bit of that he was once more able to speak. "Well, that's the devil of it, begging your pardon, I'm sure. Because while we were supposed to be following after the *Essex*, she was delayed in *Canton* and we got ahead of her. Had I known she was there, I'd·have delivered the message then. As it was, I was not made aware of it until my first mate reported it when he had already sailed. It seemed likely she'd catch up with us by the time we reached the Sandwich Islands, but that was not the case, either.

"We had a bit of a problem there, and I'm sorry to say your letter from Sir Roland slipped my mind. But when we rea hed Los Angeles, I made sure the *Essex* had not been there ahead of us, which meant she was due right behind. I was aware that your destination was Monterey, but I knew also that the *Essex* would be in port for several days in Los Angeles, taking on a shipment of hides such as we ourselves had done."

I suppressed the urge to hurry him along, for it seemed that he was taking overlong to make what must be a simple explanation. "Yes, sir," I said, by way of compromise, and he did then go on.

"I knew there was a good chance the *Durham* would reach Monterey, take on the balance of cargo here, and sail before the *Essex* dropped anchor. So, you see, I could obey one of Sir Roland's stipulations, not both. I could not deliver the letter to you in person without delaying my own sailing. So I must therefore either leave the letter with the officials at the customshouse in Los Angeles, or bring it along and leave it with the officials here in Monterey. Since Sir Roland stressed that it was to be delivered as quickly as possible, and you would be in Los Angeles a week before you arrived here, I chose to leave the message with the officials in Los Angeles."

He drew in a deep breath and bit down again momentarily on the pipe. In the interim, I spoke uncertainly.

"Then the letter is still in Los Angeles?"

"So it would seem. I have only just learned from Captain Spacy that you were at no time allowed to go ashore at Los Angeles, and that he carried no missive back to the *Essex* for you from those officials. I do not know why the man to whom I entrusted it did not see that it reached Captain Spacy, for I paid him well for this service. But the fact remains that this urgent message from Sir Roland now lies in Los Angeles. We will touch that port again on our voyage south, to take on fresh supplies, and I will see that the letter is sent on to you by the first available means. But I sincerely regret that I was not able to hand it to you in person."

"I see. Well, I have no idea what can be so urgent about the message, but I thank you for coming yourself to explain it all to me. No doubt a slight delay will be of little consequence, considering that it was written months ago," I said.

Captain Hull expelled a sigh. "I certainly hope that will be the case, Miss Stuart. I do, indeed. And I hope that you will not think badly of me for having decided as I did, thinking it was for the best, you see."

I assured him that I in no way held him to blame for the circumstances, and let him out the front door to where one of the *carretas*-waited to take him back to his ship.

How very odd, that Sir Roland should consider his message to be of such importance. But no doubt I would soon enough learn what he had sought to convey to me.

I climbed back up the stairs, and half an hour later Hester arrived home. My younger cousin was in no way like her older sister, and when later I recounted the unpleasant things that had happened that day, I added Hester's arrival to the list.

7

would never again consider myself to be unattractive, I
decided, in those first few moments of viewing Amalie's
ten-year-old sister. I was too inexperienced to realize that
those widely-set dark eyes would one day be beautiful. All
I saw was that the child was thin, that the eyes dwarfed
her face, that she consisted mostly of bones and skin so
brown she might almost have been one of the Mexicans
who were helping out in the kitchen.

But mostly what made her unattractive was the malevolent scowl upon her face as she marched into the sewing
room and snatched a length of material from Bethany's
unresisting fingers.

"Teresa told me what you're doing, and you shan't!
You shan't use the blue brocade! It's mine, you can't have
it!"

Hester's hair was an even more mousy brown than my
own, and I thought the way it was done, skinned back
from her bony face and pulled into tight braids that
wound around her head, only emphasized its lack of at-
tractiveness. On top of that, she was a regular little savage. Not satisfied with having ripped the brocade from
Bethany, she spun upon Caro.

In her haste to tear away the red velvet Caro was only
examining, the little beast raked her fingernails down my
sister's arm, drawing blood.

Bethany had stood unresisting, but Caro was made of
different stuff. Before Amalie, with a distressed cry, could

97

move across the room, Caro landed a smack upon one of the brown cheeks. It turned pink in the outline of Caro's hand, and brought the young tigress to a halt.

Hester stared in outraged astonishment. Clearly she was not used to being disciplined in such a manner.

"Oh, Hester! Stop, you're being—"

Hester ignored her sister, staring up at the taller Caro. "How dare you! How dare you lay a hand on me?"

"You deliberately scratched me," Caro said, holding out the arm on which four parallel marks were only too visible. "In my family, people get slapped for such rude behavior."

"Rude! When you're taking the materials Mama got for me, when you're using them all up for dresses for yourself—!"

I had thought it marvelous that the household was so well supplied with dress goods, but it hadn't occurred to me why. I stepped into the melee before Hester again earned herself a slap. "Wait a moment, please. There is considerable misunderstanding here. We had no intention of taking over anyone else's dress goods, and we have no desire to make an enemy of a new cousin."

But Hester was not to be pacified. She clutched the velvet against her, bosom heaving, the handprint starkly outlined on her cheek. "Miss Strang had no right to say you could have any of my dresses. I shall report to Mama at once, and she'll tell her to stop!"

With that she spun on her heel and rushed from the room, skirts flying. Amalie stared after her, then turned back to us with hands held out beseechingly.

"I'm sorry! No one had time to explain to her that the materials will be replaced, that we only need a few things to tide you over until we can obtain more dress goods. I'm afraid Hester rather runs wild, and Papa dotes on her so he will scarcely allow anyone to correct her—"

She need say no more about how spoiled the child was. Caro and I exchanged glances, needing no words.

"No doubt the storm will blow over," Caro said, bend-ing to pick up the pins that had been spilled during the confrontation.

"Yes, of course. Mama will set her right," Amalie agreed.

Of course the incident took a good deal of our pleasure out of the dressmaking. Amalie assured us that she had discussed the situation ahead of time with her mother, that the materials which were being given over to us were not any of Hester's "special" ones, and that it would all be smoothed over.

Even seeing how much nicer my own simple India muslin looked with the pink ribbons and the bunch of cleverly contrived satin roses at the waist I was uncomfortable, although none of the ribbons had been planned for anything of Hester's.

Miss Strang inspected me critically. "You'll do, I think. Quite an improvement."

It was, indeed, for just changing the sleeves made me feel quite modish, more dainty. I, who was far too tall for daintiness.

"You look lovely, India," Amalie said, smiling. "I wonder—have you tried wearing your hair any other way than that? It is so heavy that it pulls itself out straight from its very weight, but I wonder if it might not be induced to curl if you cut it?"

"Cut it?" I echoed, horrified. My hair had never been cut.

"Oh, India, truly this is the wrong climate for such long hair! I should have thought it was in Calcutta, too—wasn't it very hot there? Mama says I am very clever with the scissors, and there is a picture in one of Miss Strang's magazines—here, let me find it—" She burrowed into a heap of materials on a table and emerged triumphant. "See, look at this! It would suit you admirably, India, I'm sure it would!"

I gazed dubiously at the printed page. The young lady staring out at me had her hair in soft curls all over her head, and it was indeed attractive on *her*. I, however, was something else altogether.

"But hers curls. Mine does not."

"No, except for just a little, the short hair right around your face. But don't you see, it might, if we cut it off so that it was not so heavy?"

"She's right, India," Caro chimed in, peering over my shoulder. "Why don't you try it? It looks quite charming."

"Papa would never have allowed me to cut my hair," I said slowly. "And what if we cut it and then find that it doesn't curl at all? I shall look like a dog that has just come in from the rain!"

In the end, I was persuaded to allow Amalie to try. An old sheet was draped about me, to protect my clothes while I perched on a stool; Amalie swooped about with the scissors, while the others watched and Miss Strang stitched. I prayed earnestly that I would be transformed into someone Mr. Peltier would be happy to dance with.

At last the ordeal was over, and a mirror was held for me to examine the results. I stared at a transformed creature, all right, but not in the manner I had imagined. I gave a wail of chagrin, for in spite of the fact that I had never considered mouse-brown hair to be a crowning glory, it was better than no hair at all! It did not even reach my shoulders!

"It will be better once we've set it," Amalie said firmly. "We will dampen it and tie it up on rags, and then we will proceed with the dancing instructions. Mama is waiting for us."

And so, ludicrous as I was with rags all over my head, we moved out of the sewing room and into the schoolroom. It had been chosen because it was the only place suitable for dancing except the drawing room downstairs; that was now being prepared for the evening's entertainment, so was out of bounds.

Brice popped in long enough to observe my haircut: "What did you do that for? You look like a clown!" he said crushingly. And then, "I'm not going to do any of that stuff," about the dancing.

Aunt Maudie spoke from the deep chair brought across

from her own room in the other wing of the house. "Everyone in California dances. Almost every occasion is an excuse to dance—a wedding, a birthday, a holiday, the birth of a baby, anything at all. You will be rather left out of things if you do not learn to dance, my boy."

Brice shrugged. "What I want is to learn to ride a horse. Ramón says there are lots of horses at Rancho Hermoso. When can we go there?"

Aunt Maudie had brought her box of chocolates, and she lifted one to her mouth and chewed thoughtfully. "This household of females does not appeal to you?"

"Oh, females are all right. But I'd rather learn to ride a horse. Major Graham said there were horses."

"Ah, yes. But ours are not used to being ridden by small boys who don't know even the rudiments of riding. I had thought *that* part of your education could wait until Amalie's wedding was over, but perhaps that is too long for a boy who is nine and impatient. Perhaps I shall speak to Ramón about it this evening, when he comes. If I can get him away from Amalie long enough for a few words."

Brice stood up straighter. "Would you, Aunt Maudie? Can I learn tomorrow?"

Maudie laughed, showing those blackened teeth, but I was beginning to get used to them. "Well, I won't promise *tomorrow*. But we shall see."

"May I learn to ride, too?" Bethany asked. She stood quietly beside Aunt Maudie's chair, her little hand resting upon the arm of it. I had thought she might be timid of this woman who was so different from anyone we had ever known, but she was not. Indeed, she seemed quite fascinated with Maudie. "Papa said you and he used to ride together when you were children."

"Oh, did we not! We rode like the wind across the moors, my Juddy and I! Once we took out our own papa's stallions, which we were forbidden to go near, for they were dangerous, you see. But it was very early in the morning, before the grooms were about, and we did not think we would be caught."

101

"Were you?" Brice edged nearer, his dark eyes round in admiration.

"Caught? Ah, in a way. For Juddy managed to control his beast, all right, but I was too small, not strong enough, and I was thrown. It knocked all the wind out of me, so that my chest hurt most unbearably; I could not even speak for some minutes, and when I did, I began to cry. And do you know what your precious papa did?"

Maudie slid another chocolate into her mouth and made us wait while she ate it. "He got down beside me, with tears on his cheeks until I started to cry. And then he said, 'Maudie, if you've broken any bones, I'll kill you.' And he made me get up and get back on the horse, and we rode home. Papa discovered someone had been riding his stallions, for they were in a lather and he never allowed his horses to be turned out that way. Of course all the stable boys denied they'd touched the animals. For a time it seemed we'd have to 'fess up, because he said he'd sack the lot of them. But your grandmother persuaded him that would be unwise, since he could not be sure which, if any, of them, was guilty. And it would not have been easy to replace them, all at once. So all I was punished for was my clothes—they were a complete mess, and I suspect Nannie guessed how they had got that way, but she never told."

Maudie's eyes were bright and knowing as they rested upon Brice. "If you learn to ride, you must promise to obey orders. You will be allowed to ride stallions when you are a man grown, when you are strong enough to handle them. Every man in this country needs to know how to ride, but getting a broken neck is of no use to anyone. You must do precisely what you are told."

"I will," Brice assured her, and I knew that he was already dreaming of the stallions.

"I will, too," Bethany said, nodding.

"You'll never be able to ride a stallion," Brice informed her. "Only a ladies' horse, on a sidesaddle. Isn't that right?"

"Why? Why can't I wear trousers and ride astride, the

same as Brice?" Bethany wanted to know. "It would be ever so much easier and safer."

"Because you're a girl," Brice said, smirking. "Girls don't wear trousers."

"Hester sometimes does," Amalie said unexpectedly. "Not in public, of course. But we're so far away from everyone, and skirts are such a nuisance for some things."

"Could I? I could wear some of Brice's old trousers, couldn't I?" Bethany begged.

"We'll see. Now it is time to learn to dance," Aunt Maudie decreed. "Amalie will demonstrate, and then you will all try it. We will begin with *la jota*."

And so, at last, we learned to dance. Oh, not well, and not the more complicated dances. But well enough, Amalie assured us. And before the wedding, when there would be *real* dancing, we would have time for more practice.

Hester did not join us. And nothing was said about the use of the goods that had been intended for her.

Our session ended in late afternoon when Major Graham suddenly appeared in the doorway of the schoolroom. Our laughter died when he cleared his throat, addressing his wife.

"So you are well enough to instruct our visitors in the dance," he said. Something passed between them, I could not guess what; this speaking with the eyes was a thing I had not yet learned. "How fortunate for them."

"They do tolerably well," Maudie said, and with calm deliberation selected another chocolate.

"You will join me, then, to welcome our guests this evening."

"Of a certainty. I would not miss welcoming Amalie's future family into our home, not even for a toothache," Maudie assured him.

His gaze flicked over the rest of us. "They are all presentably turned out for the evening?"

"Oh, yes. Miss Strang has done wonders. She is truly a marvel, Miss Strang, worth every cent we pay her. You

103

have perhaps heard of the misfortune that befell the children's trunks after they were put off the *Essex*?"

"I did, indeed. A disgrace. I have never heard of such a thing happening before." This time it was I the cold eyes sought. "And to what purpose? Did you carry anything but clothing and personal belongings?"

"There was nothing of value in the trunks," I said truthfully.

"A disgrace," he repeated, and shook his head at the depravity evident in the act of breaking open the trunks. "I have not come upstairs to commiserate upon that matter, however. We will have another guest for dinner this evening; I have instructed the servants in this regard. In fact, I have invited him to stay with us, here in a civilized household. In the few days he has been in Monterey, he has been staying at the Delgados', if you can imagine! An English gentleman!"

"Scarcely the place for an English gentleman," Aunt Maudie agreed, unperturbed, licking at a finger where the chocolate had melted. "Who is this gentleman, and where does he come from?"

"His name is Millay, and his uncle knows the Prince of Wales! He has been traveling and is on his way home to England, but his business will not be concluded before the *Durham* sails. Rather than leave him to the mercies of the Delgados for whatever the length of his stay, I have offered him our hospitality. I trust this will not inconvenience you in any way?"

"Not at all," Maudie assured him. "We do run rather short of space, however; I believe there is only the corner chamber to the east still empty? Have you given orders regarding it?"

"I had hoped that Amalie would find time to make certain our guest has whatever he needs," Major Graham said. "I will see you all at dinner, then."

There were still several hours until this time, however. The servants had been heating water and carrying it upstairs, as everyone would bathe. Amalie, who guarded the hall to make sure that I would not encounter the new guest with my head tied up in these ugly rags, was all smiles.

"How lovely, that there are two young Englishmen now in Monterey! They will certainly both be included in all the festivities. Of course Caro is rather young, and Mr. Millay is even older than Mr. Peltier; I should think twenty-seven or twenty-eight, at least. But they will no doubt add a great deal to our good times, as they will be dancing partners."

Caro was nearly ecstatic at the prospect of the coming evening. I viewed it with combined alarm and pleasure, for until the rags came out of my hair, I was not sure that I would be fit to be seen at all. I worried that Amalie had dampened my hair too much, so that it would not dry in time; when the rags were removed, only dry hair could be expected to curl. What had possessed me to allow it to be cut? Regret already overwhelmed me.

Even the children were expected to be at the dinner table. "These Californios," Amalie told us, "dote on their children and include them in everything. Even the babies come to the fiestas! Of course tonight we entertain only Ramón's immediate family, but there are so many of them. Don Esteban and Doña Isabel, and then he has a brother and a sister, Cristóbal and Manuela. There were others, but they all died. Don Esteban wanted a very large family, and he says he is very happy that I am to become his daughter, now. You'll like Don Esteban, he is very different—" Amalie stopped speaking and pretended she had dropped something that required picking up.

Different from her own father? I wondered.

Since dinner would be very late, we were served a light meal in our own rooms, so that we shouldn't starve while waiting for the formal repast. Then we were all urged to rest until it was time to go down.

Rest! When our excitement made it impossible even to sit still for long! Yet we tried, all but Brice and Bethany, who had gone back onto the beach.

Caro and I took our turns in the marvelous tin tub, our

first full bath since we had left Calcutta months earlier, and a rare treat it was. Our clothes were laid out ready to put on, and we stretched out on the bed in our shifts until we should be called.

Amalie arrived half an hour before the guests were due, to comb out my hair. She was exquisitely dressed in a white gown with scarlet ribbons, another of which had been used to tie back her dark hair, and tiny scarlet slippers for dancing. I stifled my envy and tried to sit still, without looking into the mirror, while my cousin worked over my hair.

From the corner of my eye I could see Caro, her long fair hair brushed until it shone, seated demurely near the window. Her color was high—no need to pinch anyone's cheeks tonight to make them rosy. The simplicity of her India muslin was relieved somewhat by lace and pale green velvet bands. Oh, what I would give to look like either Caro or Amalie tonight, I thought wistfully. To walk down those stairs, and have Mr. Peltier look up at me, and see his face light in a smile of admiration!

"Is it dry?" I asked anxiously as the first rag was removed from my head.

"Quite dry. And it's curling, India, I do believe it's going to come out beautifully!"

Caro twisted about to watch also. "She's right, India. I can hardly believe it's you, you look so different!"

And then at last I was allowed to stand and move to look into the mirror at my own reflection.

Surely it was not I who stood there beyond the glass, this creature in a party dress decorated in a becoming pink, this young lady with glowing hazel eyes and cheeks to rival her ribbons!

And the hair! I was prepared for shock. I did not look like the lady in the magazine, but with soft short curls all about my face, even the shade of my hair did not seem so mousey as it had.

I was almost pretty.

"And now we must go down," Amalie said. "For Papa

wants to introduce our house guest to the family before the others arrive. Hurry, they will be coming any time now!" And so, in mingled anticipation and trepidation, we descended for our first party.

8

The rest of the family was already gathered in the drawing room when we arrived. One of the maids had seen to the twins, it being obvious that Caro and I had enough to do to get ourselves ready; I gave them a cursory glance and decided that all was in order.

But my primary attention was for the tall, dark-haired man talking to Major Graham.

My uncle turned smoothly, smiling, although his eyes were as glacial as ever. "Ah, here are the rest of the family! My daughter, Amalie. My wife's nieces, India and Caroline Stuart-Brice. Our guest, Sherard Millay."

Mr. Millay took my hand and lifted it to his lips, barely touching it, but that touch sent shivers up and down my spine. He did not reveal that we had met before. "Miss India," he said, and his dark eyes met mine briefly before he turned to Caro.

He had already been introduced to everyone else. Hester was there, looking a little less ugly in her animation, in what I thought a totally inappropriate dress for a ten-year-old; it was so covered with lace and flounces and ruffles that she could have been a doll rather than a child. But she clung to her father's arm, looking up at him, demanding his attention, and I saw a different side of Henry Graham; there could be no doubting that he was fond of his younger daughter.

Aunt Maudie appeared on the ground floor for the first time since our arrival; she was ensconced in an oversized chair, and for once the box of chocolates was not in evidence, although when I came close to her I could still smell chocolate on her breath. Miss Strang had done wonders with a gown whose yardage must have been adequate for a small circus tent. Apparently undaunted by her own bulk, Maudie had chosen a vivid blue brocade; she made a startling splash of color in the rather staid drawing room.

Sherard Millay regarded her unblinkingly, a polite smile on his lips. "It is very kind of you to have me here, ma'am. I must admit that the quarters in town were far less comfortable. I hope that I don't inconvenience you in any way."

Aunt Maudie fluttered a fan of intricately carved ivory, which had certainly come from India. "Not at all. Our household is, at the moment, a bit of a madhouse, I'm afraid. It will be a relief to have our Amalie married and off to Rancho Hermoso; then we shall settle down to normal." Her eyes rested upon Caro and me, and she smiled. "Which now has grown to include three more daughters and a son. Pity me, Mr. Millay, with all those weddings coming up!"

"They're coming," Hester announced loudly, and turned from her post at a window. "All the Alvarados, they're here!"

This celebration dinner was only for the immediate families, I had been told. Yet we were thirty-two at the table. Ramón's finery tonight would have put the Prince Consort himself to shame, I thought; for he wore deep-red velvet trousers and jacket with gold buttons and gold embroidery, and there were heavy gold rings on his fingers.

He introduced his family enthusiastically. Don Esteban was beginning to be slightly stooped, but he stood tall and obviously proud of his son. He, too, wore velvet, but his was black and silver; I thought it the most elegant apparel I had ever seen, setting off his white hair to perfection.

His wife, Doña Isabel, was much shorter, with hair faintly streaked with gray; she wore rustling black taffeta, unrelieved except for white lace at her collar and cuffs.

She was comfortably rounded, smiling, and, unlike her husband and children, spoke no English, but she nodded all around and beamed upon everyone.

The younger Alvarados were as handsome as Ramón; it was soon evident that Hester had a crush on Cristóbal, two years her senior. He behaved in a manner far more mature than hers, however; his manners were impeccable, which is more than could be said for Hester, although his brown eyes had a look about them that made me suspect a lively sense of humor.

And there was Manuela, the Alvarados' only surviving daughter. At sixteen she was a rare beauty—were Hester and I the only mice in this entire gathering? I wondered. And then I caught a glimpse of myself in one of the tall mirrors, and felt a little better. No one would take me for India Stuart—or Stuart-Brice, as the major had restored to us the part of our name that Papa had dropped.

Manuela's English was halting, but delightful. It did not seem to bother her when anyone laughed at her mistakes, for she laughed with us, throwing her head back in a gesture much like Ramón's. She, too, had rings, on almost every finger, and a gold cross at her slender throat.

"You must come to Rancho Hermoso with our Amalie," she invited, taking my hand in hers. "You are always welcome—our home is your home!"

And then there were the others in the "immediate" family—I remembered Ramón's Uncle Roberto, who might have been Don Esteban's twin except that he had a wonderfully healthy mustache in addition to the thatch of white hair; I was instructed to address him as *Tío* Roberto. He kissed my hand in a most courtly way, and spoke Spanish words I did not understand, but everyone else laughed and nodded approvingly, and I took it to mean that he had in some way complimented me.

The others I did not sort out that evening; there were too many of them. *Tíos* and *tías,* a dozen of them, and a cousin and her two small children. I was dazzled by their smiling faces, their gaudy but undeniably beautiful clothing, their jewelry, their friendliness. Even those who spoke no English (these were among the aunts and uncles) made us feel as if we were part of this fabulous large family.

Nathan Peltier and Sherard Millay seemed almost obscure amongst all the peacocks, except that even Mr. Peltier stood half a head above any of them except Major Graham. Mr. Millay was seated across the table from me and two seats down; several times our eyes met and he smiled at me, as if in secret amusement at all these chattering Spaniards.'

I should have liked to sit next to Mr. Peltier, but whoever arranged the seating had put him between Caro and Manuela. Caro was a bit shy at first, but since he devoted himself equally to each of them, she soon warmed and talked vivaciously.

I sat beside Tío Roberto, who solicitiously assisted me with everything from my wine glass to retrieving a dropped fork; since I did not understand what he said, I could only smile and nod.

To my left was the cousin with the young children; she, too, smiled at me a great deal, but was too busy with her little boys to exchange more than a few words in her halting English.

After dinner, there was music and dancing in the drawing room. Ramón claimed me for the first dance, leaving his betrothed to Tío Roberto, and, except for the one time I trod upon his foot, I felt I did very well for one who had only that afternoon been introduced to the dance.

"There can be no pain inflicted from so tiny a foot," Ramón said cheerfully when I would have stammered an apology, which I thought a most gracious thing to say.

Caro danced with Nathan Peltier, more agile than I, her pretty face upturned to his with delight.

I turned from contemplation of my sister to find Sherard Millay at my side.

"I'm sorry, did I startle you? I've been looking for a chance to talk to you all evening," he said. "Would you

111

like to dance, or could we perhaps appropriate some of those chairs over there and rest for a moment?"

In the company of an attractive young man, I was happy to do either. But we both admitted to being unused to all the exercise, and we chose the chairs.

"A most extraordinary family, the Alvarados," Mr. Millay said. "So gay, so energetic. I understand they do this sort of thing all the time."

"Perhaps English blood runs a bit cooler," I suggested, feeling flustered at this first opportunity for small talk. And then, as Manuela and one of her younger uncles whirled by, laughing, I sought for a safe subject. "She's a lovely girl, isn't she?"

"Lovely," Mr. Millay agreed, but he didn't look at Manuela. His gaze was fixed on me. "I prefer a quieter beauty, however, a young woman less flamboyant."

There was surely no mistaking his meaning. I felt the warmth rise from my lowered neckline into my throat and cheeks.

"Your new hair style is most becoming," he told me. "I've never seen anyone wear it quite that way. On anyone else it might be considered almost boyish, but there is nothing boyish about you, Miss India. Quite the contrary." And then, no doubt seeing that I was embarrassed and did not know how to respond, he turned the subject. "The Grahams are most hospitable hosts, are they not?"

"Yes, of course," I said quickly. Perhaps too quickly, I thought then, for his tone changed perceptibly to one of solicitude.

"It's difficult, naturally, to be thrust upon one's relatives in your circumstances. I hope it is not an uncomfortable situation. Excuse me, that sounded as if I pry into your affairs, or put you in the position of having to explain, which of course you do not have to do. However, I realize some of the difficulties in being left alone in the world. I, too, am alone, except for two elderly uncles I seldom see. I do have the advantage of having a sufficient income so that I am not dependent upon anyone else's charity, however."

The heat in my face must have been clearly visible to him, even in this poorly lighted corner.

"And now I've put my foot in it again, haven't I? Damn it, I confess I don't know how to word what I want to say! India—Miss India—I only want you to know that if you need a friend, someone outside this household, I should like to be that friend. I'm going to ask you straight out, and please don't take it amiss that I do, for it's only out of concern for a lovely young girl left homeless. But you do not bring a fortune of your own, do you? You must rely upon Major Graham's generosity? Or am I mistaken, jumping to a completely erroneous conclusion? Did your late father leave you well provided for?"

I could not meet his eye any longer. I stared, sightless, out across the crowded room, at the colorful swirling dancers. "I do rely on my uncle's generosity," I said painfully.

He sighed. "I feared as much. The plight of an orphan is bad enough, but to be penniless as well—" He broke off, "Enough of this, we are celebrating tonight, and here I sit depressing the most charming young lady in the room instead of trying to entertain her. I say, they're playing a waltz!"

The musicians, soldiers borrowed from the Presidio for the occasion, had indeed swung into familiar music, but I nearly panicked. "I—I do not waltz, sir! I'm sorry!"

"Not waltz? But it is the most delightful of dances, Miss India!"

Was there no end to my reasons for blushing? "It is only that until today we had no lessons in dancing at all, and we've not yet got around to the waltz!"

His dark face broke into a smile. "Ah, if that's all! Well, come, you shall have your second lesson in dancing, and this one will be the waltz! I'm sure you will have no trouble with it!"

Even had Amalie not later informed me that Sherard Millay was the most accomplished dancer in the room, I should have known. For he took me, insignificant wisp that I was, and transformed me into a graceful, gliding,

113

happy creature. And when Nathan Peltier claimed the next waltz half an hour later, the joy must have been shining from my face.

He smiled, whirling me out onto the floor, and I prayed that I would manage as well with him as I had with Mr. Millay, for I trembled inwardly at his touch.

Except for greeting me, with the others, when he arrived. Mr. Peltier had not come near me earlier in the evening. Indeed, it seemed to me, observing from across the big room, that he was quite entranced by both Caro and Manuela, putting himself out to keep them both laughing.

And now he was smiling at me, and my hand was in the warmth of his, as he guided me in the increasingly familiar pattern of steps.

"Your sister tells me that you've only today learned to dance, Miss India. You're doing so beautifully, it's obvious you must have a natural rhythm and grace. And you look as if you're having a good time. Are you?"

"Yes! Oh, yes! It's all lovely, isn't it? All the candles, and such a beautiful room, and so many people having a good time!" I caught myself, aware that I was gushing.

"You're not sorry you came here, instead of returning to England, then. To your grandparents."

Perhaps the wine I had had at dinner loosened my tongue, for I'm sure that his proximity might otherwise have had the opposite effect. "I have no particularly happy memories of my grandfather. I remember my grandmother as a kindly lady, but she was completely dominated by Lord Stuart-Brice and so could seldom act on her own. No, regardless of what we found here, I think we would have no desire to go to England."

"You've hardly been here long enough to know how well you like your relatives, I suppose. Major Graham seems—well, not a warm man, even when he is being hospitable."

"But Amalie is lovely," I said. "Already it seems that we are sisters."

"Ah, yes." He guided me around so that I could see

114

Amalie, with her beloved Ramón, both of them virtually glowing. "And the little Hester, what do you think of her?" There was amusement in his tone.

"I don't think Hester likes us. But perhaps she can be won over."

At that he laughed. "Perhaps. Although you sound disinclined to work at it as hard as might be necessary." His laughter faded. "And the pretty Amalie will soon be gone to a home of her own, to a life that will undoubtedly be very busy so that she will not spend much time in this house again. I hope that Casa del Mar will be a happy place for you, when Amalie is gone. It might be that you will eventually consider a trip to England. Your grandparents must be quite elderly by now; there will not be many years more in which to rejoin them. They are quite wealthy, I believe."

This last was said casually, with some delicacy, yet it brought a flush to my cheeks, a touch of spirit to my voice. "If you think I would try to worm my way into my grandfather's good favor for the sake of his fortune, sir, you are mistaken. He has not cared to do anything for us all these years, not even so much as to send us a letter. I hardly think his wealth is of any concern to us."

"I didn't mean to imply that it was," he said gently. "Yet it cannot be easy, to be dependent upon—other relatives."

"What difference does it make which relatives we are dependent upon? I am—" I stopped, appalled, as I realized I had almost blurted out my age to him. "I am old enough to be thinking about marriage, and within a few years Caro, too, will be of an age to marry. Surely, like Amalie, we will find husbands in this land and go to homes of our own, and when we go we will take the twins with us. And if I don't find a husband, well, then, no doubt I shall make the best of my situation, whatever it may be, without resorting to calling upon my grandfather."

"I think that finding husbands will be the least of your problems," Nathan Peltier assured me. "Two such lovely young ladies, in a land where there are far more men than women. But there is surely no hurry about that. You should have an opportunity to enjoy yourselves for a long time before you settle down to matronly duties."

The dance came to an end, and I to the end of my breath. This dancing was indeed something for which one needed to be in good physical condition. Yet I was reluctant for it to end, much as Cinderella must have been at the ball when she danced with her prince.

"Would you like something to drink? I believe the servants are putting out a cold supper for us, and there is excellent wine."

I knew that the single glass of wine I had already had, more than I was used to, was at least partially responsible for my euphoric state. But I did not want Mr. Peltier to walk away and leave me, either.

"That would be very nice," I said, covering my reluctance.

There was a general movement of the dancers back toward the dining room, where indeed the servants had been busy. There was a large salmon, a fish I had never eaten, which had been baked whole, and rested upon a platter in such a position as if it were still swimming. Mr. Peltier helped me to a serving of the chilled fish, and also to the other delicacies, some of which I could not even identify, including salads and fresh fruits.

Small tables had been set up in the drawing room as soon as the dancing came to an end, and when Mr. Peltier brought me a goblet of some pale, clear wine, I sipped at it recklessly, as all the others were doing.

It should have made a delightful ending to the evening, for ending it was. The Alvarados and their guest would be heading home, a considerable ride in the night air, and we . . . Luckily there were servants to see to the cleaning up, and we could go to bed.

And, suddenly, I was more than ready for that. The wine, I thought, so different from the sweet red variety we had had with dinner, the wine was making me feel most ~culiar. I ought not to have had so much.

116

I glanced over at Caro and Manuela, who had certainly taken as much as I; they were laughing and animated, not at all unwell.

I pushed my chair back from the table. "Excuse me," I said, and scarcely saw Mr. Peltier's face turned toward mine; he spoke, but his words did not register. My only thought was to escape before I completely disgraced myself.

I nearly ran through the back part of the house, seeking a door onto the cool evening where I might be sick without the humiliation of being observed.

I reached the gardens, and none too soon. The wine, and the excitement, and the unaccustomed exertion and rich food, combined to empty my protesting stomach. In the aftermath of this upheaval, shaking and weak but already beginning to feel faintly better, I clung to one of the stone benches provided for those who would watch the sea. But tonight I was not interested in moonlight on the water; I sat still, resting my forehead on still-trembling arms, until the worst of the sensations subsided.

I must go back into the house. No doubt our guests were beginning to depart by now, and what must Mr. Peltier think of me? Did everyone realize what had happened?

I straightened and inhaled deeply several times, realizing at last that the night air was cold. Could I navigate properly now? Without further making a fool of myself?

The fresh air helped. I stood and made my way back toward the house, to where I had left a door ajar in my urgency.

Somewhere off to my right, I could hear the chattering of the Indian women in the kitchen, their language unintelligible to me. And from the front of the house gay voices, laughter, and a shout of *"Olé!"* drifted back to me.

Did I have my nausea under control? Dared I rejoin the guests until the farewells were said? Or should I, coward but safe, retreat to my upstairs bedroom and lie down?

Someone would come looking for me if I took the latter course. And I should miss seeing Nathan Peltier before he left. Would he think worse of me that I had drunk so much wine it made me ill, or that I had crept away without saying good-bye?

For a moment dizziness again assailed me. A door closed, shutting off the source of light which had penetrated to this rear hallway, and for a moment I was disoriented, not quite remembering the layout of the ground floor.

The stairs were as lost to me as the rooms where the party was taking place. I began to inch my way forward, hands outstretched to guide me along the passageway and to prevent collision with any obstacle.

When I first heard the whispers, I was engrossed in my own discomfort and they did not register. Vertigo washed over me, so that I was forced to stop and bend my head, waiting for it to recede, praying that I would not have to turn about and race again for the garden.

And then the whispering voices gradually intruded on my own private misery. I caught a word:

"—dangerous."

And the reply, also in a whisper, so that I could not identify this voice any more than I had identified the first.

"You're a fool. She doesn't suspect a thing."

I continued to cling to the wooden strip at the top of the wainscoting.

Dangerous . . . doesn't suspect— What were they talking about? I inhaled deeply, willing the nausea to pass. And the whispers continued, but the speakers must have lowered their voices, or turned away, for I could not make out the words, until I heard my name.

"India is the one—"

The one what? Were they talking about me, or about the country I had come from? And who were they?

There were doors off the corridor on both sides; the speakers must be in one of those rooms, although I did not detect light under any of the doors. Perhaps the carpets were deep enough so that there were no cracks. Or

118

perhaps the speakers were simply having such a private conversation that they had not lighted any lamps or candles, because they did not want anyone to come upon them.

Were they talking about me?

I caught one final word. "Fool."

My groping hand encountered a door handle, and almost without thinking I turned it.

The room onto which the door opened was completely dark, as all the rooms were at night when the heavy draperies were drawn against the night air. Yet there was someone there, in that darkness; I sensed it, thought I even heard their breathing.

I opened my mouth to ask who was there, and suddenly the import of those words struck me with an impact that made my question impossible.

"Dangerous."

"You're a fool. She doesn't suspect a thing."

And, *"India is the one—"*

Fear, irrational but compelling, sent a chill through me, and I reacted instinctively. I drew back, pulled the door shut, and hurried along the passageway toward the part of the house where sounds indicated the party had not yet dissolved.

My outstretched hand bumped, painfully, into a closed door at the end of the hall. I jerked it open and nearly fell through the doorway into the rear part of the foyer.

The front door stood open, the cool of the evening tempering the warmth of a room overcrowded with people. Tío Roberto was the only one I recognized immediately, and then the twins and Hester came racing through from the area of the drawing room.

I snatched for my brother, spinning him around; he looked up at me in annoyance and tried to pull free.

"Don't, India! That wretched girl has taken Bethany's ribbon, and I'm going to get it back for her!"

"Where is everyone? All the family, everyone else?" I demanded.

For suddenly it had become imperative that I know

119

who I had overheard, whispering there in the darkened room.

He looked at me as if I'd taken leave of my senses. "What do you mean, where is everyone? They're all over!" He gestured toward the gaily clad Alvarados, and then toward Major Graham, who came out of the dining room with Don Esteban and with little round Doña Isabel in tow. "Who do you want?"

I didn't know. I couldn't even be sure if the voices had been male or female.

Listening to the voluble Spanish around me, I thought that the voices had spoken English without an accent. But beyond that I knew nothing.

Brice broke out of my grasp and dashed after the little girls; I did not turn to watch them scrambling up the broad stairs to the floor above.

"India? Where have you been?"

I spun around and reached for the edge of a door frame to steady myself when Caro spoke. She was flushed and excited, thoroughly happy-looking. "Mr. Peltier wanted to say good night to you."

Disappointment stabbed through me. "Has he already gone, then?"

"Just a moment ago. He said he'd see us again, of course. We'll be going to the Alvarado ranch, I think, within the next few days. Cristóbal has agreed to teach Brice to ride a horse—under Ramón's supervision, naturally. Are you all right? You're looking rather pale."

"I felt—unwell," I admitted. "Caro, where are the rest of the family? Where have they been for the past ten minutes, five minutes? Not the children, but the others? Major Graham and Aunt Maudie and Amalie? And Mr. Millay and Mr. Peltier?" For those guests, too, spoke unaccented English.

"I don't know. I haven't been paying any particular attention. Mr. Peltier just left, only a moment ago. I haven't noticed the others, especially. I've been showing Manuela the music room; she's trying to persuade her father to buy

120

her a piano and she wanted to look at ours. Aunt Maudie's, I mean. Why? India, is something wrong?"

"I'm—not sure. Caro, I need to lie down. Make my excuses, will you? I—I must go upstairs."

Concern was etched on her pretty features. "Do you w..nt me to go with you?"

"No, no. I only need to rest." I turned away and nearly ran up the stairs, but when I paused at the top no one was paying any attention to me. Everyone who was still there was now packed into the crush in the foyer, women adjusting shawls, several of the men retrieving their hats. Aunt Maudie was speaking with Doña Isabel, smiling, taking her hand; it was the first time I had seen my aunt up and moving about.

Major Graham was bidding farewell to his guests. Amalie was there, reluctant to take her leave of Ramón; they touched hands briefly, unnoticed by anyone except me. Sherard Millay came from the direction of the drawing room, with Manuela Alvarado beside him; he bent his head to listen attentively to her chatter, and they laughed together.

Who? Who had whispered about me? What had they meant?

I felt too numbed to even attempt to figure it out. I turned away from the guests taking their leave and went on to my own room, picking up one of the candles left burning at the top of the stairs for that purpose.

The room was cool and quiet when I let myself in. The bed had never seemed more inviting. I saw my reflection in the mirror, lighted by the candle I held. Perhaps it was just as well Mr. Peltier had not seen me to say good-bye; my face was chalky and my eyes overlarge, overdark, in that pale oval.

I set the candle down and opened a drawer to get one of the nightshifts a maid had put away for me only that morning. Dear heaven! Only that morning? It seemed eons ago.

I turned when the door opened, but it was Amalie, not

Caro. She, too, bore a candle, its glow sufficient to show that *her* face, at least, was still rosy and happy.

"India? Caro said you'd come up already. Are you ill, or only tired?" She carried a glass in her hand, more of the light, pale kind of wine; even the sight of it was enough to make me feel queasy again.

"I think I tried to do too much for my first party," I admitted, feeling foolish. "Papa used to allow us a tiny glass of wine at dinner, but no such amount as I had tonight. Did anyone notice, do you think?"

"Both Mr. Peltier and Mr. Millay asked about you, but I don't think anyone was aware of anything out of the way. Mr. Peltier did seem puzzled when you left the supper table without warning, but then one must occasionally withdraw for personal reasons—" She lifted the glass and looked at the wine. "I thought you might be overexcited and I brought you this to help you sleep. But I think it is not what you need." She giggled, and I had to laugh with her.

"No, I think it is not," I agreed. "I'm sure I'll be asleep before I can even undress, if I don't hurry. I wonder which drawer has my—"

"If you don't need it, I'll drink it myself," Amalie said, and lifted the glass to her lips to drain it.

I thrust a hand into the drawer of the dresser, fingers closing over what I sought. And then I felt it, something strange and unpleasant and—frightening? Yes, frightening, for I jerked back and stared.

On the back of my hand was a creature such as I had never encountered, but one had only to look at it, even by candlelight, to know that it was deadly.

It had a round, shiny black body, and long legs—spider legs?—and as I stood paralyzed, it began to move toward my arm.

9

My choked cry brought Amalie around, the goblet poised in her hand. "What is it? India, what—oh, my God!"

My own horror increased as I saw her face. This insect, if insect it was, of such a size and malevolent shape, was not unknown to Amalie.

She came toward me in a swirl of garments, her voice sharp, crisp. "Put your hand atop the dresser!"

I do not know how I managed to do so, for I was hypnotized by the fat-bodied, evil thing—so light a touch against my skin, but so terrifying. I had not thought I could move, either to brush it off or to crush it; instinct told me that its bite would be poisonous, perhaps fatal.

No sooner had my hand been placed flat on the polished surface than Amalie moved with the wine glass. I felt the last few drops of moisture as she dropped it, upside down, over the creature, and quickly slid it off from me, onto the dresser.

The creature moved there, angrily, in its crystal prison, with a candle on each side of the glass.

I began to shake and knotted my hands into fists. "What is it?"

"A spider. A black widow spider. They're very dangerous, very—" Amalie was shaking, too, watching the angry thing in the glass as it searched for a way out, tried to climb and could not. "One of the men at Rancho Hermoso was bitten one time, on the hand. His entire arm swelled up so that he could not even put on his clothes— he very nearly died, he was sick for weeks."

"Are there—many things like that here in California?"

She was calming down now, more quickly than I. Amalie shrugged, putting a hand to her throat. "I have only seen two, in all the years we've been here. I think they don't usually venture into houses unless they are old, abandoned ones. They don't like people, Ramón says, but are often found in outbuildings. Once, years ago, Ramón says, a child was bitten and died in severe pain. We've never had one in this house. I can't imagine how it came to be in the dresser drawer—but it didn't bite you, thank God!"

"No, it didn't bite," I said, but I scrubbed at the place where it had been. "What are we going to do with it?"

"I'll call someone to dispose of it. Are you all right? Perhaps now you do need the wine to help you sleep!" She was no longer amused about the wine, but serious.

I shook my head. "No. No more wine. But I'd be grateful if someone took that thing away."

I did not prepare for bed until Caro came back with Amalie and the man Carlos, who was Teresa's husband. He took no chances with the spider, but slid it into a container by moving the goblet to the edge of the dresser top so that the creature fell over the side and was trapped in yet another prison.

"I will kill it," Carlos assured me. "Is very strange—the spider does not often come into an inhabited house, señorita. But this one will cause no more trouble."

The house was very quiet when he had gone. Caro and I undressed and got into bed; I silently, she chattering away.

"It was a lovely party, wasn't it, India? Everyone was dressed so beautifully! And the food, and the music, and the dancing—you know, much as I loved Papa, and miss him, I resent what he did to us, to deprive us of a normal social life! I was young, perhaps—at fifteen I might not have gone to adult parties. But you, you ought to have had a chance years ago, to meet young men—don't you think Nathan is an extremely attractive man?"

"Nathan?" I echoed, hesitating before I blew out the candle.

"Mr. Peltier, then! But he said we could call him Nathan, Manuela and I. He was very friendly, and he danced with me ever so many times! He told me all about his family in England, they sound like great fun, even his parents, not stuffy at all, although his grandfather sounds somewhat like Lord Stuart-Brice—rather prickly, I mean. Maybe one gets that way when one is old. Nathan said you remind him of his little sister, Susan, a bit."

I blew firmly on the small flame and was glad my face was hidden in the darkness. His sister? I didn't want to remind anyone of his sister, let alone Nathan Peltier!

"I hope it's months and months before the next ship comes, bound for England, don't you? Neither Mr. Millay nor Nathan will leave until then—Manuela says there are not many English ships, and it may be spring before one comes. Imagine what fun it will be, to have parties and handsome young men to dance with, all through the winter!"

My throat nearly closed. Of the two of them, Millay and Peltier, it was the latter I was drawn to. But he had danced only once with me, many times with Caro. And he said I reminded him of his sister!

"It was a marvelous party, wasn't it?" Caro said again, and I murmured something she took for agreement.

"You're not still upset about that spider, are you?" she asked, snuggling deeper under the covers.

"No," I said. "Go to sleep, Caro."

But for all my weariness, I could not sleep. Long after my sister dreamed beside me, I lay awake looking up into the darkness, listening to the surf beyond the open windows, thinking.

In spite of what I had told Caro, I was still upset about the spider. It was the most singularly unpleasant thing I had ever come in contact with. I should have thought so even if Amalie hadn't told me how dangerous it was.

But how had it come to be in the dresser? Its normal habitat was away from human beings. Granted, the dresser might have been empty for some time, but only that very day the servants had had all the drawers open, had packed away our clothes in them. Surely they would have noticed anything so big and black and horrid, if it had been there then.

Hester was a strange, unlovely, unlovable child who resented our presence in this house. Was she capable of so vicious an act, of putting a deadly spider into the drawer where anyone would have known I must go for my nightwear?

But if she knew a black widow was dangerous, dangerous enough to kill, would she have dared to do such a thing? Would she have been brave enough to handle it herself?

Carlos had handled it, I remembered. He had kept it safely inside either the glass or the container he brought to dispose of it, so that the danger to himself was minimal. Might not Hester have done the same thing?

Even now the thought of the spider sent a chill through me. Its very name was evil: *black widow.*

Yet Hester, having grown up in a country where such creatures abounded, might well have felt no qualms about handling it, so long as she took precautions to protect herself. And yes, I thought, I could believe she might have wanted to frighten me very badly, might even have been willing to risk having me bitten.

I might have written it all off as a childish, though vicious prank, except for one thing. Those whispering voices I had heard, the words that I had not been intended to hear.

For the whisperers, whoever they were, had not included Hester. They had been adults, angry sounding, urgent. No prank there. Whatever it was they discussed, it was quite in earnest.

Considering that I had overheard so few words, a surprising number of them were ominous. *Dangerous. Fool. Doesn't suspect.* And even my name, *India,* had taken on a sinister overtone.

What was dangerous? I? Did I pose some danger to

someone in this household? But how could I? I had only just come, seeking shelter, nothing more. *Fool.* That had been directed at one of the whisperers, *"You're a fool, she doesn't suspect a thing."* Who was *she*? I, who did not suspect a thing? What was there to suspect? And whatever it was, would suspecting it make me dangerous to someone?

Might one of the whisperers have put the black widow into my dresser?

Not a joke, from however warped a sense of humor, but a serious intent to harm me?

But why?

And by whom?

There had been two voices. Two people, who thought I was dangerous?

The Major? And Aunt Maudie?

Who else was there, who spoke English without a Spanish accent? Only those two, and Amalie, and Hester, and the two Englishmen who had been our guests this evening, Nathan Peltier and Sherard Millay. And, just possibly, Ramón, although I did not think so; his English was good, but it retained the flavor of his own language.

I wrestled with the problems, with my suspicions, but I could come to no conclusions. There was too little to go on. And when at last I slept, it was to dream that black widow spiders came at me from out of every corner, every crevice.

The household slept late the next morning. I roused only when Caro crawled out of bed and stood at the window, slim and beautiful in her thin nightgown, to inhale the cool sea air.

"There's a fog," she said, turning back to the bed. "But Amalie says there often is, in the morning. By afternoon it will have burned off, and the day will be glorious. I'm starving, aren't you?"

I groaned, feeling as if I had sand in my eyes, as if instead of sleeping I had spent the night in unpleasant struggle with spiders and unseen dangers. "Some tea

127

would be nice, but I don't know if I have the energy to get up and get it."

Caro suddenly spun about the room, her long hair flying, and then collapsed upon the bed beside me. "Oh, wasn't it wonderful, last night? I dreamed of it for so long, and when it happened, it was even nicer than dreaming! Nathan says—"

I scarcely heard what Nathan had said, for it was painful to me that he had said so many things to Caro, rather than to me. Yet I could do nothing to destroy her happiness, for did not she deserve it, and need it, as much as I?

All through the day there would be a continuous stream of "Nathan says" and "Ramón says" from the two girls who were my companions; neither of them seemed to notice that I contributed so little to the conversation.

We ate, the three of us, in the breakfast room. The twins and Hester had come down hours ago, Teresa told us, smiling, and had all gone to the beach.

"Together?" I asked. If it *had* been Hester who captured the black widow and left it for me to find, was it safe for her to be with Bethany and Brice?

"Oh, *sí,* all together, the three of them. I think that the little ones are good for the *niña,* she is too much alone, too used to doing everything her own way. This will be difficult to do, with those two around."

"If they don't kill one another," Amalie said, sipping at her tea, and although it was said lightly, it was hardly a reassuring follow-up to my own musings. "I suppose Miss Strang is expecting us in the sewing room as soon as we've finished here."

"That is what she said," Teresa confirmed. "There is much sewing to do, no?"

"There is much sewing to do, yes. Ah, good morning, Mr. Millay. Did you sleep well?" Amalie lifted a smiling face to our house guest, who smiled ruefully in return.

"I might have slept better had I not taken quite so much of your California wine last night. It is more potent

128

than what I'm accustomed to, I'm afraid. Is that fresh tea?"

He joined us at the table, as Amalie explained about the wine. "Nearly everyone in California makes his own wine. We do not, for we have not the grapes, but the Alvarados have great casks of it, and everyone drinks it every day. There are many vineyards inland, and to the north of us; the fathers brought grapes with them many years ago, when California was first settled."

"The fathers?" Caro echoed.

"The Catholic priests, the missionaries, the ones who built the missions and civilized the Indians," Amalie said. "One day we must ride over to San Juan Bautista, for there is a most beautiful church there which you would enjoy seeing. Of course it is now only a parish church, the fathers do not have the power they had before secularization. There has been a mission in San Juan Bautista since, oh, 1797, but the church is not quite so old. I believe it was completed about thirty years ago, and unlike many of the buildings in the valley it was not damaged in the big earthquake in 1818."

"Earthquake?" The other three of us said it together.

"Oh, yes. We often feel the tremors, and there have been two quakes that I remember well when the plaster fell from the ceilings and the chandeliers were set to swinging and did not stop for more than five minutes."

Caro shivered. "How terrifying!"

"It is frightening, but it is over so fast one scarcely has time to be afraid until it is all over. One gets used to the tremors."

"I won't," Caro said positively. "The very idea of the earth shaking beneath my feet is dreadful!"

"I hope that we can organize an excursion to this mission, this San Juan Bautista, while I am here," Sherard Millay said. "I would like to see as much as I can while I am in California. Once I've gone back to England, I will probably never come this way again. Would it be asking too much to know if any of you ladies are free to explore a bit with me today?"

He said *ladies*, yet it was to me that he looked with expectation. Had it been Nathan Peltier who asked, my heart might have quickened more than it did. But Mr. Peltier had clearly shown his preference for Caro, had he not? And Mr. Millay was quite handsome, quite charming.

He awaited a reply, and I looked to Amalie. "I believe that we are required to be available for fittings and so on, are we not? And to help Miss Strang with all the sewing that will be necessary before Amalie's wedding. So I'm afraid that exploring, at least for today, is out of the question, Mr. Millay."

"I'm sorry to hear it, but we'll do it another time. And please—must we continue to be so formal, since we are all to share the same roof for some time to come? My friends call me Sherry, and I implore you all to consider me your friend and do likewise. And I should like, if I would not be thought presumptuous, to address you by your given names, as well. Would we be thought quite outrageous if we did so?"

Our discussion of this question was brief. In England it would not at all have been the thing, but in California things were different. People were more informal, more friendly.

We left Sherry drinking more tea, and withdrew to the sewing room, where Miss Strang had already been at work for some time. All three of us were pressed into service with needle and thread, under her direction.

Caro and Amalie chatted away as they stitched, and occasionally I added a comment when I was directly addressed. But sewing is a task that can be done without thought, and so my imagination had plenty of time to run wild, and I did not like the thoughts I had.

There were things that frightened me more than the prospect of an earthquake.

Had I been alone with Caro, and had she not been bubbling over with "Nathan says" and delight in the previous evening's festivities and her anticipation of the ones to come, I might have confided in my sister as I had always done in the past. However, the fact that we were both drawn to the same man, who had seemed to indicate more interest in Caro than in me, had a dampening effect on my conversation.

No one appeared to notice, however, that I was in less than good spirits. Either that or they assumed that I had not fully recovered from my indisposition of the previous evening. At any rate, both Caro and Amalie chattered away so that there was no lapse in the conversation, no uncomfortable pauses for me to fill.

When at last Miss Strang indicated that we had finished for the day, we were only too eager to escape. Amalie retired to her own room, but Caro and I decided to seek out the twins and make sure, as Caro put it, "that Hester hasn't done them in, nor they her."

"Poor mite, she's not nearly so pretty as Amalie, is she? Bones sticking out in every direction, and that unfortunate hairstyle! You'd think Amalie would take her in hand, since Aunt Maudie has not."

"I suspect that taking Hester in hand is something one does at considerable risk," I said dryly as we walked down the sandy slope toward the shore. The three children were there, building sand castles close to the water's edge. "They all seem to be intact so far, making friends better than I had thought they might."

When we arrived at the construction scene, however, we learned that the friendship was more like an armed truce.

Bethany confided the facts to us, out of earshot of the other two, who were working farther down the beach, building elaborate edifices in the damp sand.

"It's a contest," she said. "Brice says I'm to judge which is the best, but Hester says I won't be fair, so we must have someone else judge. Perhaps Carlos."

"I'm sure Carlos will be impartial," I told her. "Have you been enjoying yourselves?"

Bethany made a face. "Hester always wants to do everything her own way, and she thinks we are stupid because we don't know about things she does. Brice says she would be just as stupid if she went to India. And she threw sand in Brice's face when he told her that she was rude and horrid. She *is* rude and horrid."

"And what did Brice do when she threw sand in his face?" I asked uneasily, although since Hester was only a hundred yards away she certainly had not been seriously injured for her foolishness.

"He hit her. I know Papa always said he was not to hit girls, but really, India, she is so hateful! I think he left a bruise on her arm. Do you think she'll tell Aunt Maudie, and then we'll be punished?"

"I don't know, I'm sure. But since she provoked the disagreement, perhaps she won't want to talk about it. Why aren't you making a castle too?"

"It's too much work. I'd rather wade in the waves and watch them wash out my footprints."

Caro had wandered toward the castle builders, and Bethany lowered her voice to make certain that it did not carry beyond ourselves. "Hester pinches. Very hard. On my arm, and on my bottom. Brice told her if she pinched him again he would hit her in the mouth and make it bleed. But I'm afraid if I did that, she would do something worse to me. Hester says they didn't want us to come here in the first place, and that she wishes we would go away. Do we have anywhere to go, India?"

I put an arm around her shoulders and hugged her against me, but the bleakness came through in my tone. "Not unless we go to Grandfather in England, and we haven't really the means even to do that. Perhaps when Hester gets used to us she will feel differently about us."

Would she, though? She was skinny, but bigger and bolder by far than Bethany. What could I do to protect the younger child? When Brice was around, he was quite capable of protecting them both. But there would be times when Bethany would be alone. If Hester had been responsible for the black widow in my dresser drawer, what else might she be mean enough to do?

"I think," Bethany said, snuggling against me, "that I will simply stay away from Hester as much as possible."

And that was as good a solution as I could think of, myself.

10

Aunt Maudie, after the efforts of the previous day, retreated to her room and had her dinner there alone. However, she sent word by Teresa that she wanted to see all of us after our own meal was concluded.

Major Graham had not been present; no one knew exactly what his business in Monterey consisted of, but I assumed that it had something to do with his hopes for the governorship, should the British take over the government of California. How realistic those hopes were I had no way of knowing, but I was grateful for anything that kept him away from home. Certainly the dinner table was a livelier place without him.

Sherry Millay put himself out to be entertaining, relating anecdotes about his experiences in Calcutta, where he had been sent on business for one of his elderly uncles.

"He hadn't the decency to come and ask me himself to travel around the world. Nor even to summon me to him, which would have been quite reasonable, considering his age. No, he does not care for me overmuch and so communicated only through his solicitors. But so long as he sent passage and expense money, why, I was just as pleased not to have to deal with him in person. He's a bit of an ogre."

"And do you stop in Monterey on business for your uncle, too?" Amalie asked.

"Yes—and for myself, as well. California has great potential as a producer of hides. If there were any practical way to get it to England, it would be valuable for the meat, too; now, I understand, virtually all the beef except what can be used locally is wasted. India, if your evening is not already spoken for, would you care to explore the library with me? I believe that you are a reader, as I am; we might find something with which to entertain the entire group, reading aloud."

Again he had singled me out for attention. I was flattered, and yet I could not help wishing that it was Nathan Peltier, instead, who sought my company.

"I will see what my aunt wishes," I temporized. "Perhaps she has something she wants us to do."

But Aunt Maudie, resting comfortably against her pillows with the inevitable box of chocolates at her elbow, had only an announcement to make.

"Tomorrow there will be an excursion to Rancho Hermoso for anyone who wishes to go. Miss Strang is agitated about the amount of work to be done before your wedding, Amalie, but I have promised her that if you take the day off tomorrow, you will all work harder after that. And Doña Isabel has promised us the loan of her own seamstress since there are now so many to sew for.

"Ramon has promised to send the *carretas* for you, bright and early, so you must all go to bed early tonight. They will leave Rancho Hermosa at dawn, so you must be prepared to go as soon as they arrive and the drivers have had time for a bit of refreshment. The *rancho*," she explained to us, "is a good two-hour trip by cart, although it can be done much more quickly on horseback, of course. Ramón will supervise the instruction of all who wish to learn to ride horses. And the Alvarados have been kind enough to invite Bethany and Brice to stay with them between now and the wedding, so that they may learn more quickly. If they care to stay, they should prepare tonight with all their belongings. What do you think, India?" she asked, deferring to me as the eldest.

It seemed to me an excellent, if temporary, solution to the problem with Hester. And the twins were eager to go.

So that was agreed to; Bethany would come back before the wedding for the final fitting of the dress she was

135

to wear to the ceremony. The other things she would need would have been left until after the wedding, anyway, for Amalie's trousseau must come first.

The packing, and the early hour of the next morning's departure, gave me the excuse I needed not to join Sherry in the library. Amalie gave me a sympathetic glance.

"He is quite taken with you, India. Isn't it marvelous, that you have only just arrived and already found a champion? Each of you?"

So Amalie, too, had relegated Nathan Peltier to Caro. I tried to keep my voice level.

"But when the next ship sails for England, they will both be on it," I reminded.

"Who knows? In the meantime you may fall in love, and if Sherry asked you to go with him, back to England? Wouldn't you want to go?"

"I'm in love already," Caro announced. "And if I'm invited, I guess I would go to England. Although I've begun to love it here—it's so different, so wild and free! I like that, being free!"

I did not want to continue the conversation, and turned away.

The trip to Rancho Hermoso took the full two hours Aunt Maudie had said it would. We had hoped that Ramón and Nathan would come with the men who drove the *carretas* to get us, but they did not. However, we were all to go, Caro and the twins and Amalie and Hester and I, and Major Graham rode beside us at a leisurely pace, to be sure that no harm befell our party.

The carts were reasonably comfortable; we rested upon sweet-smelling hay, and so long as we kept Hester in one cart and the twins in the other, there were no problems. Caro went with our cousins, in the lead *carreta*, and I could hear the babble of their voices without being able to make out what they said over the creak of wheels and the sounds of the horses' hooves.

Our way wound inland, away from the Pacific; we had

136

started out warmly wrapped against the morning fog, but soon left it behind as we dropped into the valley beyond the low hills.

Brice asked dozens of questions I could not answer, about the grass and the cattle in the distance and a multitude of other things. It did not bother him that I did not reply most of the time; he was so excited about visiting the ranch and learning to ride horses that nothing could have dampened his enthusiasm.

We had risen early, and I was still tired; once I had adjusted to the movement of the *carreta*, I lay back and fell asleep until Brice's shout roused me.

"There it is, India! Look, look at all the buildings!"

Rancho Hermoso, from a distance, looked more nearly a village than a ranch. The buildings gleamed white in the sunlight, most of them with red-tiled roofs. The house, which we learned was called a hacienda, was very large, two stories, and with a shady veranda across the front where Manuela and Cristóbal awaited us.

There were corrals and outbuildings of all kinds, and horses, enough horses to send Brice into raptures. Clearly, in this country, every man had at least one horse, and they were beautifully cared for and expensively saddled.

My eyes swept over those assembling to welcome us, seeking the fair head amongst all those dark ones, but I did not see it. Ramón was not there, either; I heard Amalie's cry of disappointment.

But Amalie would soon be married, she would have her Ramón forever. I pulled myself together and began brushing hay off my clothes. I would let nothing spoil this excursion, certainly not envy of someone who deserved the happiness soon to be hers.

The Alvarados met us in force, even the black-clad Doña Isabel appearing, plump and smiling, in her doorway.

And then, at the last moment, Ramón and Nathan Peltier appeared from the direction of the corrals. Strong arms lifted us from the *carretas*, and my spirits soared when, for a few brief moments, Nathan's hands were

137

upon me. He was laughing, welcoming us, and swung Bethany off her feet, then turned to the other cart, and to Caro.

"Come in, come in! After so long a ride, you must be ready for something to eat!" Ramón cried.

We had eaten before we left, but we were ready to eat again. We tromped across the wide veranda, past its inviting hand-fashioned chairs, and into the hacienda itself.

"This is what a house should be like in this country," Ramón told us cheerfully. "Everyone will make it their own home, for whatever time you are here! Manuela, show our guests where to wash up, and then there is food for everyone!"

The house was of adobe, like the buildings we had seen in Monterey. It was all freshly whitewashed, and we were amazed at the thickness of the walls, at least three feet through.

"It is to keep out the heat," Amalie said when Caro commented upon this.

"And there was a time when the walls also served to keep out enemies, although it is some years since we have had any difficulty with those," Cristóbal said. He was a fine-looking boy who would grow into as handsome a man as his brother; though only three years older than Brice, he stood a head and a half taller.

The *sala*, or living room, was an enormous one. Here, too, the walls were whitewashed, a startling contrast to the darkly paneled walls at Casa del Mar, and they were brightened with pictures and gaily colored mats or rugs. The tile floor was softened with scattered, vividly woven rugs.

There were dogs and cats everywhere, and half a dozen young children. Two of them I recognized as belonging to Ramón's cousin; the others were apparently the offspring of the servants, of whom there seemed to be countless numbers.

The coolness of the house was welcome, and I found that I liked it, the uncluttered spaces designed for comfort and convenience rather than for elegance. Indeed, the simplicity had an elegance of its own.

I never did learn exactly how many people lived in the hacienda; I don't think Doña Isabel herself could have said without counting them off on her fingers. There were uncles, aunts, cousins, and an ancient grandmother who had not attended the dinner party at Casa del Mar; she was a tiny, wrinkled lady addressed as *Abuelita* Rosa by the family, and as señora by the servants.

We were taken to Manuela's room, where we washed and combed our hair; I was pleased with the way the curl had stayed in fairly well in spite of the way the wind had blown through it during the journey. I would make as good an appearance as it was possible to make.

It was then that I saw how the Spanish built their houses, and it was a manner both practical and attractive. It stood in a hollow square around a courtyard, or *patio*, in the midst of which a fountain played. So far as I could tell, every room in the house opened upon the courtyard, with covered verandas running around the entire interior at both first- and second-floor levels.

The patio was full of growing things, was green and blooming in a profusion of late-summer flowers. Amalie caught my eye and smiled. "It is beautiful, isn't it? I can hardly wait to come here to live."

"But not for the fountain and the flowers," Caro teased, and we all laughed when Amalie blushed.

The Alvarados cooked as they did everything else: with great generosity and enthusiasm. The "little breakfast" set out for us included every sort of fruit I had ever heard of, freshly baked bread and flat, unleavened cakes called *tortillas* wrapped around assorted fillings, none of them identifiable except a strange variety of pinkish bean, great platters of fried eggs, and a beverage that was new to us.

It was called coffee, and we drank it hot and sweet with sugar in it, cup after delicious cup.

The twins could hardly wait to be done with the food; Bethany was allowed to change into a pair of her brother's trousers in preparation for the riding lesson.

139

Hester, of course, already rode; she was superior in her expertise and offered a good deal of advice, most of it unappreciated. Once I saw Cristóbal wink at Brice after Hester had made a particularly stinging observation, and I felt better about them. Between the two of them, the boys were more than a match for Hester.

Major Graham joined us for some of the coffee, then was off to talk with Don Esteban before he continued on in his way to Monterey. Whatever our uncle's actual possibilities, he was certainly making every effort to prepare himself for the high office to which he aspired, and no doubt the support of an important man like Don Esteban Alvarado would be of great value.

Enough value, I wondered suddenly, to make it worth his while to encourage the marriage of his daughter to the Alvarado heir? But it was an unworthy thought, for there were plenty of indications that Major Graham was fond of his children, and that he saw to their comfort and their needs as Papa had seen to ours.

We were to participate in the riding lessons, too, but not until we had had a chance to rest a bit, which we were only too happy to do. Manuela and Amalie showed us about the hacienda, including the suite of rooms—a bedroom and a sitting room—which would be Amalie and Ramón's private quarters after the wedding.

"Mama and Papa have always had their own separate rooms," Amalie said, brushing slender fingers across the crocheted spread on the bed, "but Ramón and I have already decided to do it the way *his* parents do, to share a room." And then her face flushed a deep pink, in embarrassed pleasure.

"Manuela, come along," Cristóbal called from the veranda. "If anyone is going to ride, Ramón says it should be done now, before it gets any hotter! Pancho has been given orders about the horses, and they are ready!"

We had no riding habits, of course, and at our ages could not expect to ride astride as Bethany was going to do. But the Alvarados came in all sizes and shapes, and

Manuela found costumes for Caro and me; Amalie, naturally, had her own.

As soon as we emerged from the house, I could see what Ramón meant about the heat. It was going to be very warm, here away from the cooling sea air.

The younger members of the family were out of sight somewhere; once we heard a whoop of laughter that I knew meant Brice was enjoying himself. I smiled, glad we had come.

Hester was not with them, but had climbed onto the rail fence that surrounded one of the corrals where the animals had been prepared for us. I had not been apprehensive until we got close to them and saw how large they were.

Pancho was a small brown man with a luxuriant mustache and only a few teeth, which were clearly visible when he smiled. He did not, we learned, speak much English, and that badly, but we would make out.

Caro was mounted first, and Pancho indicated, with gestures and his few English phrases, how she was to hold the reins, how she was to hook her knee around the pommel of the saddle; the reins were then given over to a rather dirty little boy, to lead the horse around the corral to begin with.

Pancho then turned to me. "And thees is the señorita India, no? *Este caballo por la señorita!*"

I gazed mistrustfully at the beast he held ready for me to mount. It was enormous, and it rolled its eyes at me as if to signify that it found me lacking as well.

But Pancho was gesturing with his hands, showing me how I must climb the mounting block and then position myself on the horse.

Hester watched from the corral fence, her thin mouth twisted in an expression of derision. It was that which decided me, and I moved to follow Pancho's bidding.

The next few moments are rather blurred in my memory. I had mounted the horse, I had correctly positioned my right knee, but instead of leading the beast

141

about as the boy was doing with Caro's horse, Pancho handed up the reins.

"*Bueno, bueno,*" Pancho said, and I felt the animal tremble beneath me, the heat of his flanks reaching through my garments, and then the horse shied away from the fence.

Behind me, Hester let out an explosive and unladylike yell. The next thing I knew I was fighting to retain my seat as the horse reared and bucked.

I went off, hitting the hard, dry earth with such force that all the wind was knocked out of me and I could not even cry out. The horse kicked, and for a moment I saw those deadly hooves over me; had it been possible to do, I would have rolled to one side, but I was stunned and could only wait for the trampling I was sure would come.

The next few moments were confusing. I heard someone scream, and Pancho's exclamations, which I could not understand but were certainly profane.

My head had struck something and my vision was imperfect, my eyes refusing to focus, and the pain in my chest grew with an excruciating, fiery agony. And then vision faded altogether, and the only sensation that remained was pain.

11

I was not really knocked out, they said, for the blackness lasted no more than moments; I might have wished it to last longer, for as consciousness returned, so did that searing pain when I tried to inhale the air I so desperately needed.

There was a great babble of voices, most of them speaking the Spanish I could not comprehend. But tone of voice seems to be universal, for I was dimly aware that the words showed concern.

"Get that damned horse out of there!"

That voice I recognized, as a moment later I knew who was kneeling beside me, hands gently probing. When my vision began to clear, it was Nathan Peltier's fair head above me, his face close to mine, the clear brown eyes showing relief when I made a gasping noise.

"India? Where are you hurt?"

His arm assisted me to a semi-sitting position and steadied me against him, so close that I could feel his breath on my forehead.

Speech was still beyond me, but at least I was breathing again, uncomfortable as it was to do so.

"Do you think you've broken any bones?" Nathan asked.

I groaned. It felt as if I'd broken every one I had, but I was not yet able to say so.

"Bring her into the hacienda," Ramón said worriedly. "I don't understand how she came to be put up on that

143

stallion, he is not fit mount for a woman, and half the men on the place wouldn't ride him!"

He turned on the hapless Pancho with a barrage of rapid Spanish, and the poor man hunched his shoulders and spread his hands in the universal gesture of disclaiming knowledge or responsibility.

The next thing I knew, Nathan Peltier was lifting me in his arms and carrying me across the sunburnt earth toward the house, with half a dozen people bobbing along beside or running ahead of us. I didn't care about any of them; I turned my face to my rescuer's chest and closed my eyes, still feeling too dreadful even to be aware of humiliation.

In the great *sala* I was put gently upon a sofa, and while the women of the household clustered around, murmuring, Nathan did not release my hand but knelt beside me. "India, do you hear me?"

"Yes," I muttered thickly.

"Good. If you like I will carry you upstairs and the women will put you to bed. There is a doctor at the Presidio, one of the men can ride to fetch him—"

I swallowed. "No. I don't think—I need a doctor. I only need to—breathe." Suddenly I remembered the story Aunt Maudie had told, how she had ridden the forbidden horse and been thrown, with no damage done except the wind knocked out of her. And I remembered, too, what Papa had said to her—*Maudie, if you've broken any bones, I'll kill you.*

To my own astonishment, I laughed.

For a few seconds the expression on Mr. Peltier's face wavered, as he considered, no doubt, that I was on the edge of hysteria. And then he, too, smiled. "I think she's going to live," he pronounced. "Are you going to tell us the joke, India?"

"Papa," I said, the effort of the speaking still painful. "When Aunt Maudie was thrown—from His Lordship's stallion—"

Caro and Amalie, then, both chimed in with the rest of the story, and Nathan grinned with them. Relief was

144

clearly written across the faces of those who understood what I had tried to say, for if one still had a sense of humor, one could hardly be mortally injured.

Ramón, however, hovered at the end of the sofa, his handsome face a thundercloud. "Miss India, I can't tell you how sorry I am that this thing has happened on my *rancho*. It was some dreadful mistake, one that should never have happened. Pancho is not very bright, but he is good with horses, and I thought he could be trusted to see that you were given a beginning lesson in riding. I cannot quite make out who told him what, but it seems that he thought you were an accomplished rider! He knew your sister was not, and he put her on a proper old nag, as he should have. But he insists that someone told him you would be insulted if he gave you less than a spirited horse, and he chose a stallion that has never been ridden by a woman!"

His distress was evident, and I wanted to assure him that since I had survived I did not blame anyone, but he did not give me the opportunity.

"Pancho is easily confused, and now he is frightened and upset by your fall, which makes him even more stupid than he usually is! I know that Major Graham spoke to him about the lessons and, I'm sure, explained that you were both novices. And Miss Hester, too, knew that you had never ridden before. But apparently a good many people offered advice, some of it in a humorous vein, and poor Pancho misunderstood something—his English is poor—or took literally something said as a joke, and now he is prostrated with remorse. As are we all, that you should be hurt on a visit to us."

Even then, while pain was the thing uppermost in my mind, there was yet room for an emotional reaction to two other things; one was the fact that Nathan Peltier still knelt beside me, holding my hand, and that there was concern in his face. Second was the suspicion that someone might have told Pancho, in all seriousness, to mount me on that wicked stallion.

Breathing was somewhat easier by now, and I would

undoubtedly be bruised and sore for days to come. I must pull myself together and reassure Pancho that I had not been killed because of his error, and let my hosts know that I did not hold them to blame for my accident.

This I tried to do, and all the faces looked a little less distraught; it was taken for granted however, that riding lessons were finished for the day.

This did not apply to the twins, and I thought they were safe enough with Cristóbal since he spoke excellent English and knew perfectly well that neither of his students had ever sat a horse before. No one, however deliberate the intent, could mislead him as Pancho had been misled.

Yes, that is what I thought. For while it was perfectly possible that an old man, with orders issued to him in a language only half-understood, could have made such a mistake, I could not believe that this was the case. Had it not been for that black widow in my drawer, for those whispering voices in a darkened room, such thoughts would never have occurred to me. But once having arisen, suspicion would not be put aside.

I said nothing, of course. Not even to Caro. For the first time ever, there were others than myself to be her companions, and it was obvious that except for her fright over me, she was enjoying this visit tremendously.

So I lay back in a hammock, an ingenious and amazingly comfortable contrivance in a shady corner of the garden, and simply rested while the others went up to Manuela's room. Occasionally I heard their voices or their laughter, and I envied them their innocence and their happiness.

Perhaps, I thought, we should go on to England and Lord Stuart-Brice. Certainly there we would be safe, and he could hardly refuse to take in his grandchildren once they'd appeared on his doorstep. We had no money, but perhaps Captain Spacy could be persuaded to take us, since he was bound for England anyway and had as yet no new passengers to occupy our cabin, knowing he would be paid once we reached our destination.

The urge to flee was strong. I had no proof of anything, but I felt convinced of a malevolent force around me; even His Lordship caused me less apprehension than dealing with spiders and "accidents."

I fell asleep, and woke to find Nathan Peltier sitting in a chair only a few feet away, watching me.

I scrambled to sit up, wondering if I had let my mouth fall open, or if my skirts had been immodestly arranged, but he waved me back.

"No, no, be comfortable. I hope I didn't disturb you, but I'd had enough of either Ramón's energetic excursions or those silly schoolgirls chattering, and I've not adjusted to the Spanish custom of siesta. Everyone else is asleep." His smile was relaxed, friendly. "I'll admit, though, I hoped you'd wake up and talk to me."

Mildly flustered, I didn't know how to respond. Silly schoolgirls? And he did not put me into their class? I pushed with one foot and set the hammock swinging gently.

"This is a beautiful spot, isn't it? I see why the Spanish like their courtyards."

"Not quite like English gardens, but lovely nevertheless," Nathan agreed. "It's a very different way of life they live, indolent by English standards. Yet everyone seems prosperous and contented. I envy Ramón and his Amalie; they have much to look forward to, and I'm sure they will be very happy."

"They are very lucky," I said quietly.

"And you, India? What do you look forward to?"

"I? To the same things every girl does, I suppose. To—to being like Amalie, to making a good marriage and having a family." I could not say, *to falling in love*, but surely he could read that into my words for himself. "I have been thinking about England, wondering if we made a mistake to come here instead of returning to Willows Hall—"

"Why do you think this might have been a mistake? Aside from the fact that poor old Pancho mistakenly gave you the wrong horse?" It was asked with a smile, but I remembered his concern when he bent over me there in the corral, when he lifted and carried me to the house, and I did not take it amiss.

I could not explain, either. I could not tell him the things that disturbed me, things that just possibly might have no significance at all.

I shook my head. "It is sometimes hard to know what is the best thing to do. This is a beautiful land, but so many of its people speak a different language, which we will have to learn if we hope to remain here, or we will be forever strangers. We lived too long in Calcutta without ever becoming part of that world, and I don't want to make that mistake again. I have no money for passage to England—" Embarrassment warmed my face at this admission to a man who was, after all, little more than a stranger. "But I wonder if Captain Spacy would consider taking us; I'm sure my grandfather would pay him once we were delivered there."

He had been in the act of tracing an irregularity in the wood on the arm of his chair; his fingers stilled for several seconds before he spoke. "I'm afraid it's too late to ask Captain Spacy about it; the *Essex* sailed this morning, shortly after dawn. And the *Durham*, of course, had already gone."

So. It was already too late. I had not even attempted to send a message to my grandfather, for I knew that Sir Roland had already done so, months earlier, right after Papa's death. By this time Lord Stuart-Brice knew where we were, and that we were impoverished and existing upon the beneficence of Aunt Maudie and Major Graham.

For the first time it occurred to me to wonder if Aunt Maudie, too, had been cut off from her family, or if she corresponded with them after all these years.

"Well. That is disappointing," I said, making my voice light. "But I don't suppose Caro and the twins would have liked leaving California, anyway. I think they are all quite willing to learn to speak Spanish and ride horses and take siestas."

"And you?" His voice was soft, kindly. "How do you feel about those things?"

I sighed. "Cowardly. Very cowardly." And then I wondered what had possessed me to make so frank a statement (for all that it was true) to a man I wanted to impress.

He did not seem put off by this statement, however, but grinned at me much as Papa used to do when he was pleased with me, although perhaps I misinterpreted it. For what was there to be pleased about?

"Well, I can't help you with the Spanish, God knows, for I've only picked up a smattering of it myself. They all speak so rapidly I'm not sure I could interpret their words even if they spoke English. And siestas, I suspect, are easily learned, especially if one is kept up late at night eating, drinking, and dancing. A nap during the day is simply a way to survive. About riding a horse, now, though. I am quite accomplished at that, having taken my first spill, such as yours, a good many years ago. There is a common belief among riders that the thing one must do when one is thrown is to get up and immediately get back on the horse. Not, of course, until one has his wind back, but directly thereafter. I would be most happy to teach you to ride, India; and we have no language difficulty to allow for any further mistakes such as this morning's. Would you permit me to do that?"

For a moment the enormity of his offer struck me dumb. I only just kept from letting my lower jaw drop.

"I am sure Ramón will provide horses—appropriate horses, not dangerous stallions. And I would, of course, ride over to Casa del Mar to undertake the lessons. Please say you will do this, it would give me great pleasure."

"I—I—That is very kind of you, sir."

"Not kind at all. Having something to do, in the company of a young lady, is much better than having nothing to do by one's self. I am a visitor here, with no skills of any value to my hosts, all of whom have work to do, business to attend to. They put themselves out to see to my comfort and my pleasure, yet there are long hours on

149

my hands. The ride to Casa del Mar is a pleasant one, and instructing you in the art of riding a horse would be an even pleasanter task. Please say yes."

I forgot my aching chest and limbs as a surge of pleasurable warmth washed through me. "I should be very happy, then, to agree, sir."

His grin made him look suddenly younger than the twenty-five years Caro had learned him to be. "Good! I'll be over, oh, say in midmorning? Tomorrow? And please, since we are going to be friends, and I don't quite have the hang of this señorita business, may we not be on first name terms? Nathan and India?"

"Were I in my grandfather's castle, I doubt that would be thought proper. But in California, it seems, one can dispense with some of the more rigid rules."

We sat there, smiling at one another, until Ramón came to summon us to join the others, and I was well content.

We rode home in the early evening, Amalie and Caro and I, with Hester sulking because she had not been allowed to remain and visit with the twins. Ramón and Nathan rode with us, and it was a merry group, for we laughed and sang and were in such a mood that we might almost have been thought inebriated when we reached Casa del Mar.

Aunt Maudie and the major and Sherry Millay were just about to go in to dinner. Amalie expressed surprise that her mother was joining the others so soon after the dinner party. "She tires so easily, and it is an effort to get up and down the stairs, but no doubt the company is stimulating, with a guest in the house, and she feels she must make the effort."

Make the effort she had, and she was elegantly gowned in heavy green satin, her plump hands laden with jewels which flashed when she gestured, as she did frequently.

"You'd be better off for a change of clothing and a freshening up," she told us, plucking a bit of hay out of

Amalie's hair. "But since the meal is about to be served, I believe we will put up with you the way you are. India, whatever has happened to you? There is a dreadful bruise on the side of your face!"

"I fell from a horse," I said, and watched their faces, the major's and Aunt Maudie's. For once I had reentered this house, my suspicions returned full force.

No one reacted any way but normally, however, with concern and gratitude that it had not been any worse. Amalie explained to her father.

"It seems that Pancho thought you—or Hester, or someone—told him India was an accomplished rider, and he gave her this great brute of a stallion. Ramón says few of the men would care to ride him!"

Major Graham met my eyes directly. "The man is an imbecile! Granted my command of the Spanish language may not be perfect, but it was sufficient to indicate to anyone but the feebleminded that the girls had never ridden before! I don't know why Don Esteban keeps the man on—he's obviously dangerous! At least India was not seriously injured; I've known people to break their necks falling from a horse."

"It is possible to survive," Aunt Maudie said, moving toward the table where the servants were hastily adding more places, "without riding a horse. I haven't been on one in nearly ten years; no, longer than that. Before Hester was born. India will manage without riding except in a carriage or a *carreta*, I should think."

"But I'm going to learn to ride," I said.

My words dropped into the stillness like a pebble into a pond; I could feel the circles widening until they had touched everyone in the room. I was not sure how I knew it, but I thought that someone—more than one?—felt a strong reaction to what I had said. But I did not know for sure what the reaction was.

"Mr. Peltier is going to ride over tomorrow for the first lesson," I said. "He has time on his hands, and as he said, there is no language barrier, so there will be no misunderstandings."

"There are horses in our stables," Major Graham said. "But they are too spirited for a beginning rider, and except for Amalie's and Hester's horses, they are not used to being ridden by women."

"Mr. Peltier said that Ramón would supply appropriate horses."

The major grunted, leading the way toward the table. "In that case, there should be no problems. Come along, let us eat before the food is cold."

Hester, still sulking, had little to say during the meal. But everyone else made up for it. Amalie and Caro were full of their day, of the beauty of the hacienda at Rancho Hermoso, of the friendliness of the Alvarados, of Ramón and Nathan.

"Do you think Nathan would teach me to ride, too?" Caro asked. "After all, I didn't get much of a lesson today. As soon as you were thrown, everything came to a stop."

"I don't know how much time he will have, nor how many horses," I temporized, but I devoutly hoped that the lessons would be mine alone. Selfish I knew it to be, but Nathan had, after all, referred to the others as silly schoolgirls, which seemed to indicate that he did not regard me in the same light. Perhaps he was not, after all, completely taken with my sister.

"You can borrow my horse, if you like," Amalie offered generously. "After taking this day off today, I will have to spend the rest of the time until the wedding in the sewing room, I expect."

By this time my bruises were making themselves felt. I was lame and sore, and only too ready to go up to bed shortly after dinner. Mr. Millay was at the foot of the stairs as I started up, his expression one of concern.

"I can't tell you how sorry I am that your excursion today was spoiled by an accident with the horse. And how glad I am that you weren't hurt beyond a shaking up."

I thanked him, pausing only briefly, then went on up the stairs, but Sherry came with me.

"This Peltier fellow, do you know anything about him?

Other than that his father knew Don Esteban years ago, or some such thing?"

"Only that his family lives in Essex, not far from my grandfather's."

A frown was etched faintly in his forehead. "I see. Well, I suppose there's no harm in riding lessons, no matter what sort he is. I mean, the lessons will take place close to home, and since everyone will know you're together, he will surely not try to take advantage in any way."

I nearly stumbled on the stairs. "What do you mean? Why should he try to take advantage of me?"

"He seems quite a charming fellow," Sherry said. "From a young lady's point of view, I mean. But I should hate to see you hurt in any way, India."

My face felt frozen into a stiff mask. "Why should I be hurt? He is only going to teach me to ride a horse."

Suddenly he smiled. "Yes, of course. And I'm sure he's an able teacher. He grew up, I believe, as a member of the British aristocracy, and riding was a major part of that life." He made it sound useless, as well, and I had no response to this. We had reached the head of the stairs. "Good night. I hope your unfortunate accident today won't prevent a good night's rest."

I walked away from him, down the long passageway toward my room, my mind churning. Was he warning me against an emotional involvement with Nathan Peltier?

Well, to be quite fair, such an involvement was what I hoped for, wasn't it? It was true that in a country of such vast distances it would be most convenient to know how to ride, and certainly such a skill would make it easier for me to get off by myself, to widen the field of freedom I had just begun to taste.

But it wasn't because of that my heart had leapt when Nathan made his offer. Not at all. I hoped that closer acquaintanceship would ripen from friendship to love. I longed for the relationship that Amalie had found with Ramón, the romance I had dreamed of since the day I read my first novel, half my lifetime ago.

153

I knew that Nathan intended to return to England. But he might change his mind, during the months before the next English ship arrived in Monterey. I did not know what a young Englishman might do to occupy himself in California, but surely if he desired to remain he would find something.

Was that what Sherry was warning me about? That Nathan might trifle with my affections and then sail off to England without me?

I was puzzling on it, increasingly troubled, when I entered the room I shared with my sister. Caro had lighted a lamp and her reflection looked out at me from the mirror, highlighting her lovely hair. But there was a frown on her face.

"I always thought I should enjoy living in an English manor house. Perhaps it would be different with English servants, rather than Indians or Mexicans."

"What ever do you mean by that? The servants are all most helpful, and very friendly, I thought."

I closed the door behind me and leaned against it, as if to shut out the memory of what Sherry had said to me, and my own reaction to it.

"Well, look at this." She tilted up the delicately made case which had been Mama's, to show me the jumbled collection of trinkets. "Someone's been poking around in here, the chain is so tangled on this pendant I haven't been able to straighten it out. And the earrings were all in their places, in pairs. Look at them now!"

I walked across the room to examine the contents of the box. "Why do you assume that the servants did it?"

Caro looked at me sharply. "Who else would have done? I'd be inclined to blame it on that insufferable Hester, but she was gone all day, the same as we were. And I'm sure Aunt Maudie is above such snoopings, even if she got about easily, which she doesn't. Amalie says she almost never leaves her own room, except for something special like the dinner for the Alvarados."

I shrugged. "All the Californios seem to appreciate

154

beauty. No doubt whoever looked at the things was simply admiring them. There is nothing missing, is there?"

"No." Alarm suddenly quickened in her face. "India, you still carry the pearls on your person, don't you? They're safe?"

"Certainly they're safe." Unconsciously, I rested a hand against them. "Caro, you haven't told anyone about them, have you?"

"No. Never a word, although I don't know why they should be such a big secret. After all, the whole point of giving them to you was as a dowry, wasn't it? Dowries are to attract husbands, aren't they?"

"I don't want a husband because I own a valuable necklace. Indeed, unless I sold them, of what use would they be to a husband? They're to be worn."

"But you haven't worn them. Do you know what I thought, when you fell from the horse this morning? After you'd begun to come around, so that I knew you hadn't broken your neck, I mean? I was afraid they would take you into the hacienda and perhaps undress you, put you to bed. Even just to examine you, to make sure there were no more serious injuries. If they had, they'd have discovered the pearls. What would you have done then?"

"It didn't happen, so why worry about it now?" I asked, but of course it was a matter for thought.

"You're going riding again tomorrow, and probably every day, for a time. What if you fall again? What if you're injured, and brought in unconscious?"

"Oh, for pity's sake, Caro! As if I weren't nervous enough about getting up on a horse again—"

"Well, there's no telling, is there? I don't think you ought to carry the pearls around on your person the way you've been doing. You ought to hide them."

"And where would you suggest, so that they wouldn't be found? The house is full of servants who poke into everything in the very nature of their work. Probably one of them was dusting the jewel case and couldn't resist taking a look into it, and then fingering what they saw. I suspect the pearls are not gaudy enough for the tastes of most of

155

them, but I wouldn't want to risk putting them in the jewel case."

"I'm not suggesting you should. But there must be many places in a house the size of this one to hide something, if you insist on keeping the pearls a secret."

"I'll think about it," I promised, and got out the rags on which to curl my hair, putting an end to the conversation.

But there was no putting an end to my thoughts. And after I had gotten into bed and blown out the lamp, my anticipation at meeting Nathan tomorrow was overshadowed by those thoughts.

Had it been simply an inquisitive but harmless servant who jumbled the contents of the jewel case? Or was the act tied in, more sinisterly, with the break-in of our trunks, when our clothes had been examined and scattered?

But if Caro hadn't told anyone, and I believed that she spoke the truth, then how could anyone know there was anything valuable to search for in our belongings?

12

My days took on a pattern. Breakfast with Caro and Amalie, and sometimes Hester, in the room overlooking the garden. An hour or two of sewing with Miss Strang and the others. And then the riding lesson with Nathan.

Caro begged to be included in the lessons, but Nathan brushed her aside, lightly, smiling, but firm. "I can't teach two people at once; I should be distracted from one while I attended the other. If there is time, when India is sufficiently accomplished, we may do it then. Or India herself may be qualified to do it."

Caro was disappointed almost to tears, but there were plenty of things to do, and both Amalie and Sherry Millay were available to her for company. I stifled my own sense of guilt and simply enjoyed the lessons.

Not that I was not terrified, the first day, when I must again mount a horse. But this one was a far cry from the great stallion that had thrown me, a gentle mare who stood patiently while I mounted and, after the first few minutes, calmed my fears.

Those rides were the high point of my day, for once the lesson had been completed, when I returned to Casa del Mar in a state of exhilaration, I spent hours in a euphoric daze with the mountains of sewing in Miss Strang's domain.

We were usually dismissed from those tasks an hour or so before dinner, when there would be time for reading or music—Caro, Amalie, and I all took turns at the piano, often with Sherry listening in contentedly—and then there would be dinner itself. Aunt Maudie did not participate having returned to her custom of having a tray in her room.

We saw Maudie every day, however, for we must report our progress with sewing and lessons. I became accustomed to the smell of chocolate and the soft sounds of the insides being sucked out of them, although I never ceased to wonder that she could eat regular meals in addition to the quantities of candy that she ate. She never offered any to anyone else, and I never once saw Major Graham in her room, nor, indeed, in the same corridor where it was; he kept to the ground floor or his own suite at the far end of the house, strengthening my impression that theirs was less than a love match.

Maudie seemed to like to talk, and we would all sit about in the oversoft chairs and listen. Mostly she recalled humorous episodes from her childhood, and admitted freely that she had caused a great deal of trouble and that Papa, or Juddy as she called him, had had his work cut out for him, protecting them both from His Lordship's cane.

Sometimes Hester, too, sat in on these sessions, but I think that she resented mention of Juddy as much as she resented us. She was such a sour-faced little thing. If she happened to be with Aunt Maudie when we showed up more often than not she would leave, without so much as excusing herself. She had, as Caro remarked tartly, no manners at all.

Sometimes, in the dusk, I liked to wander by myself on the beach. There was something wonderfully soothing about the play of the surf on the shore; it put things into proper perspective, somehow, to know that the ocean had been occupied thus for thousands of years and would continue to go on for thousands more, no matter what mere human beings did or did not do.

Perhaps I also used those evening walks as a hedge against an increasing intimacy with Sherry, for he seemed to take every opportunity to be with me. He did nothing objectionable, actually, only talked about ordinary things,

158

but he made me uncomfortably aware of a pressure I did not know how to handle.

More to my liking was the time I spent with Nathan. Again, nothing really happened, except that we talked more easily, also of ordinary things. But I felt we were becoming friends, and perhaps that might lead to something deeper than friendship.

The trousseau grew and was finally completed, a stunning array of finery that included everything from evening gowns to riding costumes, from underwear with tiny tucks and ribbons and lace to exquisitely detailed nightshifts of the finest silk. Amalie was busy with the wedding plans and spent less and less time with us.

The wedding would be held in church. But instead of returning to Casa del Mar for a reception, they would go from the church to Rancho Hermoso.

"There are so many who must be included, you see, and there is not room for them all here. They will come from miles around, and as the festivities will last for days, there will have to be sleeping space for them all."

"I thought all Ramón's relatives already lived at the ranch," Caro observed.

"No, no, those are only the *closest* relatives. There are many cousins and another set of grandparents and distant relations. Also, there are many friends. Everyone in Monterey, everyone in the valley, will be invited. It is the custom. There will be eating and drinking and dancing; Manuela says there will be plenty of romancing, too, since a celebration such as this is the only chance many young people have to meet and get acquainted. Papa did not feel that we should follow the Spanish customs, but Mama insisted we were Californios now, and that we should not offend any of the Spanish community by sticking to our staid English ways. When she put it that way," Amalie said with satisfaction, "Papa had to give in. He is very conscious of his position and the respect the Californios have for him."

I wondered if Aunt Maudie knew of his ambitions to be governor of California, and wondered at how cynical I had become, to be so totally convinced that the major capitulation had been in his own interests, rather tha Amalie's.

When Amalie's trousseau had been completed, with th assistance of the seamstress from Rancho Hermoso, ther was a little time left to attend to the needs of the rest us.

Gowns for the bridal attendants were all made alike; had begged Amalie to reconsider about the matter of th maid of honor, and so Manuela remained with that dut Caro and I would be co-attendants, which was enough f us who had so recently come into society. Hester and Bet any, with their late summer flowers in dainty white ba kets, would also be dressed alike.

Manuela sent an invitation to Caro, proposing that a ter the wedding she should prolong a visit at Rancho He moso.

"Do you think I ought to stay?" my sister aske brightening perceptibly. I wondered if she were intrigue by Manuela or the prospect of being under the same roo with Nathan Peltier, and then decided this was unworth of me.

"Why not, if you'd like?" I said it quietly, and Car immediately looked at me more closely.

"Well, for one thing, it would leave you here alon Amalie will be gone, and the twins are apparently intenc ing to stay on at the ranch indefinitely—there would b only you and the major and Aunt Maudie and Hester."

My voice was dry. "That does sound dreary. Howeve if we're to live here—I'll have to get used to it, won't And you were the one who was invited, not me."

"It's not that Manuela doesn't like you," Caro sai "She thinks you're so much older, and more mature. Yo don't like to do the silly things that we do. Amalie's clos to your type, only of course she won't be wanting con pany for a while—"

"Not on her honeymoon," I agreed. "Don't wor about me, just go and enjoy yourself."

"I do worry about you, though." Her eyes narrowe

taking in my appearance. "You've always been slim, but I think you've lost weight." She tugged at the waist of my dress. "See, it's loose! And there's been something about you, you're not yourself. You don't really like it here, do you, India? You seem almost—almost afraid of something."

For a moment I hesitated. Although we had been sharing a room, and a bed, ever since our arrival, we had talked very little, considering how we had for years confided everything to one another. But at Casa del Mar we had been very busy, and there were so many other people to talk to—and I was reluctant to put my suspicions into words.

Yet now—now I heard my own words, reluctant, yet carrying a conviction that was reflected in my face as well, for I saw myself in the mirror and turned away.

"Something is wrong, I think. When Major Graham talked to me that first evening—I didn't understand what he said, what he meant. I thought he didn't want us here, he went on about how he was not a wealthy man, and something about—" I stopped, remembering that he had warned me to say nothing of his aspirations regarding the governorship. "About his business plans, none of which meant anything to me. I thought perhaps he meant to send us on to England, but he didn't do that."

"Aunt Maudie and Amalie have been most hospitable," Caro pointed out. "And except for the fact that someone was poking about in our jewelry case—and"—she frowned thoughtfully—"I think in our drawers, too, since then, but that surely was inquisitive servants, and nothing's been taken, well—we've certainly been treated like family."

"I heard someone talking, the night of the dinner party," I said slowly. And I told her what I had heard. And after that I related what Ramón had said, that old Pancho was sure someone—my uncle?—Hester?—had urged him to provide me with a spirited horse. "And the black widow—how could it have gotten into the dresser if someone didn't put it there?"

161

"India! You can't believe that because they don't want us here, the Grahams are trying to—to murder us!" Caro was incredulous. "Or even to deliberately make us frightened or uncomfortable! What would be the point? If they truly don't want us here, why not have simply sent us on to England on the *Essex*?"

I didn't know, of course. I had hoped that it would make me feel better to confide in my sister, but somehow relating my fears had only strengthened them, not allayed them.

"It might be that little wretch of a Hester. She's capable of being rather vicious, I think," Caro went on more thoughtfully. "But surely she wouldn't seriously intend to get you killed!"

"It wasn't Hester I heard in that darkened room," I reminded. "That was adults, I'm sure."

"But you don't even know for sure whether they were men or women? And what was it they said, something about someone not suspecting a thing? It was an engagement party for Amalie, maybe they were planning a surprise for her."

But they had also mentioned danger, or something being dangerous. And I had either heard my own name, or someone referred to the country in which I had lived for so many years.

I had related all this to Caro, so I didn't belabor it now. I tried to assume a more cheerful air. "Perhaps you're right. At any rate, go ahead and accept Manuela's invitation. It's what we always wanted, isn't it? A chance to make friends of our own age? And Manuela can teach you Spanish, and more about life as a Californio."

"And Sherry will be here. I'd forgotten Sherry. You do like him, don't you, India? He's quite taken with you, I'm sure he is. He watches you all the time, and even when he talks to me, it's mostly about you."

"Oh? What does he say about me?"

"He asks, mostly. About what you like to do and read and so on. He does try to please you. Don't you feel anything for him at all?"

162

There was a painful ache in my throat, quite unexpected. "I think he is very attentive, and very kind. Of course I appreciate that."

"But you aren't falling in love with him." She was disappointed, but I couldn't help that.

"No, I don't think so."

Caro sighed. "Well, there will be other men, no doubt. Amalie says there are far more men than women in California, and more coming all the time. Some of the Americans are quite handsome, Manuela says, although her parents think them rather rough and uncouth. I suppose they haven't had the advantages of education such as Nathan and Sherry have had; the United States is such a primitive country as yet. I can't wait to fall in love—I could do it now, easily, with Nathan, but I'm afraid he looks upon me as a schoolgirl. Is fifteen too young for a man of twenty-five?"

The pain intensified, but I managed to speak past it. "Probably. I'm going back to the sewing room, Caro. I've a hem to finish."

"India!" Her tone held me back. "There's something—You're going to have to find somewhere to put those pearls before the wedding."

I turned, staring at her blankly, still thinking about Nathan. "What do you mean?"

"I mean if you aren't going to be brave enough to wear them, then you'll have to hide them somewhere. The dress you'll wear for the wedding is cut in such a way that you'll never be able to disguise that pouch beneath it, the way you do now. I felt it when I touched you just now, and sooner or later someone else is going to be aware of it, too."

I hadn't thought of the style of the new dresses, but she was right. The gown was fitted at the waist; there were no concealing gathers.

"I'll think of something," I said, and went on down the passageway to the sewing room.

Miss Strang sat bent over the garment on which she

stitched; she straightened and rubbed at her back when I entered the room.

"It must be very difficult," I said, suddenly compassionate, "to spend all your time sewing."

"It's hard on the eyes," she admitted. "But I've been doing it for more than thirty years, ever since milady was a young girl. I wouldn't know how to do anything else."

"Milady? You mean Aunt Maudie? You've been with her for over thirty years?"

"A lovely little thing she was, much like Miss Amalie." She bit off a thread and made a critical appraisal of her work, then began to rethread the needle. "She had such beautiful clothes, she did. Lady Stuart-Brice always had the best of everything for her."

"And you were at Willows Hall?" I had no memory of her, but then as a small child I had taken little notice of anyone save my own nanny, and I scarcely remembered her.

"From the time milady was ten," she confirmed. "Oh, she was a spirited one, she was. Had Miss Amalie's looks and Miss Hester's bit of deviltry."

I wondered if she'd admire Miss Hester's bit of deviltry if she knew it included black widow spiders and dangerous horses for inexperienced riders, but I forbore to ask. I was more interested in something else.

"Then you knew Papa! You were at Willows Hall when he was a boy, too!"

"Oh, yes. I remember Judson very well, although of course I did not see as much of him as I did of milady."

She was not looking at me, and I thought there was something odd in her tone.

"Didn't you like my father, Miss Strang?" The question was out before I could control my tongue, and at that she put down her work and looked at me across the lapful of pale pink satin.

"Like him? Yes, I liked Mr. Judson," she said, and bit off another thread. "I felt very badly when he was sent away from Willows Hall. Very badly indeed."

"Sent away?" My mouth was suddenly dry.

"Why, yes. I thought you knew it; it was certainly no secret within the family." She looked me fully in the eye, then, and there was something there I could not identify but which chilled me, nonetheless. "Lord Stuart-Brice covered it up, so that there was no open scandal, no prison sentence. Mr. Judson was sent away because he stole Lady Montague's star sapphire."

13

For a few moments it seemed that my breathing, painfully stopped, could not be restarted. Papa? Stole a sapphire?

It was impossible. I knew my father. He would never have stolen anything. And then, at once, suspicion rushed in to fill the void within me. Papa, a remittance man. *Was that why he had kept us cloistered at Willows, because if we had moved in Calcutta society someone would have told us?*

Even as my thoughts took the traitorous turn, my lips denied. "I don't believe it. Papa would never have done such a thing."

Miss Strang stitched grimly. "He was very young then. Very foolish."

Not that young. And never that foolish.

"I don't believe it," I said again, with less force. "Did he admit it? Did he say he had stolen something?"

"I don't believe he ever did. But then, Juddy often did not own up to his misdeeds, even as a child."

"But he had a brutal father—yes, he was, and don't deny that to me, because I remember my grandfather, Miss Strang! And he used to strike out with that dreadful cane, I remember him nearly breaking my hand because I picked a tulip! A tulip, one tulip, when there were hundreds!"

"His Lordship was a stern disciplinarian," the seamstress conceded.

"What happened to this—this star sapphire that was stolen? What was Papa supposed to have done with it?"

"It turned up, eventually. Mrs. Montague got it back."

"But then why——? I don't understand. If it was stolen, and he was punished for it by being sent away from his home, even away from his country, then how did Mrs. Montague get it back?"

"It was delivered by a messenger. No note with it, nothing like that, and the fellow was gone before anyone could question him. A common sort, a paid emissary, no doubt."

"Before or after Papa left Willows Hall?" The pain of it was awful, and I continued to struggle against the things she told me, yet I could not give up hearing them.

"The day before, I believe." Miss Strang paused to sip at a glass on the table beside her, and I realized she was drinking wine. At this hour of the day? Before lunch?

Having lubricated her throat, she went on. "But His Lordship was adamant that Juddy should leave; no member of his family who was a thief should get off unscathed, nor remain in England to further disgrace the name."

"But Papa was a married man with a wife and two small children! And if he said he was innocent, how could they believe——?"

"The stone was missing. While Lady Montague was a guest at Willows Hall. The facts were quite convincing." The look she gave me, then, revealed that she had harbored a resentment against Papa all these years, that she held him responsible for——what?

"Did Aunt Maudie believe he was guilty?" I demanded.

She took another sip of the wine, and I wondered if she'd be talking to me at all if it hadn't been for the wine. Certainly she had said almost nothing to me of a personal nature since I had been in this house, until now.

"Milady begged and pleaded and cried for her brother," the woman said slowly, remembering. "And when we heard that the gem had been returned, milady thought that would be the end of the furor, that Juddy would be allowed to stay. Only His Lordship said it made

167

no difference, the deed had been done, the guilt was there."

My lips were so stiff I could hardly speak. "So Papa was forced out, with his little family, and was never allowed to go home again."

"But his was the guilt! And he was not the only one who suffered for it! Her ladyship was heartbroken, but there was nothing she could do; and she lost both her children! Yes, both of them! Because in a rash moment of rage milady Maude swore that if Juddy were to be banished, she would leave as well, and she would never return to Willows Hall until Juddy was welcomed back, too. Which, of course, never happened. Lord Stuart-Brice is not the forgiving sort, not even after thirty years.

"So I packed everything for her, and for *him*, and we moved out, too, bag and baggage, from the only real home I'd ever known. You don't know what it was like, living in those cramped quarters provided for the military, after living at Willows Hall! Only a few servants, where there had always been dozens! Watching the pennies, when there had never before been any need!"

I had gained a small clue from her emphasis on the word *him*, whom she had packed for—him, being Major Graham.

"They were living at Willows Hall, too? Aunt Maudie and Major Graham?" I didn't remember them at all.

"Yes, certainly. Oh, they were off and about a good bit, but I still had my own room, my own things about me. Miss Amalie was in the nursery, or often at her grandmother's—Mrs. Graham was not gentry, but she was a gracious woman with a decent home and an income of her own, and she doted on Amalie. His Lordship could not abide crying babies, and your own mother managed to keep you reasonably quiet, but Miss Amalie had the colic and cried a good bit, so her other grandmother saw to her a good bit."

She sipped again at the wine, and the glass was now empty. I wondered how much of the stuff she had already had, and if she often drank up here in the sewing room by herself.

"So you see why I hold it against Juddy to this day, the ruin he made of milady's life. For she'd have been happy there in her old home. As I was happy there, with my own room and the privilege of having an old friend in for tea occasionally."

Yes, that would have meant a great deal to a woman like Miss Strang, that she could invite friends to the castle and be served tea by a white-capped maid. Still—still—

"But how can you hold Papa responsible for Aunt Maudie leaving if she decided it for herself? She saw how unfair it was, and she tried to support him—"

"She vowed to go in a moment of passion. She was always a passionate young woman, milady was. For all the good it did her, married to *him*." Again there was no mistaking the bitterness when she spoke of Major Graham. "And so we ended up here, in this godforsaken foreign land where there are no gentry, only peasants, peasants who cannot even speak the king's English! I have no friends to visit nor to entertain, and milady, what does she have, poor thing?"

She looked at me, her eyes big and dark and touched with a glaze that came from the wine, and I could not doubt that she believed the truth of what she said.

I had no answer for her, of course, and so she provided her own. It seemed that once started, this woman, who had probably been unable to confide in anyone for years, could not stop. The words literally spilled from her lips.

"She was so beautiful, once. A lovely, slim young lady. She had so much to give, so much, but she fell in love with a man her father said was not appropriate to her station in life. She would have married him anyway, although I advised against it, since he had scarcely a penny to his name, being the second son and having to depend upon himself. But milady was sometimes wild and reckless, and she swore she loved him. She was too young to know that love is not everything in a marriage."

My voice sounded rusty. "Yet a loveless marriage cannot promise much, either, surely."

"Oh, that's what she got, all right! Her father said the only way to put the foolishness out of her head was to see her married to someone of her own sort, and he brought home Major Graham. He wasn't a major then, but his prospects were good, and he came of a suitable family. Milady raged and wept, saying that he was so old, and she did not love him. But Lord Stuart-Brice was a man who had his own way, and the wedding took place. I made her trousseau, as I've made Miss Amalie's, but it was not a happy task, I tell you."

She sniffed, and a surprising tear fell upon the satin lying limp across her knees. "She was like a wild woman. She refused even to stand for the fittings, but a physician was called in and she was given something to quiet her. She begged me to help, but what could I do? I had no funds, no way to help her. I loved her as if she were my own, I did, but there was no way to go against His Lordship when he made up his mind."

"And so she was married to a man she did not love." The ache in my throat now was for Aunt Maudie.

"Did not love, and came to hate. Yes, that's not too strong a word to put upon it! Miss Amalie was born, and that was a joy to her, for she was a beautiful, if sickly, child. Milady was able to insist that the infant's needs came first, and for a time he allowed it. And then he got her with child again, and she wished it dead, and it was. It was born alive, but only survived a few hours, and she wept until she made herself ill, and thought that she had killed it by hating it because it was *his*. I tried to convince her it was not so, but she would not be consoled for the longest time, poor thing."

By now the tears were dripping, unheeded, spotting the satin. I ought to have taken it away from her, for it was Caro's dress for the wedding that she was hemming, but I did not want to chance interrupting the flow of words. Painful or not, these were words I had to hear.

"Two more babies came, and both died soon after they

170

were born. Oh, how guilty she felt, as if her hatred of their father had caused it! Even her physician assured her that this was not so, but *he* blamed her." The loose skin at her throat trembled with her emotion and she picked up the glass, but it was empty.

"And then you see what she had to do, at last and so dreadfully, to escape from him. After she knew that she was to have Miss Hester, of course. 'This is the last one,' she said to me. 'I'll not continue to produce babies that die.' We thought that Miss Hester would go the way of the others, for she came early, and she was so tiny and so ugly, poor mite, but milady fought fiercely for her. And strangely enough *he* didn't find her objectionable, although he certainly had not taken all that great an interest in Miss Amalie when she was an infant. Indeed, he made her the spoiled, pathetic child that she is now, poor Hester; he would not allow anyone to lay a finger upon her no matter how naughty she was."

She gasped for air, as if the telling were taking everything out of her, as no doubt it was; yet it was therapeutic, too. Would she regret, tomorrow, what she had said to me today?

Yet she must not be allowed to stop; I must learn all that I could, and I think that had the bottle been there I would have poured her more wine to further loosen her tongue.

"And you see what milady's become? What she's made of herself, so that he would leave her alone? So that she was so unattractive to him—no, even repulsive, he finds her now—that he did not protest when she moved into a room of her own? To eat and eat until it's a wonder she hasn't killed herself with eating!

"Oh, he was furious, he was, when she began to get fat! Tried everything, even to cruelly locking her into her room to keep her from eating. But even after all that had happened to her, milady retained her spirit. Each time he thought he had starved her into submission, and each time she came out she managed to get the food he had forbidden her, and eventually it was he who gave up. Not milady. Not my Maudie.

"And so she has peace from him, at last, but look at her! Look at her! Her beauty's gone, and her health, too, no doubt! It broke her heart when the letter came about Juddy. I thought she would never stop crying. Finally even *he* took pity upon her and called the physician from the Presidio to sedate her. You wouldn't know it, from the way she greeted you, I'm sure, she's adjusted to it somewhat by now, but I never heard her cry worse, not even when her babies died!"

Miss Strang snuffled noisily and groped about for a handkerchief, into which she blew explosively.

"And it all stemmed, you see, from Juddy taking that wretched gem. Can you blame me that I blame him?"

I could not reply. I was too shaken by the revelations she had made.

Certainly I understood how she felt about Aunt Maudie. And her own world had been turned topsy-turvy, as well, when she had to leave Willows Hall.

But Papa a thief? No. He could not have raised us the way he had, had he been a dishonest person.

Yet a sickening suspicion remained.

How had Papa come by the maharani's black pearls?

14

To say that I agonized over Miss Strang's disclosures would be to understate the case. Both Caro and Amalie noticed that my behavior was abnormal, and commented upon it. I put them off by saying that I was simply not feeling well, that I had had too much activity and not enough rest.

This left me with time to myself, but lying alone in my room was hardly reassuring. It only gave me time to think, and my head fairly spun as I tried, without success, to sort it all out and find something I could accept and live with.

The night before the wedding I had come to no conclusions at all; indeed, it was only with an extreme effort that I put aside the physical malaise my agitation had engendered and tried to enter into the spirit of the coming celebration.

I had spent as little time as possible downstairs for some days, and Sherry Millay finally cornered me that evening after dinner, as I was about to escape again.

"I hope you're feeling better, India," he said. "I've been concerned about you, very concerned."

"I'm feeling a little better," I said, which was hardly the truth.

"Well enough to participate in the wedding? I know Amalie is counting on you, but I'm sure she would understand if you didn't feel up to it."

"I wouldn't dream of disappointing Amalie, and I'm sure I'll hold up," I assured him. He had rested a hand on

173

the newel post at the foot of the stairs, effectively blocking my way. "Excuse me, please, there is one final fitting of my gown to see to."

"Surely Miss Strang isn't still sewing at this last minute!" he protested, but he did drop his arm.

"No. But the gowns have all been pressed and made ready for wearing. We try them on this evening to be certain there are no last-minute adjustments."

"I see. Well, I will look forward to seeing all of you in your splendor tomorrow."

I said good night and mounted the stairs. I was the first in the sewing room, except for Miss Strang. She flushed slightly, then turned her attention back to something she was doing with Amalie's dress.

I knew that she was mortified beyond words at how much she had told me that morning I found her drinking the wine; mortified, and perhaps angry, too, that I had allowed her to rattle on with so many family secrets.

Yet they were my family secrets, too, and I thought I was entitled to know them. And even if Miss Strang hated me for having been persistent when her control slipped, and in spite of the turmoil her revelations had caused for me, I was glad it had happened. It was only right that I should know.

I undid the buttons on my gray cashmere and stepped out of the dress, careful that the pouch I had carried for so long made no sound, nor was visible, when I laid the garment across a chair. Woodenly, without speaking, Miss Strang helped me into the gauze and satin confection I was to wear tomorrow, and I stood in front of the tall mirror to admire the fit.

Truly the woman was a genius with her scissors and needle. For a moment I forgot about everything except that I was wearing the most exquisite gown I had ever seen. Prettier even than Amalie's gown, I thought, for hers was a creamy white, while the delicate pink satin in this one was far more becoming to my coloring.

My hair would be curled before tomorrow, and I would wear Mama's locket at my throat—not the pearls!—but if ever a man should see me and be taken with my looks, it would be in this dress, even as I was tonight.

We heard Amalie and Caro on the stairs, and then their laughter as they came toward us down the passageway. The seamstress looked at me critically, and then reached out to pinch my cheeks.

"You are so pale the dress eclipses you," she said, and it was true that a bit of color in my face was an improvement, but I could not help thinking there had been a unwonted ferocity to the pinch.

"Oh, India, you look beautiful!" Caro had come to a halt on the threshold, her hands clasped at her bosom. "Oh, Amalie, it's going to be the most beautiful wedding ever!"

I turned about, and then about again, and everyone pronounced the dress to be perfect, in no need of additions or alterations.

"Now yours," Caro said to Amalie, and I slipped carefully out of my new gown and hung it up so as not to let it trail on the floor nor crease in any way.

I did not stay to see the others at their final fittings. Caro was right about the pearls, and I would have to find somewhere to hide them, at least during the wedding.

I had been thinking about places, but none of them seemed quite right, quite safe enough. I wondered now if the reason I had not told anyone but my sister of the pearls was that I could not admit to having them if there was any chance Papa had not come by them legitimately. Had I, even before we left Calcutta, suspected that he might not have done so?

The problem of a hiding place remained. Where? The pouch was not large, it would take only a small cubby in which to hide them, but I must be sure no one else would look there before I could retrieve them.

Not in my own room. I had decided that some time ago, for I was sure that someone, whether the servants or some other member of the household, had on several occasions investigated the contents of our wardrobe and our drawers. And if we were to be gone for the wedding and

175

the festivities following at Rancho Hermoso, the room would be totally unguarded.

The doorway to Aunt Maudie's room was open, and she called out to me. "India! Child, stop a moment and tell me: How is the new dress? Does it please you?"

I stepped into the room, which she always kept so warm, in which the air was so heavily scented, the whole overlaid with the fragrance of chocolate. It was not yet dark outside, but with the draperies drawn she always needed lamps in here.

"It's lovely," I said, and did not have to feign admiration for it. "It's going to be a beautiful wedding."

"And a happy one, I hope." She beckoned me nearer, indicating the chair beside her bed. "My Amalie is a very lucky girl to have a man who loves her as Ramón does."

I nodded, summoning a smile. "She deserves happiness."

"Yes. Hand me my knitting basket, will you, pet? I will work on it a little tonight, and then probably not for weeks again, until all this celebrating is over and we can get back to normal. I don't know how well I'll stand up to a wedding that lasts for days, but the Alvarados have most kindly offered to provide me with a private chamber, so that I may participate as I like, and rest when need be."

"And my uncle? Will he stay with the Alvarados, too?" I felt a new surge of warmth and compassion for this aunt of mine, knowing as I did something of her story.

"I think not. He does not like to leave Casa del Mar empty for long, although so far as I know there is little that could happen here. There are no longer any warring Indians in this part of the country; the Spanish fathers saw to that. Of course all the servants will attend the wedding and the dancing afterward, we could hardly deny them that. I need another ball of wool, my dear—would you fetch it for me? The scarlet. It's in the top drawer of that chest against the far wall, or maybe it's the second drawer."

Just getting to the chest she pointed out was like running an obstacle race; I pushed aside a chair, clambered over a footstool, and squeezed between a pair of tables. Since Maudie had chosen to shut herself away here in this room, she had obviously brought everything in with her that had any meaning for her.

I didn't envy the maid who tried to keep this place tidy, I thought, nearly sprawling over another low stool hidden in the shadows. The chest she spoke of was covered with mementos: a jewelry box of some light wood, painted with Japanese figures, some books, a tiny lamp, an ancient doll, a bowl of hard candies thick with dust, a box containing a child's marbles. In fact, everything atop the dresser was so dusty it made me sneeze. Obviously the maids didn't worry too much about the corners where Aunt Maudie herself seldom went.

I pulled open the drawer and began to look for the wool. There was every other color, but no scarlet.

"Try the second drawer, then, pet. And sit poor Tilly up straight, will you? She's been leaning farther every day, she's about to slide off."

"Tilly?" I echoed, turning about.

"Yes, my doll, Tilly. I've had her since I was four, and though there were many dolls after her, none of them ever meant as much to me as Tilly. You can see where she had a broken arm; that was so your father could play doctor and put her in a splint."

I looked at the doll, ancient Tilly, whose eyes were so faded she looked blind, and whose painted head had suffered many injuries over the years.

"Neither of my girls wanted to play with her; Amalie thought she was pathetic, a hospital case, and Hester thinks she is ugly. Which may be just as well, since she's lost half her stuffing and I've never gotten around to mending her, poor old dear. Yet I can't bring myself to throw her out."

I touched Tilly, improving her posture, and the idea was there. A doll no one liked, no one touched, not even to dust. A doll who had lost half her stuffing.

My heart began to beat more quickly. No one was

177

likely to come here, certainly no one would expect me to hide anything valuable in this room, if they guessed that I had anything valuable.

Poor Tilly toppled off the chest onto the floor, striking her head once again. I made some small exclamation and dropped to my knees, well hidden from the bed by the intervening rubbish.

For a moment I couldn't get the pouch free from my hampering skirts. And then I heard the material rip slightly, and I probed for the opening in the side of the doll, under her dress, where even now a bit of the stuffing oozed out.

"Are you all right?" Aunt Maudie asked, and I pushed myself to my feet.

"Yes, quite all right. I knocked the doll off, but nothing broke, and I cracked my head." I put a hand to my forehead, rubbing at it. "Now where is the scarlet—? Ah, here it is!"

Triumphant, I brought the wool to her. I do not remember what we talked about in the five minutes I remained in the room. It was only after I closed the door behind me that my heartbeat slowed to normal.

For now, the black pearls were safe.

The morning of the wedding dawned with only a trace of mist floating in from the sea. Long before we were ready to set off for the church, the sun had burned its way through the fog and we had clear, gloriously blue skies.

Amalie, though smiling radiantly, was very nervous. We would dress at the church, since our journey might result in damage to some of the fragile fabrics, so we were loaded into our carts (Aunt Maudie occupied one by herself) and the major rode horseback.

It was not until our cousin began to instruct us on the coming ceremony, and the part we would play in it, that we realized that the wedding would take place in the Royal Presidio Chapel, a Catholic church.

"It's the only church in Monterey, and the Alvarados

178

are all members of the parish." Perhaps it eased Amalie's nervousness to talk. "I, too, will come here after Ramón and I are married, and our children will be christened here." The pink deepened in her cheeks, and she gave us some of the background of the Royal Chapel. It was one of the oldest in California, having been founded by Father Junípero Serra and Father Juan Crespi in 1770. She explained that it was no longer run by the fathers as a mission, but a priest still officiated there for the benefit of the local citizens.

Until secularization, when by law it was deprived of them, the mission had encompassed much land and many buildings which supported the Indian natives the fathers had come to teach and to civilize. Now there was only the chapel, a part of the Presidio.

Caro shot me a glance, making a face that was so much like Mrs. Forsman when she was giving us her view on Catholics that I almost laughed in the middle of Amalie's discourse. What would Mrs. Forsman think of us now!

The Royal Presidio Chapel was an imposing building of sandstone, cut at Carmel, Amalie said. It was soft and easy to work, but hardened after it had been exposed to the air, and it was then plastered over. It gleamed in the morning sunlight. There were large double doors through which we would leave after the ceremony, and to the left of them a tower with a pair of bells.

Our party made its way through the streets of Monterey, and the citizens who were about waved and smiled. We did not enter through the main doors, but through the right transept portal, a smaller door set in gracefully molded bas-relief plaster design.

The interior of the church was far larger than we had expected, and quite beyond our experience, for I had only memories of the chapel at Willows Hall and the country church at the neighboring village, neither of them on such a grand scale as this. Our feet echoed on the tiled floor and I felt lost in the vastness, for the ceiling was many feet over our heads. Caro looked quickly at the statues in

179

their niches, then back at me, remembering no doubt what the Forsmans had said.

Miss Strang had come along as a guest, of course, but her first duty was to see that we were all properly dressed. "Come, come, let us begin; it won't do to have the bridegroom arrive before we are ready. I will see to Miss Amalie first and then to the rest to you."

Candles had already been lighted, dozens of them. The younger members of our group were more subdued than was usual with them, and Bethany whispered to me.

"Is this where they worship statues? Like Mrs. Forsman said?"

"We're not going to worry about what Mrs. Forsman said," I told her firmly, putting down my own misgivings. "It is a beautiful church, and it was built to worship God. I don't know about the statues, but I do know that we love Amalie, and she is to be married here, and all that is expected of us is to support her. Come, turn around, I'll do your buttons."

From that moment on we were too busy to remember to be nervous, about either the ceremony to come or the fact that we were in a Catholic church. We were buttoned up, hair recombed by Miss Strang, and pronounced ready.

The building was filled when the ceremony began; the faces and the colorful costumes were no more than a blur as we moved down the aisle toward the front of the church.

Someday I, too, might be moving down an aisle this way, toward a man I loved, I thought, and matched my footsteps to Caro's and Manuela's and wondered if Nathan was watching me and if he thought me attractive.

The priest, a soft-spoken old man, said nothing I could understand except their names—Amalie and Ramón. And since I did not have to listen to his words, I could watch the others, and I saw the tenderness in Ramón's smile, the joy in his eyes, and I envied Amalie as I had never envied anyone before in my life.

And then it was over, and the solemnity, the formality, were forgotten. The twin bells chimed out the news, and we all surged out into the sunshine, and the frivolity began.

Of course we still had miles to go in the *carretas*, to Rancho Hermoso, but no one was prepared to wait until they got there to begin celebrating.

I found myself in a cart beside Hester, and to begin with I did not pay much attention to her. My gaze drifted through the crowd, searching for Nathan Peltier. When I found him, he was not alone; Manuela had captured his arm and was laughing up into his face. He saw me, and smiled and called something I could not make out, but then he turned to help Manuela into a *carreta*. I turned away, swallowing disappointment.

I did not see Caro anywhere. She would be caught up in the joy of the moment; she had never looked lovelier than she did today, in the white gauze over pink satin, her pale hair caught back with a pink ribbon. There would be young males aplenty eager to talk to her and dance with her, I thought.

Our *carreta* started with a jerk, throwing us all backward, and as I reached out to steady myself I heard a strangled sound from Hester. I looked down, then, to the small brown face a few inches below my own, and saw tears coursing down her cheeks.

"Why, Hester! What ever is the matter?"

She rubbed an angry hand across her eyes and looked away, not answering. I followed her gaze and saw Amalie, laughing face upturned to her bridegroom, before they were swallowed up in the crowd of well-wishers, and I thought I understood.

"You aren't losing Amalie, Hester," I said quietly. "She loves you, and she'll visit you often. And no doubt you'll spend a lot of time at Rancho Hermoso, too."

She said nothing, her spine rigid.

"And someday, in a few years, it will be your turn. You'll have a lovely wedding, and go to a home of your own, and have your family, just as Amalie is going to do."

She looked at me, then, dark eyes flashing with impotent fury, I thought. "You don't know anything about it," she said. "I've lo t her, it will never be the same."

I was ashamed, then, of the platitudes I had offered, although indeed I did not know what else to do. For she was right, of course; it would never be the same after today.

I felt sorry for Hester, for all that I could not bring myself to like her.

But the day was too bright, the mood of those around us too joyful, to allow myself to be depressed by poor Hester. Especially when Nathan galloped up alongside our *carreta* and bent over to call to me.

"There are things to do at the ranch, so I ride ahead! But save the first *jota* for me!"

After that, it didn't matter that he was gone, for I knew he would meet me when I reached the ranch.

We had heard about the Californio hospitality, and about their capacity for celebration. But our expectations were exceeded by the reality.

The hacienda was cleaned and polished and there were delicious odors everywhere; in the kitchens many smiling women worked, and over the great outdoor spits turned sides of beef, and everywhere there was wine and laughter and ribald jokes (which I was glad I did not understand, although the implications were clear even in a foreign language). And there were people. Dozens and dozens of people.

I danced with Nathan. And with Cristóbal, and Tío Roberto, and Sherry Millay, and many others whose names I never knew, whose smiles and dark eyes mingled and ran together in my memory.

The Spanish language, of which I had learned only a few words as yet, seemed to me a beautiful, liquid speech. Romantic. Exciting. It flowed around me, broken occasionally as someone tried to communicate with me in my own language. Dance. Eat. Drink. Lovely, lovely, lovely. Only they said it *bella*, or *hermosa*, or *lindísima*.

I should have been quite content to spend the entire day with Nathan, but there was no chance of that. He was

182

too much in demand, and the Alvarados introduced him to their friends and relations, as he went from group to group, danced with girl after girl.

And Sherry would have been content to spend *his* afternoon with *me*, for every time I turned around he was there, smiling, waiting for me. Yet I did not have to make any effort to escape his attentions, for there always a young man at my elbow, asking in his mellifluous Spanish if I would care to dance.

I did not even notice when the light faded from the sky, for there were so many lanterns and bonfires and torches about, and the pace of the activity so intense, that day blended into evening and evening to night, and it seemed there would be no end to the merrymaking.

Aunt Maudie, however, who had sat on the veranda watching the festivities, finally caught my attention with an upraised hand. "India, my dear!"

I smiled an apology at the young man I left standing as the music began again, and moved toward my aunt. I sank onto a chair beside her, suddenly aware that I was overheated and overtired.

"Ah, it's good to rest a moment! How much longer will it go on?"

"Until they are all too drunk or too tired to dance any longer," Aunt Maudie said dryly. "But it has gone on too long for me. I'm ready to go to bed. Would you be so good as to come with me, let me lean on your arm? My room is on the second floor, and those stairs are a chore to climb."

"Of course. Now that I've stopped dancing, I'm not sure I can begin again. I may look for Caro and see if she isn't ready to call it a night, too, although she's having such a marvelous time I may have to drag her away. Do you think I should?"

"If not now, within an hour or so," Maudie said, heaving herself to her feet. "Soon Amalie and Ramón will withdraw, and after that the serious drinking will begin, I think. That is the time for young females to turn in, and I

183

trust that you will see to your sister. Hester and the twins are still running about, too. Once you've gotten me safely tucked in, you may play the little mother again and find them, see that they go off to bed. Remember how you used to play the little mother with Caro when she was an infant?" She smiled, recalling it.

"You remember that?" I offered my arm and she took it, although she did not put any real weight against me. "It's odd, but I can't remember you or Major Graham being at Willows Hall at all, nor Amalie, although she was a baby there when Caro was born, was she not?"

"Oh, well, my father did not like crying infants about him, so we often took her to her other grandmother's, and when we were at the Hall we kept to our own quarters. His Lordship was an easy man to quarrel with, and my husband did not approve of my standing up to him." Her tone was somewhat flat when she spoke of Lord Stuart-Brice. "Ah, it is somewhat quieter in here, isn't it?" We had entered the grand *sala*, which was lighted but deserted, and the thick adobe walls somewhat diminished the sounds of the music and the voices. "Doña Isabel was apologetic that they could not provide me with a bed-chamber on the ground floor. She knows I do not climb the stairs at home any oftener than I have to."

It did not seem to me, however, that she had any difficulty with the stairs, other than that she paused halfway up to rest for a moment and catch her breath. She was a grossly fat woman, yet she moved easily for all that, I thought.

The room that had been turned over to her was at the far end of a short corridor that was lighted by several candles set at intervals in niches in the walls. We reached the door and used the nearest of the candles to light one in her room. This was cool and pleasantly furnished, so totally uncluttered that I wondered how the contrast between it and her own room at Casa del Mar should strike her.

The shutters were open, and she moved to close them,

further reducing the sound, although we were on the patio side of the house and I did not think she would have any trouble sleeping through it.

"Undo my buttons, will you, pet?" she requested. "Miss Strang would have performed that task for me, but she was quite worn out, poor thing. She's been devoted to me for years, and has seen me through many things. Childhood, girlhood, a marriage, births and deaths, and now another wedding, a happy one this time. She has earned the right to go to bed when she pleases. She did not really want to stay here the night, but we persuaded her that it was impossible to return home alone. Ah, that's good, thank you, pet."

I did not want to stay and watch any further disrobing; those mounds of quivering flesh were unnerving to me.

"Do you need me for anything else, Aunt Maudie?"

"No, no. I shall manage from this point on. Go round up the little ones; they won't have sense enough to know they're exhausted until someone makes them retire. And Caro, too, of course. Once Amalie and Ramón have withdrawn, you should both do so too."

I murmured compliance, and went out into the corridor, closing the door behind me.

To my surprise, all the candles had gone out.

I hesitated, wondering if I should go back and get the one from Aunt Maudie to relight them, but the idea of viewing her in a state of undress stopped me.

It was, after all, only a short corridor. There were rooms off it, with closed doors, and all I had to do was walk along it until I reached the head of the stairs. Then the light from the *sala* would allow me to descend safely to the ground floor.

There was nothing frightening about it. Candles often guttered and went out in a draft. I strode confidently toward the stairs.

I heard nothing, no opening of a door, no footstep, no breathing. Yet suddenly an arm went around my waist and I was jerked off my feet; even as I opened my mouth

185

to scream out a protest, a hand closed over it in a cruel clasp.

Incredulous, I realized that I was being pulled into one of the rooms, that a door was kicked shut behind us, and that my attacker was attempting to tear off my clothes.

15

Outraged indignation lent strength to my struggle. Aunt Maudie was right, the drinking had surpassed the bounds of decency and common sense, and some drunken lout had decided I was fair game.

It would have been impossible, in the weeks of preparing for my cousin's wedding, not to have learned a little about relationships between men and women. While I was still largely ignorant of the finer points of the marital state, I was not as innocent as I had been upon leaving Calcutta.

Indeed, the stirrings of my own body since meeting Nathan Peltier gave me some clues to the things no one had put into words for me.

And so it was that after only a few moments I realized that this brutality was not an attack upon my virtue, at all.

It was, I recognized in astonishment as the one hand effectively prevented any outcry and the other roamed over my person, a search.

It was a man who held me, a man's strength that overcame mine, a man whose grunt of determination came so close to my right ear. I was pinned against him, and the fullness of my skirts prevented my kicking backward in an effort to strike a vulnerable spot that might make him loosen his grasp.

I tried desperately to lunge away from him, to break his hold, and for a second I thought I had gained a slight advantage, for my mouth was momentarily freed. I sucked in a much-needed breath, whether preparatory to screaming for help or simply to avoid asphyxiation I could not have said, but the sound warned him.

The hand came back, this time covering my nose as well, and I knew what it was to be suffocated. I heard the material of my new dress tear, and felt him probe beneath it, but it wasn't modesty that caused my panic.

I was dying, I was going lightheaded from lack of air; that lack even made me forget the pain inflicted by the cutting fingers.

He was going to kill me.

And then, suddenly, he muttered a curse and flung me away from him. My head struck something solid and I lay, stunned, fighting to draw air into tortured lungs.

I did not know how long it was before I was able to lift my head, to drag myself to a sitting position.

He was gone. Had I even heard him leave, close the door behind him? I didn't remember. But I knew I was now alone in the room.

Outside, the sounds of celebration were unabated. From a long way off, I heard the shouting and the increased laughter, and wondered if the well-wishers were sending Amalie and Ramón on their way to bed.

I no longer had any speculations about what would take place between them, there in that beautifully prepared room, on their wedding night. I was too shaken to think of anyone but myself. I got to my knees, and then, reaching for what turned out to be a bedpost, hauled myself to a standing position.

I was not the victim of an attempted rape, but of a search, a very thorough and personal search, by someone who expected me to be carrying something valuable.

How could anyone know about the pearls?

Yet why else should I have been subjected to this? If the man had, indeed, intended rape, there was nothing to have stopped him from going through with it. He had effectively silenced me, had at all times been in control. Even had I managed a scream, no one would have taken any notice of it with all the other racket going on.

It had to be the pearls. Someone knew about them, knew their value, knew I carried them under my clothes.

As I rested, trying for the second time within a few short weeks to recover from a near-fatal lack of air, I tried to think it through.

Not servants who had looked through our jewel case and our dresser drawers, but someone who knew about the pearls. Not children or ordinary vandals who opened our trunks upon the beach and all but turned them inside out, searching, either.

Someone knew. Knew I had the maharani's pearls, and deduced that since they were not hidden anywhere else, they must be on my person.

Who?

I made my way across the unfamiliar room, totally dark since the shutters had been drawn, and opened the door. The candles had not been relit, but the darkness was not so absolute, either, for a dim glow emanated from the direction of the stairs.

I stood for a moment at the head of them to get my bearings. I could not go out looking like this, with a torn bodice and perhaps bruises beginning to show on my face. The room I had been assigned to share with Bethany was only a few yards away, and once I passed out of the short corridor, I found candles again lighting my way.

The face that stared back from the mirror was wild-eyed and frightened, color high, but there were as yet no visible bruises. My hair tumbled across my forehead as the curls escaped Miss Strang's careful arrangement.

The dress. The beautiful dress had been torn, exposing chemise and bosom, and automatically I clutched the material into its proper position.

I must put on something else and go down the stairs and find the children, and Caro. I turned away from the mirror and toward the clothes we had brought with us.

I was still fastening buttons with unsteady fingers when someone tapped lightly on the door; a moment later Caro's bright head popped through the opening, and I saw that Manuela was with her.

189

"India, there you are! We couldn't imagine where you'd gone, you're missing all the fun! You should have seen the major learning to dance the—what was it called again, Manuela?"

I could not understand the giggled response as the door opened all the way to permit the two to enter the room.

"How long ago?" I asked, and did not recognize my own voice.

"How long ago what?" Caro's eyes swept over the discarded gown, unaware of its significance.

"How long ago did the major learn to dance the whatever-it-was?"

"I don't know, ten, fifteen minutes, I suppose. He's had ever so much to drink, I couldn't believe it!" She started to laugh again, but at last my appearance must have relayed some message. "Is something wrong, India?"

"Yes. Did you see anyone leaving the house, coming down the stairs, as you came in? A man?"

"There are people all over the house, men and women. Why? What's the matter?"

"I was attacked only a few minutes ago, in the corridor where Aunt Maudie is sleeping. By a man."

They were suddenly silent, all humor drained out of them as it had been drained out of me. Manuela muttered something in her own language, and I did not ask what she had said, sure that she only expressed horror that once more something had happened to me as a guest at Rancho Hermoso.

"Are you hurt?" Caro demanded.

"Only bruised." I looked directly into her eyes, warning her, and she knew at once what I meant.

"I must tell my father," Manuela said. "We will search for this—this fiend who preys upon our guests. We must search him out and—"

"Wait." I stopped her. "Tell your father, of course, because he has a right to know what goes on in his own household. But do not disturb Ramón, and do not let it interrupt the festivities. I am not eager to let it become public knowledge that I was—subjected to this abuse.

And I do not know who the man was, I did not see anything, I have no clue. There will be no way to identify the man who attacked me, and to make a public announcement would be to throw suspicion on every man here."

Manuela hesitated. These Californios had their own code of honor, and for all I knew it called for immediate and violent action against a man who would cause harm to a guest in their house.

"Perhaps you are right. It would be a shame to spoil Amalie and Ramón's wedding celebration."

"A great shame," I agreed.

"But this is a serious offense. The family should know, should be on watch to prevent the man from molesting anyone else."

I knew perfectly well that there was no danger to anyone else from the man I had met in the dark, yet I wanted Manuela to go, I wanted to talk to my sister. "So you must tell your father. But ask him to consider my wishes."

"*Sí, sí,* of course. I will be back," Manuela said, and fled.

Caro regarded me in the candlelight. "Are you really all right? He didn't hurt you?"

"It hurt at the time," I admitted. "I thought he was going to suffocate me."

"You weren't carrying the pearls."

"No. I hid them at Casa del Mar, last night."

"In a safe place?"

"In a safe place."

Suddenly she shuddered, and reached out to hug me. "Oh, India! How did he know about the pearls? I told no one, no one! I swear it!"

"Nor did I."

"Then how——?"

"I don't know."

"What are we going to do?"

"I don't know that, either," I said slowly. "Try to remember, Caro. Where everyone was, say in the ten minutes before you entered the house."

191

She drew back, startled. "Everyone?"

I made an impatient gesture. "Everyone who speaks English. This was not done by a friend of the Alvarados, nor a member of their family. The man was bigger than most of them, for one thing, I'm almost sure of that; he was certainly taller than I am, for I bumped my head under his chin at one point. But I believe whoever it was also searched our trunks on the beach, which could have been anyone, and also our room at home. Which means he is one of those who speaks English. The major, Nathan Peltier, Sherry Millay."

Caro stifled a cry of protest. "India! Never Nathan, he wouldn't do a thing like that! And even the others—"

"Someone did it," I said coldly. I was beginning to think logically again, to recover from the shock. "Where were they? Can you say positively that any of them was within your sight all of the last ten minutes before you came into the house?"

Her hesitation was brief. "No. I saw them all, off and on, all evening. But I can't say exactly when, not the last ten minutes. India, it sounds as if the man was waiting for you, put out the candles after you brought Aunt Maudie upstairs. How did he know you'd be doing that?"

"I don't know." *Unless*, I thought, *Aunt Maudie herself had asked for my assistance simply to get me into that darkened passageway.* And that would mean she was in league with the man, whoever he was. The major? A man she despised? But I did not voice this suspicion. "I suppose that Don Esteban will insist upon talking to me, for all the good that will do. I cannot rejoin the celebration, and someone must find the children, including Hester, and see that they go to bed."

"Yes. Yes, all right, I'll do that. But you don't want me to leave you alone—?"

"Yes, go," I said. "And see that they get to bed at once."

She was reluctant, but I insisted I did not need her to wait with me until someone else came. I had many things to think about, none of them pleasant.

I slept badly, with Bethany motionless beside me. I could not help remembering the terror of those few minutes in the dark with a man determined to wrest my secret from me. Had I still been carrying the pearls, he would have found them and taken them by force.

I was glad that Don Esteban had seen fit to tell only a few of his trusted family members, and that the celebrants as a whole knew nothing. At least I was spared that humiliation, although he insisted that eventually Ramón must be informed, as well.

My own appearance in the morning was hardly reassuring, although the expected bruises did not materialize. Yet when we descended the stairs, well into the morning, I found that I did not look all that much worse than anyone else. Most of them had been up half the night, and nearly all of them had drunk their share of the potent Alvarado wines; I had had sense enough to leave that completely alone this time.

There were not too many people stirring as yet. No one expected the newlyweds to emerge for hours, if at all, but a smiling maid informed us (through Manuela) that they had sent for coffee and fruit, so they were awake.

We gathered around the table, Manuela and Caro and I, isolated from the others by our speaking of English while they all chattered away in Spanish. I both dreaded and anticipated meeting Nathan and Sherry; would I be able to tell, when I looked directly into the man's eyes, who had attacked me last night?

But they were both, it seemed, already up and out of the house, riding or joining in one of the contests of which men seem so inexplicably fond. There was roping going on, Manuela said, and we could go out and watch it after we had eaten.

Caro and I had never imagined such feats with a rope, whirled over one's head and then with a loop dropping around the neck of a horse or a steer, such as Manuela described. We tried hard to get back into the spirit of the occasion, but it was impossible not to remember what had happened in a darkened bedroom the previous night.

193

As we emerged onto the shady veranda, where already the early-autumn heat was making itself felt, we heard a cry from one of the Rancho Hermoso hands.

"A rider approaches," Manuela said, translating the rapid Spanish. "Someone from the customshouse. Perhaps there is another ship in port, although it would be unusual to have a third in such a short time."

We all knew that a ship would mean supplies, and perhaps a demand for more hides; no one really wanted to return to work on only the second day of the wedding festivities, but the men who were out and about began to drift toward us as the rider came into the yard.

It was not a ship he had to report, however, but a message to be delivered. To me.

Clearly everyone was curious, but Don Esteban, looking none the worse for wear after his son's wedding (although Caro said he had drunk wine almost continuously, it seemed to have no effect upon him), waved the others away.

"It is a letter for Miss India," he said. "She shall read it in the privacy of the *sala*."

Only Caro went with me, the others all being sent about their own business, while the man who had brought the missive was offered refreshment in the kitchen.

The house was quiet, the *sala* a haven of peacefulness, and for a moment I hesitated with the sealed letter in my hand. I didn't have to recognize the crest in the sealing wax to know that it was the letter Sir Roland had sent via the captain of the *Durham*.

"What is it?" Caro demanded when I delayed in breaking the seal. "What is it all about?"

For a moment I had the feeling that I did not really want to know, that the news, whatever it was, would only add to my troubles. And then common sense reasserted itself and I peeled off the blob of scarlet wax and read the message.

My dear India, it began. The writing was cramped but perfectly legible. *Since your departure from Calcutta, information has come to me which, though alarming, must*

194

be passed on to you. A man was found dying in an alley less than a week after you sailed, a man who was of no significance in himself, but who was, we believe, the one who killed your father.

Caro, who was reading over my shoulder, sucked in a shocked breath; and I, too, felt a stab of remembered pain.

He was paid to seek out Judson Stuart and steal from him a necklace and earrings of rare black pearls that at one time belonged to the Maharani Mohindar of Kanpur. When she died the Maharajah Ashoka wanted no other member of his family to have them. I was at first puzzled as to how they came to be in Judson's possession, but I have now spoken to the maharajah himself, and he tells me that they were a present, an expression of gratitude. Your father protested such a valuable gift, but he accepted them because they were in the nature of repayment for the life of Ashoka's oldest son. Your father was not aware, when he saved the boy from drowning some time ago, that he was the son of a rajah, a prince himself. But Ashoka did not forget, and the jewels were freely given.

The rush of emotion that washed over me left my knees trembling. Caro reached out to steady the paper, pushing it flat onto a table top so that we might both continue to read.

The man, whose name was Nizam, was apparently murdered by his own confederate, the man who had hired him and was angry when he did not get the pearls. He did not give us this man's name; indeed, he insisted he did not know it, and he died without even providing us with a physical description. He said your father was carrying a very large sum of money, which I am sure had been raised for the business venture Judson intended to pursue with Charles Morrisey. Indeed, Morrisey confirms that Judson expected to transact their business that last evening, but for reasons known only to himself did not do so. No doubt there was some further information he needed or wanted. At any rate, he was robbed of this money, and unfortunately we were not able to recover any of it. Nizam says the man who hired him to commit the actual robbery did not believe that he had not gotten the pearls as well as the cash, and killed him for not turning them over as agreed.

The reading of this horrible tale was enough to make us both have to sit down. I felt I could not bear to go on, yet the words had a hypnotizing effect upon me so that I could not stop.

My dear India, I cannot express my concern for you, and so far away from my protection! I have worked most closely with the Calcutta authorities to determine what might be done to protect you. I'm sure that you know nothing of any of this, least of all of Mohindar's pearls, yet it is quite possible that the man responsible for your father's death thinks that you have them. For after Nizam's death we found that his living quarters had been searched in such a fashion as to be almost totally destructive, as someone looked for the gems. Since he did not find them, he might assume that they were left in the possession of Judson's family.

"Dear heaven," Caro murmured. "Oh, poor papa!"

I scarcely heard her and continued to read.

I have no desire to frighten you unnecessarily, but it could be most dangerous to leave you in innocence of all this. I am sure that your uncle can take steps to protect you in a way that is impossible for me to do. For I greatly fear that the man responsible for this dastardly crime may be following you to California. The fact that you are without knowledge of the pearls will in no way save you should he do so.

All I have been able to learn about the man who hired Nizam to rob your father (and to kill him, if necessary, to obtain what he sought) is this: He is an Englishman, and he once worked as a minor secretary in Ashoka's household.

I will, of course, pursue my enquiries in this matter; a journey to speak again with Ashoka will no doubt reveal the man's identity, for he has certainly fled from that employment by this time.

As soon as I have any more information, I will communicate it to you. But I dare not wait until I have it before sending you a warning, and I have learned that a sister ship to the Essex *sails directly, and will carry this message.*

Waste no time in informing your uncle of the circumstances, so that he may take appropriate action. The Durham *is no more than a week behind you, so I trust this will reach you well before any harm can befall you. I pray that God will protect you, as well.*

It was signed, *Your obedient servant, Roland Trask.*

I was amazed that I did not turn quite hysterical. Caro turned a white face in my direction and spoke unsteadily.

"But the *Durham* got ahead of us, and the message came so late—"

"And there were two Englishmen on that ship which sailed a week after ours," I said.

The horror written on her countenance could only have reflected what she saw on mine.

16

The remainder of the celebration, from which we could not immediately escape, was a nightmare. Suspicion consumed us. Neither Caro nor I was capable of appearing normal in behavior; we both pleaded digestive upsets and withdrew, although of course some of the Alvarados knew we had other reasons than overabundant food and drink.

We could do nothing but wait to be taken home.

And talk. We paced the room from which Bethany was mercifully absent and talked.

Nathan Peltier and Sherry Millay had both tried to gain passage on the *Essex*. Both had followed on the next available ship. Both had been guests at Casa del Mar, had had the opportunity to search our trunks and our room.

Yet so far as we knew there was no way either of them could have given an order to a confused old man so that I would be put up on a spirited horse. And it seemed unlikely that anyone other than a Californio would have resorted to a black widow spider, either to frighten or to kill.

The man in the passageway last night could have been either of them.

"Or neither," Caro said stubbornly.

"Or neither," I agreed; she could not be any more heartsick than I at the possibility.

"Are we going to tell the major?"

"No." I didn't even have to think about it. "I don't see how he could have known about the pearls, but I don't trust him. No, we won't appeal to him for protection."

"Aunt Maudie?"

Slowly, I shook my head. "Not Aunt Maudie, either, I think."

"You can't believe she would conspire to rob or do away with her brother's children, surely?"

"I don't know what I believe. Until I do, we will simply remain silent. We will tell nobody anything."

"But everyone on the rancho knows the messenger came for us, from the Presidio. We'll have to make some sort of explanation. Certainly Aunt Maudie will learn of the letter as soon as she comes downstairs, and she'll ask."

"We will say that it was from Sir Roland, and that it informed us about this man, Nizam, who confessed to shooting Papa and stealing his money. We will make no mention of the maharani's black pearls, nor the fact that Nizam was hired by an Englishman. We will remain as ignorant as we have been up to now."

For a long moment she stared at me, and then Caro nodded. "All right. Whatever you say, India. Dear God, when can we go home?"

It was not until the following day. For hours that seemed like weeks, we had to pretend, for even an indisposition on the grand order could not be extended to cover so long a period of time. We tried to eat, we lied to everyone, and when Doña Isabel assumed that grief over Papa had been renewed by the letter from Papa's friend, we were glad to let everyone assume it. That way, no one expected us to continue to dance and make merry.

Aunt Maudie's eyes narrowed as I related the supposed contents of our letter. "This Sir Roland, you can trust him? He was truly Juddy's friend? He is not in some way—" She paused delicately. "He would not cheat you out of your heritage?"

"No, of course not! He was Papa's good friend, he was there with us until Papa died, and he did everything for us afterward, when we couldn't have managed on our own!"

Maudie sighed. "Ah, well. No doubt you are right. It

199

just seemed so odd to me, that Juddy wouldn't have provided for you to the best of his ability. He must have believed that this business venture would do that, only he was prevented from carrying it through. Poor Juddy."

Poor Juddy, indeed. And poor us, too, I thought.

Sir Roland was wrong. We could not trust these relatives enough to throw ourselves on their mercies, not to the extent of revealing everything.

Possibly someone had followed us—or preceded us—from India. But it seemed equally possible to me that our enemy had not followed us at all, but had been here before us, waiting.

The children, of course, knew nothing of any of this. Riding lessons had been interrupted during the festivities; Brice could hardly wait for them to begin again, and he was a much more apt pupil than I had been. Ramón urged that all three of the youngsters stay on for a few weeks more; Hester did not need lessons, but could enjoy the company of her cousins, he said. And Amalie would not need to be completely separated from her family quite so quickly.

Hester, however, did not care to stay. I looked at her sour little face and thought that she had not enjoyed our visit at Rancho Hermoso much more than I had.

Caro, who had planned to stay on also, for a prolonged visit with Manuela, came to tell me she did not feel she should leave me alone. "I can always come later, after these—these problems have been resolved."

"Don't be foolish. To change your plans now will only reveal that we are—aware. We may learn more by pretending to ignorance. And I think it would be wise to have you here, to keep an eye on the twins."

She was persuaded, although I knew she was uncomfortable about letting me go alone. I would miss her, but there was no reason to think I would be any safer with Caro in the same house than without her. If an enemy plotted against me, a fifteen-year-old girl would not prevent his success. And, I thought, Caro might well be better off with the Alvarados, who certainly would be on guard against any repetition of the episode in their hacienda.

And so we gathered for the trip back to Casa del Mar. It took an incredible will to smile, to say the right things to everyone. I hugged Amalie, who was blooming like a rose, with genuine affection. But to the others I turned a face that was forced into a simulation of enthusiasm. The Alvarados must be thanked for a final time, and Major Graham and Sherry cantered toward us, ready to escort the *carretas* on their way.

Nathan nearly missed our leave-taking. He came toward us across the yard, fair hair blowing in the wind, and I wondered how I had ever thought him ordinary looking. Had Amalie felt this way about Ramón, before she knew that she was in love with him?

I could love him, I thought, yet even as I longed for Nathan's company, I could not forget the suspicion Sir Roland had put into my head.

Nathan was smiling, and he rested both hands on the edge of the *carreta* and looked down at me. "So you're off! Will we have a riding lesson as usual tomorrow morning?"

I spoke before I had time to think about it. "I—I think not. It has been an exhausting week. Perhaps after we've had a chance to rest—"

"All right. Send a message when you're ready to resume riding," Nathan said, but I thought his voice had gone a little flat.

And then we were off, headed for home, and I fought the prickle of tears in my eyes and did not know why I cried.

Fatigue was more than an excuse not to go riding with a man who might wish me harm; I was exhausted so that I wanted to sleep and sleep. I told myself that if Nathan wished me ill, he had had the opportunity during our earliest lessons to stage another mishap. He had not done so, so why was I afraid to go with him now?

I slept, and cried in my sleep, and wished that Caro were there to curl around me until I went back to sleep.

Sir Roland's letter had explained a few things, but left many more questions unanswered. If an enemy sought only to lay hands on the pearls, what then was the meaning of the black widow spider, the whispering voices, the "accident" of putting me up on a dangerous stallion? How could any of those things have resulted in a successful theft of the pearls?

And if I feared Nathan needlessly, how would I bear it when he went back to England, alone?

Miss Strang, too, seemed overtired and unwell. I believe that she kept to her room for several days after our return to Casa del Mar; it was only upon Aunt Maudie's prodding that Miss Strang and I finally pulled ourselves together for another session in the sewing room.

I had lost interest in clothes. Miss Strang exclaimed sharply when she saw the dress that had been torn, and gave me a searching glance. I only made some remark about the energetic dancing after the wedding, no more. I did not think she was convinced that this was how it had been torn, but she did not press me.

Sherry continued as he had been before the wedding, seeking out my company, pleased to sit and listen if I played the piano, inviting me for walks on the beach.

He, too, I looked upon with suspicion. I accepted no invitations that took me away from the house except that I yearned to walk on the beach, and several times he joined me there, in plain view of anyone who might be watching from the house.

"Is something wrong, India?" he asked. "You are so quiet, almost withdrawn."

"I am only overtired," I evaded, and hoped it would be left at that.

"I wonder about Major Graham. Surely the wedding isn't responsible for *his* malaise as well," Sherry said.

We were in the library, where I had gone to choose a

book to read before I went to sleep. I turned to look at him across the expanse of red carpeting. "Major Graham?"

"Yes. Haven't you noticed? But perhaps not, you don't join him for breakfast the way I usually do. He is certainly concerned about something, he's even worse than you are—gets up looking as if he hasn't even been to bed, doesn't hear when he's spoken to, is obviously engrossed in his own thoughts. If I thought he would not take it amiss, I'd offer my help, if there is any I could give. But the major is not an easy man to know."

"Well, he certainly hasn't confided in me," I said.

But from that time on, I paid more attention to what was going on around me.

And it was true; my uncle clearly had something on his mind. He rose early, went to bed late, and was gone a good deal of the time in between. Often he did not even come home for dinner, and on those occasions Aunt Maudie sometimes joined Hester and me and Sherry at the great formal table.

I took it that Major Graham moved ahead with his plans toward the governorship. Several times, rather late at night, men came to the house; I did not see them, but heard their voices, and knew they sat until after midnight in the library, talking and drinking brandy.

Once, when Aunt Maudie had been lured to the dinner table by the assumption that her husband would not be present, we had only begun on our soup when Major Graham appeared.

He was weary and short of temper; he waved aside an offer of soup and stated shortly that he would dispense with that and to get on with the meal. I found myself wondering how he and Lord Stuart-Brice would have made out together, each of them being so used to having his own way.

We had been having a rather lively chatter, or at least Aunt Maudie and Sherry had. Sherry attempted to maintain the mood, but it was difficult in the face of what could only be described as surly responses from my uncle.

Finally Aunt Maudie fixed her dark eyes upon him as she speared a forkful of broiled salmon and raised the tender pink flesh to her mouth.

"What is it that's creating such an attraction in Monterey? Out here in the wilds this way, we hear nothing. Yet you are there nearly every day. Is there some difficulty?"

"Difficulty!" The major swore and refilled his wine glass from the carafe at his elbow. "That damnable Larkin! It's absurd, yet he continues to work at it, trying to persuade Mexico that California should be annexed to the United States! How can one annex something hundreds of miles from something else? The Russians were driven out, and now it is the cursed Americans who think to horn in!"

Aunt Maudie chewed placidly. She washed the salmon down with wine before she spoke to Sherry and me. "Thomas Larkin is the American consul in Monterey. A perfectly civil man, in business here."

"He's an idiot!" the major declared. "To turn California over to the Americans makes even less sense than to let it remain under the rule of Mexico! Damn it, why is this cold?" He nearly flung a bowl of vegetables at a shocked Teresa, who muttered an apology and withdrew with the offending dish. "Why is it a man cannot get a decent meal even in his own house?"

So that was it. If the United States gained a foothold in California, Henry Graham's dream of being governor was over. No wonder he was upset. Yet still he said nothing to his family of his aspirations. Was it because Sherry Millay was there, or what? And why had he told *me?*

We all finished our meal in silence and excused ourselves as quickly as possible. It was dark outside now, as we moved into October, but I would have liked a stroll on the beach, with the sound of the pounding surf covering the beating of my own heart, had I not now been afraid to go there alone.

"India." I paused, looking back over my shoulder; Sherry hurried toward me. "Please don't leave me alone down here this evening. After that dreadful harangue at the table, I need something to settle my stomach. Say you'll play for me, turn my mood around."

I looked after my uncle's retreating back, as he made his way to the library for his evening cigar and his brandy. "I thought you and Major Graham got along very well."

"Well enough," Sherry said, noncommittal. "And I understand his agitation; we Englishmen are rather spoiled, I suppose. We like to think that Britannia rules the world, and certainly California is a valuable prize, whoever gets her. But I can't see spoiling an excellent meal because of politics."

I made no comment on this. I knew nothing and cared less about politics.

"Will you play? There is something about an hour of music that rounds off an evening. Your aunt says that she enjoys it, too—she leaves her door open and the music carries up the stairs."

"Very well," I conceded. "I will play for a while."

It was true that music was soothing; once begun, I could lose myself in it, forget my fears and apprehensions, and relieve tensions. Actually, since nothing had happened in the several weeks since the wedding, I had been somewhat lulled. And perhaps, just perhaps, if Nathan rode over, I would agree to begin riding with him again, I thought.

It was a pleasant evening. The only thing to mar it was, on the occasion of my pausing for the drink of chilled orange juice that Teresa had brought, the sight of Hester's angry small face observing us from the darkened hallway.

I sighed. "I don't know what to do about Hester. She is very unhappy, I think, since Amalie has gone. Yet she refuses to allow anyone to befriend her."

Sherry dismissed Hester with a gesture. "No one can be responsible for anyone else's happiness. Each of us has to find his own, and I think Hester is not yet working at it. You have tried to be friendly with her; don't blame yourself that you haven't been successful."

205

"But an unhappy child does—unpleasant things, sometimes."

"Oh, what's Hester done?" Sherry regarded me with lively curiosity.

"Maybe I'm wrong. Maybe she didn't do it at all—" I was sorry I'd spoken, yet the thought was honest and spontaneous enough so that I now felt compelled to carry through on it.

"What?" Sherry demanded.

"Well—there was a spider in my dresser drawer. Amalie said it was called a black widow, and its bite can be fatal. It doesn't usually enter inhabited buildings, so I assumed someone had brought it inside—"

His curiosity sharpened, as did his voice. "Did it bite you? No, of course it didn't, or we'd have known. Why did you think Hester would have done it?"

"Well, it was there, where everyone said it shouldn't have been. In a house, in a dresser being used earlier in the day. And—and it seemed that someone must have put it there."

"So you nominated Hester for the job? You may be right. It doesn't seem the sort of thing an adult would do. Yet I wouldn't expect the little Hester to take to poisonous spiders, either. Did you accuse her of it?"

"No. What would be the use? She would probably only lie about it."

He put out a hand to cover mine where it lay on the piano bench. "I'll see if I can find out what's troubling her, why she would dislike you enough to do such a thing. India, India, you are having a rather beastly time of it, aren't you? But I'm glad you've chosen to talk to me about it. It may be that I can help."

There was something about his hand, resting on mine; I could not have said whether I liked it or not, only that it aroused peculiar sensations within me. I swung about on the piano bench and stood up, effectively withdrawing my hand.

"Thank you. It is good to know that I have a friend,

Sherry. And now, if you'll excuse me, I am very tired. I believe that I will go up to bed."

"Good night, then, India." He smiled down at me, and then, quite unexpectedly, bent his head to brush his lips across my forehead. "Sleep well."

I scarcely remembered getting out of the room, with the touch of his kiss branding my forehead. I was glad that Caro was not waiting for me upstairs; the heat in my face would surely have given rise to questions for which I had no answers.

It was the following morning when, upon descending the stairs, I found Major Graham waiting for me in the hall. He was ready to leave the house, for he wore his riding clothes and carried his hat, but he turned in such a way as to make it clear he had only been delaying until I should appear.

"Ah, there you are, India. Teresa said you would be down shortly unless you had overslept. I wanted a word with you before I go to Monterey to see if I can stop this foolishness with the Americans before it goes any farther. It is unthinkable that California should fall into the hands of the United States—" He broke off, controlling his emotional outburst better than he had been able to do the previous evening. "I've told your aunt, she is very pleased on your behalf, as I'm sure you will be, too."

"Pleased?" I echoed uncertainly. "About what, sir?"

"Why, that we have had an offer for your hand in marriage! A request that the young man be allowed to court you, at any rate."

"Court me?" My echo was a faint one. Nathan? Had Nathan asked? I felt positively giddy, but a moment later that dream crashed about my ears.

"Yes, indeed. Very fortunate you are, I should say, that a man like Sherard Millay wishes to marry you."

There was a ringing in my ears. I simply stood there, stunned. Not Nathan, but Sherry—

The major smacked his hat against his thigh in a satisfied way. "Quite. No more than appropriate, I should say. Of course I gave him permission. You aunt thought you

207

were somewhat taken with that other fellow, that Peltier. But he comes of rather common stock, I believe. Millay has an uncle who knows the Prince of Wales, I understand. And since it turns out the Peltier fellow is already engaged to marry some girl back in England, why, this has worked out for the best, hasn't it?"

Shock waves washed over me, rendering me speechless.

"Well, he'll be making his own speeches, no doubt, and I'm late. There's a meeting this morning, and I don't want that damned Tom Larkin to have it all his own way, without even a dissenting voice! I'll be off. And my congratulations, my dear."

He left me standing there in the middle of the darkly paneled foyer, locked in my own silent struggle as the door closed behind him.

17

I moved as one in a daze, allowing Teresa to bring me a cup of the hot, sweet coffee, but unable to touch a bite of food.

Nathan engaged? To some girl in England?

How long had the major known? Did everyone know? Everyone but me? Why hadn't Nathan told me himself?

But there had been no need for it, from his point of view; cold logic soon began to assert itself as the coffee coursed through me. I was only a girl, a guest at the home of his friend; he had offered to teach me to ride, that was all. He'd made no commitment beyond that. He had enjoyed Caro and Amalie and Manuela and me, and treated us all alike, hadn't he? As if we were the younger sisters he missed, being away from his own. Why, he'd even told Caro that I reminded him of his sister, Susan.

Of course, there was no reason to explain about a fiancée in England, to a girl who meant nothing to him.

I stared through the blur of tears at the attractive tray of melon slices Teresa had set before me, and then pushed back my chair and moved toward the stairs, almost at a run.

I knew it now, I must have known it for weeks, that I loved Nathan Peltier. But at least I hadn't made a fool of myself over him—he did not know it. Thank God I had not said or done anything to reveal my infatuation with him!

I would have hurried past Aunt Maudie's room, but her door was open and she called out to me.

"India! Stop a moment, pet, and fetch me my toothache drops, will you?"

I blinked back the tears, willing them not to overflow, and retraced my steps to her overheated, overscented bedroom.

The drops were there, on a table near the door. I carried them across to the bed, where my aunt sprawled in comfort, enjoying coffee with her chocolates. I had never known her to be up so early, but she seemed wide awake. Perhaps an aching tooth had wakened her.

"Thank you, dear. Have you seen your uncle this morning?"

"A moment ago," I said, swallowing hard against the ache in my throat.

"Then you know you're to be congratulated! Sherry is such a nice young man, don't you think? Well brought up, good family, although I take it there isn't much of it left now except two elderly uncles. Untitled, but substantial means, I take it. And Sherry's the heir. He freely admits he hasn't much on his own, but one of the uncles is seventy-three and the other is seventy-eight. So long as you're here, get me another handkerchief from that top drawer, will you, pet?"

So they had talked about it, among themselves: Sherry, the major, and Aunt Maudie. They knew more than I did about Sherry's background. Did they know as much about Nathan's?

It was about Nathan that I longed to ask, but I dared not. I brought the handkerchief and asked politely if there was anything else she needed.

"No, I'm in tolerably good shape for the morning, now. Teresa will be back in a bit for this tray." She sighed deeply. "I do miss my Amalie. She's always been such a good girl, so helpful. And now it seems it won't be long before you will be going, too. You do look favorably on Sherry, don't you? Such a good-looking man. Between you, you should produce handsome babies. Oh, don't blush, pet, it's time to be thinking of such things."

She selected a chocolate with care and bit off an edge

of it, savoring the flavor. "It's the most important thing a woman ever does, the marriage she makes. If it's a good one, her life will be happy and filled. If it's bad, there is no situation so intolerable. And if you marry Sherry, you'll be able to go back to England . . ."

I had to say something, anything. "Do you still miss it, England? Papa did, to the day he died."

"Miss it? Yes, of course I miss it. England is my home, even though it's unlikely I'll ever see it again. And Willows Hall—how I miss it, even after all these years! I miss the sound of voices speaking English. Do you know that even in my own kitchen here, they never speak a word of English unless I happen to stray into it? They jabber away in their incomprehensible tongues, and it makes me aware I'm in a foreign country." She sighed again, and put the rest of the chocolate into her mouth. "You're fortunate an Englishman has come along now, at the right time. Don't misunderstand me, I had no objection to my Amalie marrying a Spaniard. Ramón adores her, and she him, and that's more than romantic, it means he'll be good to her and her life will be a happy one long after the honeymoon is over.

"But there are a limited number of young Spaniards like Ramón, ones of wealth and good family. Oh, there are plenty of men, if you aren't particular as to type, but few of them have any prospects, few of them could offer a woman a good life. The Americans have great charm—" She paused to glance at the open doorway, as if my uncle might hear and challenge her on this. "—but they are a rough lot, and most of them haven't a penny to their names, nor ever will have. They won't build homes like Willows Hall in California, I assure you. Yes, Sherry is a good catch. Even a brilliant one."

She reached out to pat my hand with her soft, puffy one. "You're a good girl, too, India, like my Amalie. I wish you happiness. And no doubt you're eager to get off to Miss Strang and get started on those pretty dresses, eh? But don't forget to stop and visit with your aunt as you come and go."

With that admonition ringing in my ears, I fled. Not to Miss Strang, but to my own room, where I threw myself across the bed in a paroxysmal spasm of weeping.

This was an indulgence I could ill afford, however. When I had worn myself out, I got up and bathed my eyes and combed my hair and dusted powder across the worst of the ugly red splotches.

Miss Strang looked at me in that sharp way she had, but she made no comment upon my appearance, and the sewing session commenced as it had done on all those other mornings.

I did not see Sherry until late that afternoon, and though I had spent the entire day imagining what I would say to him, I found myself tongue-tied when the moment arrived.

I had sought a time alone on the beach, and I walked some distance along the shore, well out of sight of the house. The surf continued its ceaseless assault upon the sands, its rhythm the same as ever, but today it did not sooth me.

What was I to do?

If it was true that Nathan was to marry some girl in England, as everyone but me seemed to be aware, then there was no hope in that direction. And everyone regarded Sherry Millay as a fine matrimonial prospect, and expected me to be overjoyed that he had asked permission to court me.

Certainly I was more strongly attracted to Nathan than to Sherry. Yet I recognized that, for all my age, I was too inexperienced to be sure what was genuine and what was calf love. I had had no opportunity to meet young men, let alone form friendships or romantic alliances. Quite possibly, if I forced myself to stop thinking about Nathan as it now seemed I must, my affections would fasten upon Sherry.

Yet there was always the possibility, however slight, that either Sherry or Nathan was the man Sir Roland had written about, the man responsible for the death of the thief Nizam and, before that, of my father.

My head was in a turmoil that even the Pacific could not calm. If only there were some way to know! It seemed unlikely to me that a thief, having followed me from Calcutta, would propose marriage (or offer riding lessons and friendship!) in the hope of gaining possession of the black pearls.

Far more likely, the one who knew of the existence of the necklace would search trunks and dresser drawers and then, in desperation, my person. And that individual, I thought, was more likely to be Major Henry Graham than either of the young Englishmen.

My uncle was, I suspected, more than a little deranged. He doted on his younger daughter to the point of idiocy, for he had made her disliked by nearly everyone but himself because he refused to teach her manners or discipline. And this business about the governorship of California—his determination to win it for himself bordered on obsession. I could well imagine him as the brutal searcher of my person, as well as one of the whisperers.

Only in the latter case, of course, he had been talking to someone, which meant he was not alone in the plans he made, the actions he took. And the only person I could imagine him conspiring with—having the opportunity to conspire with—was Aunt Maudie. Yet she despised him, and I found it difficult to believe that she wished me any ill.

My head ached abominably, just thinking about it.

I saw Sherry standing at the top of the sandy bank, his hands in his pockets, his dark hair blowing in the wind. And then he plunged down the embankment and came toward me, smiling.

"India! I wondered where you'd gone! And then I guessed that you'd want to think, and this is a good place for it, isn't it?"

My mouth went dry, my tongue was frozen. When he reached for my hands, I could not control the tremor that ran through me, and once again, I could not have said whether I felt thrill or fear. In novels the heroine was al-

213

ways trembling, and that was with joy. I did not think it was joy I felt, however.

"Your uncle has given me permission to court you, and I hope that you're as happy about that as I am." His dark eyes bored into mine, the smile continued to curve his lips, as he waited for my reply.

"I—I don't know what to say. I had not expected—"

"I'd hoped you would," he said quietly. "Because I wanted you to want me to make an offer. But I know that you are very young, and quite inexperienced, and I'm prepared to go as slowly as you need me to go. However, I've just this morning heard that a British ship is due in Los Angeles in a month's time. My business in Monterey will be completed by then, and I'd like to sail for home. I would like very much to marry you and take you with me. And that would necessitate almost immediate planning, since we would have to travel south to meet the ship."

I stared at him in consternation. A month! But that was no time at all!

"I know that isn't long, but the next ship probably will not come until spring, and I have no means of livelihood here. You would like to return to England, wouldn't you? With me?"

I did not know what to say. Indeed, I was incapable, for the moment, of any speech at all. And in the back of my mind a tiny thought intruded upon my discomfort: *Might Nathan Peltier elect to sail home on that same ship?*

But what Nathan did was nothing to me, any more than what I did was any concern of his. I had to consider my future. I had come to like Aunt Maudie, but she played a small part in the life of our household. I neither liked nor trusted my uncle, and Hester did not bear speaking of. What were my alternatives if I did not accept Sherry's offer?

Marriage to one of the rough Americans, living in a hut rather than in a place like Casa del Mar? That was what Aunt Maudie had intimated as my most likely fate.

Well, if I loved the man who provided that sort of life

for me, I thought I was sturdy enough to endure it. True, I had been gently reared, was used to servants and woefully ignorant of the things a frontier wife should know. But I was intelligent and industrious. I was quite capable of learning to do the necessary things. Wasn't I?

And there were the children. I thought aloud, then. "Caro, and the twins. I have to think of them."

Sherry disposed of them easily. "They'll be quite happy here with your aunt and uncle, won't they? Caro and Manuela have become fast friends, and now that Caro is learning to ride they can visit back and forth often. As for the little ones, so long as they have horses and companions, they will be happy anywhere."

Something must have shown in my face, for he changed tack slightly. "Of course we can always send for them later, when we are established. To be truthful, I can't promise you the sort of home I'll be taking you to, for I gave up the house in London when I sailed for India. But the uncles live in a very pretty place, not large, only a dozen bedrooms, but there are pleasant gardens and it's in good repair. It's entirely possible that by the time we reach England it will have passed to me. If that isn't the case, we'll rent a house in London. And in a year or two, we can have your brother and sisters join us, if you'd like."

A year or two! So casually he said that, as if the time were of no consequence! Yet what did I expect? That a new husband would take on three additional people at once?

"I—I am quite overcome by all this, for I did not expect anything of the sort. I don't know what to say." And that was certainly the truth! "Please, I cannot make any decision yet."

I could tell that he was greatly disappointed, but he managed a rueful smile. "Then I will have to practice patience, won't I? I've heard that it's a virtue in a husband."

Only eight months ago I had been eager to find a husband. And now, when Sherry presented himself in that role, I did not know what to do. If I had not had Sir Roland's letter, what would I have decided then? If my life had not been riddled and torn by suspicions that gave me no peace? Perhaps even now our friend in Calcutta had learned the identity of the culprit and could ease my mind, but it might be many months before he could communicate with me. And in the matter of marrying Sherry, I did not have months. I had only weeks, days.

He tucked my hand through his arm and we turned toward the house. "Think about it, India. Perhaps you are too shy, or too innocent, to be able to speak of such things. But you must know how attracted I have been to you since the moment I saw you. A girl with character and backbone, as well as a comely face. Why do you think I jumped at your uncle's invitation to be a guest here, rather than stay in Monterey? Because you were here, of course! And if you have not fallen in love as quickly as I, well, then, I will teach you to do so! It is a thing you can do, I think."

Could I? Oh, Papa, Papa, I cried silently. Would you have chosen this man, had you done the choosing? You gave me the pearls out of love for me, but I almost wish I had never seen them! Not if they cost you your life, not if possessing them is dangerous to mine!

Yet I had the pearls, and I could not give them back, and I knew that whatever happened, I would have to make the decisions myself.

There was no one to help me.

Caro returned from the Alvarados, praising everything about them, full of happy stories and joy for Amalie and Ramón, and admiration for Nathan.

"He is a remarkable man. I wish he weren't too old for me," she sighed, collapsing on the bed in a flurry of skirts that revealed her ankles.

"Since he's engaged to someone else, his age hardly matters, does it?" I asked.

Caro raised up on her elbows. "Engaged? Nathan? To whom?" she demanded indignantly.

"You've been living in the same household with him for weeks. I thought he might have told you her name," I said, and was unable to control the tartness in my tone.

"No. He's talked about his sister, Susan, and some earl's daughter he used to play with—Oh, no! Surely not *her*?"

"An earl's daughter is generally considered to be a good catch, I think." How could I speak of this, without my voice breaking? "What did he say about this earl's daughter?"

"Only that he taught her to ride, and that they'd known each other forever. He used to chase her and pull her hair."

"No doubt he got past that stage, if he's planning to marry her."

"How do you know?" Caro sat all the way up. "I never heard him say anything about an engagement!"

"I thought everyone knew it by this time. Major Graham told me first, and then Aunt Maudie referred to it, as well."

She scowled, tossing back her long hair. "And to think he never told us! Letting us waste our time, hoping! What a dirty trick! Well, I guess he did think we were only silly schoolgirls, because he remarked about our giggling. And of course he's never made any bones about wanting to go home to England. He thinks California is interesting, but he has no desire to live here. Like everyone else, he thinks the Americans are barbarians. Do you think they are, India?"

"How would I know? I haven't met any of them."

"We saw some, though. On the streets of Monterey, the day of the wedding. They were very tall, and except that their clothes were a dreadful contrast to those in the wedding party, I thought they were quite attractive. Even the bearded ones. I should think if they were shaved and dressed up, they might be quite as elegant as Sherry. How have you been getting along with Sherry while I was gone?"

I inhaled deeply and pretended to be busy searching for

217

a handkerchief, with my back to her. "He's asked me to marry him."

"What!" Caro sprang off the bed, and raced to put her arms around me in a joyful hug. "India! And all this time we've been chattering about nothing, and you're engaged! How marvelous!"

I swallowed hard. "I'm not engaged, I only said he's asked me to marry him. Our uncle has given him permission to call upon me—that's a silly way to put it, isn't it, since we're living in the same house. But I—I haven't given him an answer, yet."

"But you're going to? To accept him, I mean?"

"I don't know. There's still—I mean, there was the letter from Sir Roland, and none of that's been resolved, we still don't know—"

"But nothing's happened since you came home, has it? We don't know that anyone followed us from Calcutta, it was simply a guess on Sir Roland's part that they might. And that episode at the Alvarados, it could easily have been simply someone who'd had too much to drink, who thought to surprise you and have his sport with you, in the dark—"

"It wasn't sport he was after," I told her grimly. "He was searching me, Caro. Looking for—for the pearls."

"But no one knew about the pearls. Neither of us told a soul. And you've never been assaulted before, how could you know exactly what a man would do—?"

I allowed it to drop. Caro, rosily romantic, wanted to believe that I was allowing my imagination to create dangers and villains where there were none.

But I knew better. And I had less than a month to decide what I was going to do, and there still was no one to turn to for help. No one at all.

18

I had, of course, sent no message to Nathan Peltier that I was ready to resume my riding lessons. Yet I could not put down the secret hope that he would ride over to see.

He did not, naturally. It would have been easy enough for him to send a note of inquiry, for several times a week Amalie and Aunt Maudie exchanged communications by various riders.

Clearly he took no personal interest in my welfare. I had been no more than another of the "silly schoolgirls" he indulged as he might his younger sister.

I worked around to asking Sherry about him, in as offhand a way as I could manage. For Sherry and Nathan had traveled together aboard the *Durham*, and although neither had ever showed any partiality toward the other, they must have learned something during that long voyage across the Pacific.

In spite of my sounding as if my interest were the most casual sort, Sherry gave me a sharp look when I mentioned Nathan.

"You weren't seriously interested in him, were you? I tried to warn you off an involvement with him."

"It isn't I, it's Caro," I lied. "She's been quite besotted with him ever since they met." That, at least, was true. "I shouldn't want her to be hurt."

Sherry shrugged that off. "I'm sure she's too young to interest Peltier. He is, after all, a man of the world and accustomed to women of society. Her infatuation can be no more than calf love, and since he doesn't return it, and will no doubt return to England at the earliest opportunity, there is little to be concerned about."

"Did he mention to you that he was engaged to marry some girl in England?"

"Not to me directly, no. We didn't take to one another, I'm afraid. Perfectly decent chap, and all that, I'm sure, but I can't say we hit it off. So we didn't discuss our lady friends, nor much of anything else. However, I believe Ramón did say that Peltier was betrothed to the daughter of a duke, or some such."

"An earl," I corrected. "Caro didn't know; he never told her."

"Well, I suppose he wouldn't, since I'm sure he looked upon her as a young cousin rather than a sweetheart. To give the man credit, it doesn't seem that he made any effort to engage the affections of any young lady here."

He hadn't had to make any effort to engage mine, I thought sadly. It had simply happened. I changed the subject, for I did not think I could discuss Nathan without giving myself away.

The following evening Sherry returned late from Monterey, where his business was nearly concluded, to join us after dinner. The major was there, and from his usual bad temper I assumed that things continued to go awry in his plans for the governorship.

"I think, sir," Sherry said to him, "that I might have a word with you. I've just come from Delgado's and it seemed to me that a crisis is building up."

The major's cold eyes swept over the rest of us and dismissed us. "Let's have a brandy on it. Was Larkin there?"

"No, sir. But he's involved in it, up to his neck. It seems certain that he's negotiating with Mexico for the purchase of California on behalf of the United States. Even the price is being whispered about—forty million dollars."

They walked off and left us there, Caro and the twins and Hester and I. For a moment I stared after them, then gave Caro a little push.

"Take the children upstairs, will you? I'll be along directly."

Hester, never one to mingle, had already gone on up the stairs, presumably to visit with her mother before bedtime.

I did not even wait until the others were out of sight. I wanted to know what was going on, and there was only one way to find out, since a mere female was seldom informed about anything. Even if the Americans were about to buy California for themselves, why should Sherry be concerned? He was leaving for England on the next ship.

I reached the library only a minute behind the men. They had not bothered to close the door, on the assumption that none of us would bother to eavesdrop, apparently. I could smell the major's cigar and I heard the clink of glasses.

"If there is truly that amount of money available for such a purpose," Sherry said clearly, "it seems quite possible that Mexico will agree. All this trouble along the border puts both sides in a bad mood, and if Larkin is successful in his endeavors, California will soon fall into the American hands."

"Never! It's preposterous! I have worked for years to prevent this sort of thing from happening! There will be bloodshed before it's over, if Larkin persists in this aberration! Mark my words, we won't go down without a struggle!"

"No, sir. I was sure that you wouldn't. And that's why I'm concerned. If there is going to be trouble, and from what I heard tonight it seems certain there is, then I would like to get out of here. It isn't that I'm a coward, you understand, but if there's a fight, it is not mine. I have no interest in the matter, one way or the other, unless Britain comes into it. All I want is to take India and get out, head for home, before anything happens to her."

I stood rigidly beside the door, listening to these men who would decide my fate as well as their own.

"Yes, yes, good idea. Take her and go. The priests

aren't likely to perform a marriage ceremony on a moment's notice, but the captain of the ship you're taking at Los Angeles, he can do it. Or, if you've time to seek them out, there's an English missionary in Monterey, came on the *Essex*. He's not Church of England, some odd little sect, bit of a crackpot. But he's legally qualified to perform a marriage ceremony, I should think. The sooner you get her away from here, the better."

"Yes, sir. The thing is, sir, I'm not sure she'll go. Right off, like that. She hasn't actually accepted me, you know. And she wants to take her brother and sisters to England, which is out of the question at the moment. I've told her we'll send for them later. But if you and her aunt were to—to help me persuade her that it would be the best thing to do. An immediate wedding, get out before there's any trouble that might prevent our leaving on that next ship—we could leave for Los Angeles within the next few days, before this business comes to a head. If India can be convinced."

"Leave that to me. I know how to deal with recalcitrant females," the major said with a chilling confidence. "She will be ready to go when you are, I assure you."

"Day after tomorrow, then," Sherry suggested.

"Very good. Very good. Day after tomorrow it will be. Don't worry about it, she'll be ready, I'll see to it."

I backed away from the door then, when I heard one of them put his glass down on the table. I fairly ran up the stairs, remembering to take care going past Aunt Maudie's door so that she wouldn't call me in, but the door was closed. I heard the murmur of voices and knew that Hester was with her.

Dear God, dear God! I thought. What was I to do now?

Could they force me to marry Sherry? So soon? Would anyone listen to me if I protested, if I fought against it?

I did not know why my uncle was so eager to have me married and off to England, but I had no doubts at all about his ability to coerce me into doing what he wanted.

And Sherry—he hadn't sounded like a prospective

groom, he had sounded like a man making a business arrangement.

Dear God, was it Sherry? Did he know about the pearls? Had he followed me from Calcutta only to get his hands on them? Would any sane man marry a woman in order to obtain her jewels?

He might, I thought, for these. Maharani Mohindar's black pearls were worth a king's ransom. A man might do anything to possess them.

A man who had killed for them would hardly have any scruples about marrying for them.

Sheer terror sent me fleeing through the darkened corridors, not even pausing to light a candle to take with me.

I could not, I could not marry Sherry Millay and go to England with him.

Caro was closing Bethany's door behind her with a lilting, "Goodnight, love." She turned, startled, at my rapid footsteps, lifting the lamp she carried.

"India, what's the matter?"

"Come inside and close the door. Caro, Caro, we have to do something. Please help me."

Her face registered both astonishment and fear. It had always been I who provided the help, not asked for it. In the bedroom where I now slept by myself, since my sister had finally moved into Amalie's vacated chamber, she put down the lamp and gathered me into her arms.

"You're shaking like an aspen! India, India, what *is* it?"

I told her. I couldn't help it, I began to cry before I had finished, which shook her rather badly, I think. She clasped my hands in hers and tried to soothe me.

"There must be something we can do. If you really cannot marry Sherry, and of course if you don't love him you cannot, no one can *make* you do it, can they?"

"Would you want to wager your life on that? Would you? Knowing what the major is like? Do you think if he decides that I am to marry and go to England, that I will be allowed to do anything else?"

She gnawed at the corner of her lower lip. "What can

we do? We could run away, but we can't leave the twins behind, and besides, we have no money—"

"We have the pearls." I stopped shaking and wiped at my eyes. "We have the pearls. If they're worth a fortune as Papa said, then it should be possible to use them as security for our passage to England. No, we won't sell them—how could we, with no idea of their true value and who in this savage country could afford them? But they must be worth far more than the cost of passage to England, and we'll have to trust that Grandfather will make good on the money so that we retrieve the necklace. I did not want to throw myself on the mercy of a grandfather I never even liked, but anything is better than what the major has in mind for me. And I'm afraid here, Caro! It's true, nothing dreadful has happened since I came back from the wedding, but I'm afraid!"

"And I left you and went to stay with Manuela and have a good time. I'm sorry, I thought you would be all right. India, how are we to get to a ship that will take us to Grandfather?"

"There is one coming to Los Angeles within a month. Perhaps we can get there within that time. I know, I know, it is a long way. But we must try."

"We can't do it on foot. Not in a month, not with the twins."

"Then we'll help ourselves to horses. Don't look at me like that, I know the major will be furious, but there is no other way. We all ride well enough now so that we'll manage, somehow."

"We have no money at all. How will we exist, traveling all that way?"

"We will take what we can carry, and depend upon Providence for the rest." I said it firmly enough, now that my initial panic was over.

"Providence," Caro echoed. "You know, that might possibly be the answer. Manuela told me about the missions, the ones the fathers founded up and down the length of California. Their lands have been taken away, and they no longer care for all those hundreds of Indians.

But most of them are still operated by the priests who remain there; they have their own gardens, they are self-supporting. They might take in and feed four hungry pilgrims."

"We know so few words of their language," I said, remembering Amalie's wedding ceremony at which I had understood nothing whatever.

"The twins have learned quite a lot of Spanish, and I know a little. Enough to indicate that we are hungry, that we need a place to sleep. It might work, India. We might be able to do it."

In our innocence, we supposed that we could find our way to Los Angeles, several hundred miles to the south, simply by following the line of the shore. We brought the lamp to the stand beside the bed, and began to make our plans.

I had been concerned about explaining the circumstances to the twins, but it turned out that little was necessary. When I announced that we were running away, and that it was all to be a big secret, they took it matter-of-factly.

"We could wear boys' clothes, so that no one would know it was us," Bethany said. "In case anyone comes looking for us."

"You can wear Brice's," I conceded. "I don't know where Caro and I would get anything to fit us, though."

"Carlos isn't much bigger than you are. Teresa will do the washing, and when she puts out Carlos's clothes, we will take enough of them for each of you."

"Maybe we could steal some money, too," Brice contributed, getting into the spirit of it. "I know the combination to the safe in the library; it's behind the—"

"No, no. We won't compound our crimes in that way," I decided. "Borrowing horses and clothes are one thing; taking money is something else."

"Why are we going?" Brice asked. "I thought we liked it here, except for having Hester for a cousin."

"If we stay," Caro told him, "India will have to marry Sherry, and she doesn't want to."

"If I get married," Bethany observed, "I should like to marry either Ramón or Nathan. They are both very nice to me."

"You can't, stupid. Ramón is already married to Amalie, and Nathan is going home to England. Besides, he's much too old for you." Brice rolled his eyes to indicate his disgust at her ignorance. "Well, I don't blame you for not wanting to marry Sherry. He doesn't like noise unless he makes it himself. He tells me to be quiet."

"I hope you can be quiet about this. If they know what we're planning, they will stop us," I warned, and they bobbed their heads in unison, agreeing.

Our time was short. True to his promise, our uncle called me into the library in the morning, before he left for Monterey.

He wasted no time on amenities, but came straight to the point.

"There is trouble brewing in Monterey, indeed in all of California, and Mr. Millay feels that he should get out before it breaks into open warfare. You will pack your things and be prepared to travel on the morrow; I will loan you horses and supplies, and you should be able to reach Los Angeles before your ship sails."

I opened my mouth to protest, not because I thought it would do any good, but because it would seem peculiar if I did not. But he didn't allow me to speak.

"My business is urgent, I can't stay to argue about it. You must bow to my judgment in this, and to that of your husband-to-be. You can be married aboard ship, or by one of the fathers at the missions if you can persuade them to do it. I have told your aunt I have given orders. Teresa will prepare food that can be carried in your saddlebags, and Mr. Millay will attend to everything else. You must see there is nothing for you here; if this damnable situation is not resolved, and quickly, I will have lost any opportunity to be governor. I cannot, I will not, be

226

blackmailed by a young chit scarcely out of the nursery. You will leave tomorrow morning."

He left me standing there with my jaw sagging.

Blackmailed? What in heaven's name was he talking about? How could I blackmail him, I who knew nothing whatever about him?

It did begin to make an insane sort of sense, though. That's why he had impressed upon me, my first night in this house, the fact that he had no resources beyond what it took to support his household. He could not, therefore, be expected to pay anything to me. Although since I had not asked for anything but shelter for myself and the others, I didn't understand how he would have taken that for an attempt at extortion.

Dangerous, the whisperer had said. Was I supposed to be dangerous because I knew something that my uncle would pay to have suppressed? He could not afford any hint of scandal, or it would cost him the governorship; only if he attained that high office could he meet my demands.

It made sense, except that I did not know anything about him, and I had made no demands.

I closed my mouth. It didn't matter. All that mattered was that I get out of here before it was too late. If Sherry had planned that he and I should ride to Los Angeles, then it must be possible for me to go with Caro and the twins. And the major had even given me an idea.

Teresa was to pack supplies for us. I would see to it that they were generous, and offer to take charge of them. And then, instead of waiting for Sherry in the morning, we would leave as soon as the household had retired for the night. By the time we were missed, we would be miles away. We would even take all of the horses so that pursuit, if there was to be such, would be delayed as long as possible.

We all tried to rest during the day, although it was next to miraculous that we even managed to stay inside our own skins.

Sherry himself bothered me surprisingly little. He asked,

227

quite solicitously, if my uncle had talked to me, and assumed that I was prepared to follow orders. Once more I made my protests, and hoped they didn't sound as theatrical to him as they did to me.

"Make it an early night," he said. "We will ride at first light." And at that he bent and kissed me on the lips.

Apparently he did not notice that mine were cold and unresponsive.

Brice appeared shortly after dark, triumphantly bearing the items he had stolen from the clothesline. Baggy trousers, loose shirts. We had neither appropriate footwear nor hat; anything of our own would be revealed on close inspection to be quite different from those worn by the peasants we would pretend to be. Brice thought he might manage to acquire native hats once the servants had all retired for the night; we would simply have to take our chances regarding boots. At least from a distance we should attract little attention in this garb; certainly no one could tell that the three of us were female.

We were ready except for one thing.

I had not mentioned it, but Caro did as we lay in the darkness, waiting. "What have you done with the pearls, India? Where are they hidden?"

"I haven't retrieved them yet," I confessed. "I tried several times today, but I could never find the room empty."

"Which room are they in?"

"In Aunt Maudie's bedroom," I confessed, and put a hand over her mouth to stifle her outraged exclamation. "I know, but at the time it seemed most reasonable!"

"How are you going to get them back?"

"I'm not sure. I may have to wait until she goes to sleep and then sneak in and take the doll—they're hidden inside of Tilly."

"But she sometimes stays awake reading for hours!"

"I know. But we can't go without them. It never occurred to me, when I hid them, that we'd be running away in the middle of the night."

"In Aunt Maudie's room!" Caro muttered, and for once it was she who scolded, I who was chagrined.

We lay in the darkness, and I wondered if what we proposed to do was completely beyond chance of success. Yet the idea had been born of desperation, and the need was real.

Suddenly Caro sat up. "Listen! Did you hear something?"

"No, what?"

"I don't know. Maybe someone pounding? Knocking on a door?"

"At this time of night? I hope it's only a shutter in the wind. I think I'll go down, past Aunt Maudie's room—if she sees me I'll say I was going down for a book, that I couldn't sleep. And if her room is dark and she's breathing regularly, snoring a bit the way she sometimes does, I'll sneak in and get the doll."

"You'll never get all the way across the room without tripping over something."

"I'll move very carefully," I said, in what must have been an understatement of epic proportions.

"And what if she catches you in her room?"

"I'll think of something. I'll—I'll say I have a toothache, and I was looking for the medicine, and didn't want to disturb her."

"Oh, India—" She didn't finish, but she didn't have to. If I were caught, especially with the necklace, there would be considerable explaining to do, and it might frustrate altogether our attempt to escape.

I took a candle and moved swiftly along the hallway, praying that no one was awake. Major Graham was the one who worried me the most, and he slept in the other wing and usually retired early.

Approaching Aunt Maudie's room, I slowed my pace. The candle flame flickered, as if in a draft, although there ought not to have been one.

I stopped. Someone had a window open, or a door, which was not usually the case. I could not quite tell from which direction the air came, however, and I went on.

Aunt Maudie's door was wide open, and there was a lamp lighted within.

Maybe, I thought, heart beating wildly, she had fallen asleep while reading. It would certainly make it easier for me to cross the cluttered room quietly enough so as not to disturb her.

With the utmost caution, I peered around the door jamb.

The lamp glowed beside the bed, but the bed itself was empty.

Exultation surged through me, then, and I moved with as much speed as the crowded room allowed. Tilly sat drunkenly atop the dresser, and I dared not take time to extract the necklace; I simply scooped up Tilly and headed for the door.

And stopped, for Aunt Maudie stood there, her dark eyes unfathomable.

19

We faced one another over a distance of a few feet, I stricken dumb. *Oh, Lord, how could you let this happen to me?*

Aunt Maudie's gaze dropped to the battered old doll. "Tilly? You needed Tilly?"

I was vaguely aware of voices, men's voices, and Aunt Maudie was aware of them, too. She turned her head, then lifted a finger to her lips and moved silently back out into the passageway.

Her bulk was considerable, yet she moved silently and with apparent ease.

I followed her. Even in my present state, I could not help being curious about what was going on in the entryway below, and I realized even before we reached the head of the stairs that the draft (which put out my candle) came from the opened front door.

A moment later, I recognized one of those voices, and my fingers closed over the bannister in shock.

"Devil of a time to come banging on a man's door," the major was saying, irritation sending his voice loudly through the house. "And I wouldn't consider allowing you to speak to anyone in my household now. It's a damned intrusion, man!"

"I won't leave until I've spoken to India," Nathan Peltier said.

Aunt Maudie glanced at me, then gathered the voluminous robe about her and, with a warning shake of her head so slight I was not sure I had actually seen it, she started down the stairs.

"What is it? What's the matter? Why is the door standing open?"

They could not see me, there in the upper reaches of the house, but I could see them. Nathan looked windblown and tired, yet determined; my uncle was fully dressed, though not as carefully as was customary, which I took to mean he'd been called from his bed.

"This man is demanding—demanding, in my house!—to see India. I've told him it's quite impossible," the major said.

"Well, close the door while you discuss it," Aunt Maudie suggested, in her usual placid manner. She continued on down the stairs, carrying her own candle, although it, too, had been extinguished in the wind which chilled the entrance hall. "Perhaps, Mr. Peltier, you would be so good as to tell us the nature of your errand. The hour would seem to indicate some urgency."

"I've been in Monterey, which is in a turmoil tonight," Nathan said, and the sound of his voice set my blood to racing. "And I heard very disturbing news. I plan to return to England soon, but I must speak to India before I go. I've heard that she is engaged to marry this Millay fellow, and I can't go without speaking out about him."

"I fail to see where this is any concern of yours," the major said, in a tone that would have stopped a lesser man.

"That may be. But I think that when a man loves a woman—even if she has made it abundantly clear that she does not return his affection—he had a right, no, a duty, to protect her, even from her own actions."

Aunt Maudie had reached the foot of the stairs; she sailed like a mighty ship across the room to close the door, then returned her attention to their unwelcome visitor.

"I think we must ask you to explain yourself," she said, even as her husband moved as if to bodily eject the younger man.

232

And I, trembling (in the chill? or from the hammering of my own heart?) could not believe what he said. Loves a woman? Could he mean what it sounded like he meant? By this time, I needed the aid of the bannister to remain standing.

"I would prefer to explain to India herself," Nathan said.

Aunt Maudie's eyes never wavered from his; not by so much as a hair did she reveal that I listened up there in the darkness above them. "I think that you will first have to explain to us. And then we will judge whether or not to call India from her bed."

"This is a damned insolence, and there is no reason to tolerate it!" my uncle exploded. "I did not carry a pistol to my own front door, but, my God, I will hear no more!"

"I will," Aunt Maudie stated coolly, and her husband, who had started to turn away, was sufficiently startled to stop in his tracks.

"Well, Mr. Peltier," Aunt Maudie said, "we are waiting."

For a second or two, Nathan hesitated. He ran a hand through his fair hair, erasing the damage from the wind, and when he spoke it was not loudly, but every word carried to where I stood.

"When I heard that India was to marry that Millay fellow, I felt as if I'd been struck a terrible blow. But quite aside from my personal feelings, I've had to wrestle with my conscience. I have nothing but suspicions, I can't prove what I think to be the facts, and at first I thought, well, if India loves the man—but if *I* love *her*, can I let her do this thing? Unsuspecting? Innocent? I had to tell her, I must at least warn her—"

The major let out a howl of rage. "In the middle of the night? Are you a complete idiot, Peltier? You are totally incoherent, and all this babble means nothing to me! Nothing! India is to be married to Millay, it is all settled, and they leave tomorrow for Los Angeles to sail for England! Now go home and go to bed, and let us do the same!"

It seemed to me that Nathan's face paled in the light of the lamp that illuminated the hall. "I can't do that, sir. It's one of the reasons I came, because I, also, will leave soon for that same ship. And I only just now, an hour ago, learned that Millay and India intended to be married at once, that I had no more time to make up my mind whether to let her do it or not."

"Let her do it!" My uncle's visage took on a purplish hue. "This is nothing to do with you! You have nothing to say about it!"

"For heaven's sake, shut up and let the man say what he came to say," Aunt Maudie interjected.

That he was not used to being spoken to in such a manner was evident from the major's face, but it did give Nathan a few seconds' head start.

"Thank you, ma'am. What I have to say is this: I believe Millay to be a complete blackguard, perhaps even a murderer. I think he came to California because India came, perhaps she has something of great value—"

"What rubbish! She came without a penny to her name, blackmailing little b—"

"Henry, for once in your life, *shut up*," Aunt Maudie snapped; she seemed to swell, as if with power and strength. "If this is boring to you, I suggest that you return to bed. But I intend to hear what this is all about, and it would take far less time in the telling if you would *shut up*."

I thought for a moment that he would strike her, but Maudie did not back down. Indeed, she did not even look at her husband, but turned all her attention to Nathan.

"Go on, Mr. Peltier."

"I must backtrack a bit in order to tell this logically," Nathan said, and again ran a hand through his hair, this time leaving it standing in peaks. "I, too, came to California partly because of India, although it is true that Don Esteban Alvarado was a friend of my father's, many years ago. My grandfather and Lord Stuart-Brice are old acquaintances, and when his lordship knew that I intended to journey to Calcutta, and that I contemplated returning by way of California to deliver something my father wanted Don Esteban to have, he asked me to perform an errand for him as well."

He had their attention, at last; as for me, I seemed to have slid down the bannister to crouch at the top of the stairs, as if all my bones had melted and would no longer hold me up. Certainly, from that point on, the major ceased bellowing his interruptions.

"His Lordship is an old man. I don't have to tell you that he's an unbending one, I'm sure. But maybe he's at least softening in his old age, and he's thinking about his home and his title, when he's gone. He didn't tell me anything about why his son left England, but I had the impression that he was sent away, and that though the old gentleman continued to provide for him, he didn't keep in touch in any other way, just through the solicitors.

"So what he asked me to do was to investigate. Judson Stuart-Brice, and his family. He wanted to know what they were like, what sort of people, what his son had become. Unfortunately, his son was killed before I could make any effort to meet him. His children were walled away in such a fashion that nobody could get at them—apparently everybody in Calcutta knew there had been some disgraceful act in his past, although I didn't speak with anyone who knew exactly what it was. They seemed to think he kept his family to themselves because he didn't want them to learn about it. He told one individual, who took him to task for 'protecting' them in such a severe fashion, that when they were older he would explain things to them himself, and that he was sure they would understand.

"At any rate, I had no access to his children to see what *they* were like. It was only by chance that I learned they had booked passage to California on one of our family's ships—the Peltiers have been in trading ships for four generations—and I thought that was the perfect opportunity to get acquainted with them. Captain Spacy was none too happy with me for demanding a stateroom he had already booked to someone else, but I'm afraid that for once I used my position and insisted upon it. I thought it was important to do it, and the gentlemen who were refunded their passage money made sufficient profit so that they were willing to delay their departure from Calcutta."

His hair was taking a beating, for he kept running his hand through it, unaware of his own agitation. The cold was beginning to seep through to me, but I would not have moved if my life had depended upon it.

Which, in a sense, it did.

"This Millay fellow showed up, demanding passage, also. There was no space available, and he offered to pay the entire passage to share my cabin. That in itself I thought peculiar, since it was a considerable sum to waste when by waiting a few weeks he could have sailed for half the cost. He was very angry when I refused him. I hurried to take care of my father's business so that I was ready to sail when the *Essex* did."

A look of anger came over his countenance, and his jaw firmed. "However, on the night before she sailed, I was dragged into an alley and beaten senseless. I woke up the following morning under the care of a physician who said I was lucky, for my attacker had been frightened off before I could be robbed. That might have been the case, but I think it is more likely that my assailant didn't intend to rob me in the first place, he only wanted me incapacitated so that I would leave that stateroom empty on the ship."

"And you think Sherard Millay attacked you in order to take your berth?" the major asked incredulously.

"I don't think he did it himself, no. The light was poor, but I could see enough to know my attacker was a great brutish lout. I would like to believe I could have handled Millay, at least in hand-to-hand combat..

"I didn't connect Millay with the incident until I found that he had booked onto the *Durham* the following week, the same as I did. Then I began to wonder about him, and spoke to the captain. He knew nothing of the man save that he'd paid for his passage, but he did not think

Captain Spacy the sort who would have allowed the man to take over my berth when I didn't show up, especially since I was the owner's son as well as having stowed all my gear aboard and paid in full.

"I know all this isn't very much to go on, but I'd learned something interesting before I boarded the *Durham*, since I had questioned an acquaintance of my father's with the Calcutta police. Judson Stuart-Brice was believed to have had in his possession a very valuable piece of jewelry, something to do with having been rewarded for saving the life of a young rajah. It was not until we were nearly at the California coast and Millay mentioned in my hearing that he had once held the post of undersecretary to a Maharajah Ashoka that things began to click into place in my mind.

"What better position to be in, than secretary to a man who gives fabulous rewards to others for anything from creating a beautiful painting to saving his son's life? Yet the Maharajah did not reward Millay, but dismissed him, for reasons that were never specified.

"Might not a man harbor anger against his former employer, and, knowing of this gift to Stuart-Brice, have tried to obtain it for himself?

"I have no proof of anything, as I've said. I only know that the arm of coincidence seems overlong. I know that someone broke into India's luggage where it rested on the beach, supposedly vandalizing the contents. But it occurs to me that Millay was searching for the jewelry he did not get in Calcutta, that he thinks India has it.

"And if he's guilty of this, then he may well be guilty of her father's murder, too. So you see, even if she is in love with him, I can't let her marry without determining the truth of the situation. Is he guilty, or is he not?"

I felt suffocated, and yet there ran through me a golden thread of pure joy. Nathan, thinking I loved Sherry, had come here to protect me. And he had said he loved me.

Aunt Maudie's face tilted; she looked up into the darkness, and I did not know if she stared at me, unseen in the shadows, or toward the room where Sherard Millay lay asleep.

For once the major was speechless. It was Maudie who spoke in a voice roughened by emotion.

"How are we to determine his guilt, or lack of it?"

"I don't know. All I know is that India cannot be permitted to marry him without being warned. And with this mess in Monterey now, who knows what will happen to anyone?"

"What 'mess' do you refer to, sir?" Major Graham's voice rumbled ominously.

"Why, there is a United States naval vessel in Monterey harbor at this very moment, under the command of a Commodore Thomas ap Catesby Jones, and the governor is on his way to Los Angeles! The soldiers are in a state of total confusion, and the American flag flies over the Presidio!"

In the silence I heard my own heartbeat, the blood thundering in my ears. War? Were the United States and Mexico at war? What would that mean to us?

And then, immediately, the consoling thought: Nothing mattered, if Nathan loved me.

"I do not believe you, sir," the major said, sounding strangled. "This is impossible! The United States would not dare attack! And the governor would never have left the capitol with only a ragged handful of infantry to defend it if we were about to plunge into war!"

"Nevertheless," Nathan told him in a convincingly steady voice, "that is the situation. The United States is now in control of Monterey, and therefore, I presume, of California."

A few minutes ago, Major Graham had been a choleric red; now his face had faded to a ghastly white. His breathing was audible even from where I sat at the top of the stairs.

So much for his dream of being governor of California. Nathan, of course, did not know the magnitude of the news he brought. I wasn't sure about Aunt Maudie; had he confided his hopes, had she guessed his scheming?

The major turned like a man sleepwalking, taking no farewell, not even bothering to pick up a candle to light his way to the library. We heard the door close behind him, quietly, as if there were no more force left in the man.

"I'm sorry the news is so upsetting to your husband," Nathan said, and I thought that he controlled himself with an effort. "But that wasn't why I came here, it only adds possible complications to the situation. I *must* speak to India."

"You are distraught, I think," Aunt Maudie said, with magnificent understatement. "And India is long asleep. However, there is some merit in what you say. If Millay is responsible for my brother's death— Well, that is yet to be determined. In the meantime, I invite you to sit in my small parlor, and the servant who let you in will bring you refreshment. I will have to think about this for a time and decide what is best to do."

"I don't care for refreshment, ma'am. I wish to speak to India."

"On your own behalf, or against Millay's suit? I was not of the impression that you had told India of any affection on your part."

"I have not expressed it. She is very young, younger than most girls her age, and far younger in experience because of the peculiar way her father isolated her from society. I didn't want to rush her into anything, I wanted to give her a chance— My dear lady, give me the opportunity to say what I have to say to India herself!"

"The small parlor is over there. You may light a lamp from this one," Maudie said serenely. "I am unaccustomed to conversing with young men in my nightclothes. Pray allow me to withdraw for a time. I will rejoin you when I have made up my mind."

With that, she dipped her candle into the lamp chimney and, once again lighted on her way, ascended the stairs.

20

She did not speak until we had gained the privacy of her own room. I was still trailing the doll by one arm, and did not know it until Aunt Maudie took it from me.

"And what did you want of Tilly, pet?—In the middle of the night?"

I think I swayed on my feet. She pointed toward a chair. "Sit down. I think we have considerable talking to do. You heard the entire thing, down there?"

I nodded, wondering if I could speak, wondering if Caro were frantic by this time since I hadn't returned. She would be imagining all sorts of things, but I'd wager none of them could be as wild as what was actually happening!

Aunt Maudie dangled the pathetic doll by one flaccid arm. "What were you doing with Tilly?"

I made an odd little gasping sound before I could produce the words. "The pearls are inside her. The maharani's pearls."

For a moment she exhibited no expression whatever. Then she tipped up poor Tilly and fished two fingers into the hole in the doll's side, extracting the pouch. I sat silent while she put the doll down on the bed and then emptied the pouch onto the pillow.

Her exhaled breath expressed appreciation. "Lovely. Very lovely. Why were they inside of dear old Tilly?"

Her patience must have been considerable, for she heard me out, my halting, at sometimes incoherent explanations. Only when my faltering words trickled off into silence did she slide the black pearls back into their pouch and hand them to me.

"And you thought to retrieve them and run away. Home to His Lordship."

"I couldn't think what else to do," I admitted in a low tone.

"And what do you think now?"

Warmth flooded my face. "Nathan said—"

"That he loves you. You heard all that, didn't you? Why did you accept Sherry Millay if you're in love with this other fellow?"

"I didn't. Everybody simply took it for granted that I would do as I was told, and Major Graham told me I was to marry him. I didn't know if they could force me to do so, but they forced you—"

I stopped, but too late. Her eyes narrowed slightly. She sank onto the edge of the bed and picked up the doll, cradling it as if it were a baby.

"You must have caught Miss Strang in her cups, if you know that. Well, poor soul, she has her problems as do the rest of us, and solves them in her own way. Who am I to say that alcohol is worse than food? Yes, they forced me. Didn't you guess that if you'd told me, I would have prevented what happened to me from happening to anyone else?"

"I didn't know whether you could—or would," I said, not looking at her. A board creaked in the passageway outside, and I wondered if Caro had come looking for me and was listening.

Aunt Maudie put the doll down, very carefully, and smoothed the silken skirts.

"So you didn't trust me, either. Well, why should you?" She sighed gustily and almost as if without thought reached for the familiar box on her night table. "You've even less reason for trusting me than you thought, my dear. Unless you've guessed your father's secret. Have you?"

I brought my head up, puzzled. "Papa's secret? What do you mean?"

241

"You didn't comment on young Peltier's story about your father having been banished from England in disgrace," she said shrewdly. "Which could mean that Miss Strang told you about that, too. She must have been quite besotted. I don't think she's ever spilled *all* the family secrets before."

"She said Papa had stolen a star sapphire from a guest at Willows Hall." In spite of myself, a note of defiance crept into my voice.

"And you don't believe her? You remember your father as a good, honest man, don't you?"

She bit suddenly on her lip and I was astonished to see that it bled.

"If you heard part of that conversation down in the hall, you must have heard all of it. You heard my husband refer to you as a blackmailing little—something. Do you know what he was talking about? Did you write that letter to me, did you tell me that you knew *all about me*, with the intent of blackmailing us?"

I gaped at her, unable to fully grasp what she said. I must have looked stupid beyond measure, but it convinced her that I was innocent of *that*, at any rate, for her face softened.

"No, I can see that you didn't. I told him you knew nothing, that he was a fool for thinking that after all those years Judson would finally have told you the truth. Yet he insisted that you knew, and that your intent was to ruin us if he did not give in to your demands."

I found my tongue at last. "But I made no demands!"

"He thinks you did. He thinks you mean to ruin his chances to be governor of California, for he's convinced they would not have chosen a man with scandal in his family. It was all so long ago, it didn't matter to anyone but Juddy and me—and Juddy is dead, God forgive me, and I really didn't think it mattered any more.

"But it does matter to you, doesn't it? You don't want to believe your father was a thief, even if it was many years ago, even if the gem was returned. I've carried the guilt of it all this time, but there comes an end to every-

242

thing. If Judson hadn't told you, I was perfectly willing to do so if there was any suspicion that you knew—but then you wouldn't have been blackmailing us if your father had told you, would you?"

Now it was she who was incoherent, and she must have realized it from the look on my face.

"You didn't figure it out? After all those stories Juddy told you, after the ones even I told you? How I was always into mischief and how he was always saving me from the results of my own folly?"

Realization began to dawn, quickly followed by disbelief.

"It was—it was *you* who stole the sapphire? Not Papa?"

"I took it. Did Miss Strang tell you that I was once in love with a young man, a young man my father said was not good enough for me? And that he forbade us to ever see one another again, even arranged to have the man sent out of the country, to America? Did she tell you he then arranged a marriage with a man twenty years my senior, a man as devoid of warmth and compassion as my father was himself?"

Her voice gathered strength as she spoke, and I could see that the passion her seamstress had spoken of was still there, locked in the mounds of soft flesh.

"And then I met another man, a man who was good and kind, who would have taken me and my Amalie, another man's child, and run away with us even though we couldn't be married. It would have meant giving up his life's work, going away from England, but he would have done it. Only he had very little money—not enough, or so I thought.

"And so I took the sapphire, with the thought to sell it and join my lover. Only they decided that Juddy had taken it, and as usual my father needed no evidence beyond his own intuition. He said that Juddy should be thrown out, bag and baggage, wife and children, and the baby that was on the way. Did you know there was one, and that your mother lost it because she was so frightfully

243

upset? One more thing on my conscience, one more thing I could never make right. I don't even know if she ever forgave me for costing her that child.

"Juddy knew, of course. He knew I'd taken the sapphire, and why. And do you know the sort of man your papa was, my dear India? He told me to take it and run! He told me to go, knowing that if I did his own fate was sealed, that he'd be banished from the home and the country he loved.

"I was tempted. I'll admit I was tempted. Because I loved a man, you see, in a way that I never did before or since, and hated the one I was married to. But I knew I couldn't do that to Juddy, so I arranged to send the sapphire back to its owner."

She laughed, a bitter sound that was muffled by the heavy hangings in the crowded room.

"Innocent that I was, I thought that would make my father relent! That since no permanent harm was done, he'd leave Juddy alone. And of course it didn't work that way at all. I might as well have kept the gem, for all the good returning it did Juddy. And he made me promise, when I knelt beside him, weeping, that I would not tell. That I would not admit it was I who was the thief, not he.

"What would be the use, he said? He was already leaving, and he'd always wanted to see India, he'd read about it and loved it from afar since he was a boy. Can you imagine the state he must have been in, with his own pride and concern for his family, he still had time to consider how I must feel about it all?

"And so, coward that I was, I kept still. I let them send Juddy away. I didn't even know for sure where he was, although my father's solicitors certainly knew, and I could not even write to him. I was ashamed to write, to tell the truth. As I'm still ashamed. But now you know the truth. It was I who was the thief, not your father."

I sat for a moment in a stunned silence, and this time the ache in my throat was for Aunt Maudie instead of for myself.

"You did what he wanted you to do," I said finally, feeling the prick of tears.

"And what was easiest for me," she agreed. "And you are truly Juddy's daughter, my dear, for you try even at this late date to ease my guilt." She reached out to pat my hand. "And now I will see what I can do to help you. Naturally there will be no forced wedding. There is no need to run away. Come, we have things—"

She never completed the sentence.

We heard the shot, through two doors and up a long flight of stairs.

A single shot.

For a moment we stared into one another's faces, and then we moved toward the door.

21

The major lay sprawled across his own desk, face down in a widening crimson pool that ran and merged with the crimson of the carpet. Even without the pistol lying beneath his hand, we would have known he had killed himself.

Carlos, white-faced and shaking, spread his hands in a gesture of denial. The fumes emanating from his person indicated that he had spent the evening in a Monterey drinking place, but he was entirely sober now.

"I do not understand, señora! He heard me come in, and he called out to me, and asked if it were true! About the American ship in the harbor, the American flag over the Presidio! This man, this Commodore Jones, he has taken Monterey in the name of the United States! And I told him it was so! And then he walked back into this room, and a moment later I heard the shot. He has killed himself, señora, and I do not know why!"

What thoughts ran through Aunt Maudie's head at that moment I could only guess.

"It was not your fault, Carlos," she said after a time. "I know that you are tired, but someone must ride to Monterey. Someone must be told of this—it must be clear that my husband died by his own hand."

"Sí, sí, of course, señora! I will go! I will tell them!"

Teresa stood in the passageway, clutching a loose garment about her, her dark face for once unsmiling. "Is it true? The señor is dead?"

"Do not touch him, señora!" Carlos admonished. "I

will bring the authorities, and they will see—" He turned and fled, his wife pattering after him.

The major was dead. Aunt Maudie was free, and I was free.

I turned to look directly into the eyes of Nathan Peltier.

"India—" he said, and then seemed not to find words.

There was the sound of feet upon the stairs, and we all looked up; *poor little Hester,* was my first thought, for she had loved her father.

But it was not Hester.

It was Sherrad Millay, and he was pointing a pistol at us as he reached the bottom of the stairs.

"Where is the necklace?" he demanded.

I stood, trying to marshal my mental resources, and found them drained. Not even my tongue would function.

"Don't be a fool," Nathan said, turning to face the other man. "You can't expect to get away with it. A priceless object like a maharani's necklace, it will be recognized by any dealer in the world as too fabulous to be sold over a counter. And if the dealer isn't reputable, he won't pay you a fraction of its worth."

Sherry was perhaps a trifle pale, but perfectly composed. "I'll worry about that when the time comes. I want the pearls, India. I know you have them, and I've no time to waste. Hand them over."

"It was you who killed my father," I said, the words sounding as if they were said by someone else.

He ignored me. "The pearls. I don't want to have to shoot anyone to get them."

Anyone else, he meant. It came to me, in a quick scalding wave of awareness, that this man, whom my uncle would have forced me to marry, was a murderer. He had thought nothing of having my father shot, he had killed his own confederate, and he was quite capable of now killing me. Or one of the others.

There had been no sign of Caro or the twins or Hester.

But at any moment they might come down the stairs into the danger area. Caro, at least, was certainly awake; she must have heard the shot, must be somewhere up there, frightened, listening, trying to think what to do.

Sherry gestured with the pistol. "I'll shoot him first—Mr. Peltier. He isn't armed, but he has the look of a dangerous man." His smile was mirthless, horrible. "And then your fat aunt. It may take more than one shot for her." His cruelty must have cut deep, but Maudie stared back at him, retaining her dignity.

I heard a tiny sound somewhere above us in the big house. I couldn't help it, my gaze darted toward the shadowy upper reaches of the stairway, where a pale, blur moved, ever so slightly.

But Sherry heard it, too. He did not take the pistol off us, but called over his shoulder. "Come on down! Unless you want me to shoot your sister!"

They crept down the stairs, fully dressed, ready to run away. I didn't know how much they knew of the events of the past hour, and I ached to protect them, but there was nothing I could do short of handing over the precious pearls.

Caro, and the twins, and even Hester, her small face pinched and unhappy, although it wasn't likely she realized as yet that her father was dead. They were all white-faced, frightened, too frightened even to ask questions.

"Over there," Sherry said, and gestured again with the pistol. "You can all stand there while India produces the pearls. They're in a small leather pouch, are they not, my dear? Which you kept on your person until the day of the wedding, and then you hid them somewhere else. Unfortunately I haven't been able to find them, but now you will do it for me. You have five minutes before I shoot the first of your friends."

I looked at them all, the dear, beloved faces, and knew that no object was worth another life. I hated Sherry Millay with a passion worthy of Aunt Maudie, but I would do as he said.

I had taken one step toward that end when Caro stopped me.

"Wait. I had them last. I know where the pearls are. I'll get them."

There was something about her voice that warned me, some expectancy, some excitement that went beyond the sheer horror of the moment. *Oh, God,* I thought, *don't let her try anything that will make him shoot—*

Caro's feet were light, scarcely heard as she vanished into the upper darkness. And in well under the authorized five minutes she was back, carrying two things—the pouch with the pearls, and ragged old Tilly.

"You forgot your doll in Aunt Maudie's room," Caro said, thrusting the toy at an astonished Bethany. "Here," she said, and tossed the pouch toward Sherry.

In a reflex action, he caught it with his left hand. At the same time, Nathan lunged toward the hand that held the pistol. It went off with a sound that sent reverberations through the great open hall, and I saw that Nathan had been hit, for there was blood on the shoulder of his jacket; he staggered against the wall, then prepared for another assault.

Sherry fired again, wildly, striking nothing except the ceiling, and ran for the front door, with Nathan plunging after him.

"No!" Caro and I screamed together, for I knew that Nathan was more important than any jewels, and Caro knew—Caro knew more than any of the rest of us.

I caught at Nathan's arm, and Caro did the same from the other side; it was her words that put an end to the pursuit.

"Let him go, he doesn't have the pearls!"

Gasping, Nathan clutched at his injured shoulder and stared down at her. "But you gave him the pouch!"

"It's full of marbles," Caro said. "I found them atop Aunt Maudie's dresser. If you hadn't tried to bring him down, he might have opened the pouch and discovered the truth, but the chances are he won't look now until

249

he's a long way from here. The pearls are safe, India, they're where you had them hidden!"

I turned to look at Tilly, pressed against Bethany's bosom.

"I think," Aunt Maudie said clearly, "that I could drink a glass of brandy. After I sit down, of course."

"I'll get it, Mama," Hester said, and turned toward the library, but her mother caught her hand. "No, love, sit with me until my heart stops pounding. Caro will get the brandy." Her dark eyes met Caro's green ones over the child's head, heavy with warning.

Caro had not seen the major's body, but she had certainly heard the shot that felled him. She nodded and visibly drew herself together. "Yes, Aunt Maudie. I'll bring it."

I did not wait to see how my sister held up under the sight of a man lying in a pool of his own blood. Nathan had been wounded, and it was to him that my attention turned.

"Nothing serious," he insisted, but I persuaded him to peel off his coat so that we might be sure. The shot had grazed the fleshy part of his upper arm and caused considerable bleeding, but it did not appear to need more than a simple dressing. Unlike Papa's terrible wound, this one would heal.

We looked into one another's faces, and I felt mine grow warm. I thought of Aunt Maudie, who had lost her first love, married a man she loathed, and lost another love. I knew from the look in Nathan's eyes that my fate would be a happier one.

Caro came back with the brandy bottle and a glass; she was pale but poured for Aunt Maudie with a hand that shook only slightly, and then she offered it to Nathan.

"Maybe the rest of you could do with some, too?" he asked.

I shook my head, and saw Hester's eyes fixed upon me, resentment glowing there. Poor babe, how much more resentment would there be when she learned of her father's death? Would she blame that on me, too?

250

Suddenly I had to know. "Did you put the spider in my drawer, Hester?" I asked, but gently, for I had caused her world to change, and it would change even further, and I was sorry for her.

"I hoped it would bite you," Hester said honestly, and not even her mother's exclamation erased the animosity there. "Or that the horse would break your neck."

Aunt Maudie stared at her offspring, horrified, and swallowed the rest of the brandy.

"And are things all now explained?" Nathan asked. "I have so much to say to you, India, that I don't know where to start—"

"Begin with the earl's daughter," I suggested.

"The earl's daughter?" He stared down at me, bewildered. "You mean Hortense? What has she to do with anything?"

"They told me you were engaged to her, they all said so—"

"Millay told us that," Aunt Maudie contributed. "Both my—my husband and me. I suppose it isn't true? And that the lie sounded more convincing coming to India from us than from Sherry who obviously disliked you?"

"Engaged to Hortense? Oh, dear heaven!" For a moment amusement came through the pain. "Hortense and I played together as children, but she's been married for four years to a stuffy young clergyman and she has two young children by this time, if nature has followed its customary course! I assure you I have never been engaged to anyone!"

And then he looked down at me again and his voice changed. "Until now. If you'll have me."

It was a very public proposal of marriage, with so many bystanders. But it was quite a satisfactory one, for all that, because of course the answer was *yes.*

It was some time before we learned that Commodore Thomas ap Catesby Jones, of the United States Navy, had erred in believing his country and Mexico to be at war.

He withdrew his forces in embarrassment, and was temporarily relieved of his command because of the incident; it was not until 1848, six years later, that California officially became a possession of the United States.

Long before that time, Nathan and I had returned to England with the twins, to make our home with his family at Eagleton, in Essex.

Caro elected to stay behind with Aunt Maudie and Hester, but that is another story.

The ending to my own tale was truly one of living happily ever after.

ALL TIME BESTSELLERS
FROM POPULAR LIBRARY

☐ THE BERLIN CONNECTION—Simmel	08607-6	1.95
☐ THE BEST PEOPLE—Van Slyke	08456-1	1.75
☐ A BRIDGE TOO FAR—Ryan	08373-5	2.50
☐ THE CAESAR CODE—Simmel	08413-8	1.95
☐ DO BLACK PATENT LEATHER SHOES REALLY REFLECT UP?—Powers	08490-1	1.75
☐ ELIZABETH—Hamilton	04013-0	1.75
☐ THE FURY—Farris	08620-3	2.25
☐ THE HAB THEORY—Eckerty	08597-5	2.50
☐ HARDACRE—Skelton	04026-2	2.25
☐ THE HEART LISTENS—Van Slyke	08520-7	1.95
☐ TO KILL A MOCKINGBIRD—Lee	08376-X	1.50
☐ THE LAST BATTLE—Ryan	08381-6	2.25
☐ THE LAST CATHOLIC IN AMERICA—Powers	08528-2	1.50
☐ THE LONGEST DAY—Ryan	08380-8	1.95
☐ LOVE'S WILD DESIRE—Blake	08616-5	1.95
☐ THE MIXED BLESSING—Van Slyke	08491-X	1.95
☐ MORWENNA—Goring	08604-1	1.95
☐ THE RICH AND THE RIGHTEOUS —Van Slyke	08585-1	1.95

Buy them at your local bookstores or use this handy coupon for ordering:

Reading Fit For A Queen

QUEEN-SIZE GOTHICS offer the very best in novels of romantic suspense, by the top writers, greater in length and drama, richer in reading pleasure.

☐ DARK TALISMAN—Anne-Marie Bretonne	00240-9	1.25
☐ A DELICATE DECEIT—Susan Hufford	00398-7	1.25
☐ THE DEVIL'S GATE—Arlene J. Fitzgerald	03178-6	1.50
☐ THE DEVIL'S SONATA—Susan Hufford	00340-5	1.25
☐ DEVIL TAKE ALL—A. Brennan	00612-9	.95
☐ DRAW A DARK CIRCLE—Iona Charles	03191-3	1.50
☐ THE DREAMER, LOST IN TERROR—Alison King	00356-1	1.25
☐ FOOLS'S PROOF—A.S. Carter	00261-1	1.25
☐ THE FOUR MARYS—Rinalda Roberts	00366-9	1.25
☐ GRAVE'S COMPANY—S. Nichols	00252-2	1.25
☐ GRENENCOURT—I. Charles	00264-6	1.25
☐ THE HARLAN LEGACY—Jo Anne Creighton	03206-5	1.50
☐ THE HEMLOCK TREE—E. Lottman	00235-2	1.25
☐ INN OF EVIL—J.A. Creighton	00224-7	1.25
☐ ISLAND OF SILENCE—Carolyn Brimley Norris	00411-8	1.25
☐ ISLAND OF THE SEVEN HILLS—Z. Cass	00277-8	1.25
☐ KEYS OF HELL—L. Osborne	00284-0	1.25
☐ THE KEYS TO QUEENSCOURT—Jeanne Hines (Empress)	08508-8	1.75
☐ THE LAZARUS INHERITANCE (Large type)—Noel Vreeland Carter	00432-0	1.25
☐ THE LEGEND OF WITCHWYND (Large Type)—Jeanne Hines	00420-7	1.25
☐ LET THE CRAGS COMB OUT HER DAINTY HAIR—J. Marten	00302-2	1.25
☐ LUCIFER WAS TALL—Elizabeth Gresham	00346-4	1.25
☐ MIDNIGHT SAILING—S. Hufford	00263-8	1.25
☐ THE MIRACLE AT ST. BRUNO'S—Philippa Carr (Empress)	08533-9	1.75
☐ OF LOVE INCARNATE—Jane Crowcroft	00418-5	1.25

Buy them at your local bookstores or use this handy coupon for ordering: